Don't Make Me
Choose
Between
You
and
My Shoes

Don't Make Me Choose Between You and My Shoes

Dixie Cash

AVON

An Imprint of HarperCollinsPublishers

DON'T MAKE ME CHOOSE BETWEEN YOU AND MY SHOES. Copyright © 2008 by Dixie Cash. All rights reserved. Printed in the United States of America. No part of this book may be used or reproduced in any manner whatsoever without written permission except in the case of brief quotations embodied in critical articles and reviews. For information address HarperCollins Publishers, 10 East 53rd Street, New York, NY 10022.

HarperCollins books may be purchased for educational, business, or sales promotional use. For information please write: Special Markets Department, HarperCollins Publishers, 10 East 53rd Street, New York, NY 10022.

FIRST EDITION

Designed by Diahann Sturge

Library of Congress Cataloging-in-Publication Data
    Cash, Dixie.
        Don't make me choose between you and my shoes / Dixie Cash.—1st ed.
        p. cm.
        ISBN 978-0-06-082974-2
        1. Beauty operators—Fiction. 2. Texas—Fiction. 3. New York (N.Y.)—Fiction.
    I. Title.
    PS3603.A864D66   2008
    813'.6—dc22   2007044414

08 09 10 11 12   OV/RRD   10 9 8 7 6 5 4 3

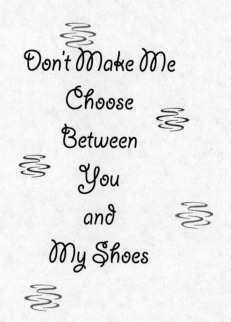

Don't Make Me
Choose
Between
You
and
My Shoes

chapter one

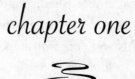

Manhattan, July 2006

He stuffed his shirt into his pants, zipped up and looked one last time into the mirror. The bathroom lighting was hardly flattering, but he didn't care. He hadn't come here to impress.

He opened the door leading to the bedroom and watched the prostitute slide her cell phone into her purse, pull out a tissue and blot the red color from her lips. He hated that greasy red shit and he had told her he wouldn't tolerate lipstick stains on his clothing or anything else.

He approached her from behind, wrapped his arms around her and jerked her body against his. His hands were large. They encircled her throat with ease. Her eyes displayed a flash of panic and a thrill rushed through him. Her head turned toward him, a questioning look on her face.

He grabbed her by the hair and threw her onto the bed. She screamed, but then he was on her, straddling her and muffling her sounds with his hand. She kicked and bit, was stronger than she looked. Before she could do more damage, he went for her throat and crushed the sound from her.

Seconds later she ceased to struggle, but he didn't let go. He knew she had only lost consciousness. It would take several minutes for her to lose life. Thank God he was strong.

Meanwhile, in a brownstone several blocks away, the prostitute's only friend received a text message sent fifteen minutes earlier from the familiar cell phone number.

B home soon. No prob. He's a cop.

chapter two

Salt Lick, Texas, July 2006

Debbie Sue Overstreet was doing her dead-level best to balance the business checkbook before customers began to arrive. Her friend and business partner, Edwina Perkins-Martin, refused to touch the computer bookkeeping, excusing herself from the chore by declaring she didn't want to catch a virus.

Debbie Sue and Edwina co-owned the Styling Station, one of two beauty salons in Salt Lick, a town of 1,232 Texan-to-their-souls citizens. The salon was different from the competition in many ways, but the most glaring difference was that one end of the Styling Station was home to a private investigation agency, the Domestic Equalizers, also owned by Debbie Sue and Edwina.

As Debbie Sue fiddled with the numbers on an Excel spreadsheet, she listened with one ear to Edwina's phone conversation on the Domestic Equalizer phone line. Everyone had a talent, and her partner Edwina Perkins-Martin's was surely talking. Curiosity was not only killing Debbie Sue, it was interfering with her ability to figure out what had gone wrong in her bookkeeping program. *Shit!*

"Uh-huh," Edwina said. "I see . . . uh-huh."

No longer able to stand the suspense, Debbie Sue left her spot at the computer and walked over to the desk they had installed in the Domestic Equalizers end of the beauty salon. "Ed," she mouthed, "who is it?"

Ignoring her, Edwina said, "Hold on, let me get a pen." The tall brunette grabbed a pen from a coffee mug that held an assortment of writing tools and scribbled something on a piece of notepaper. "Okay, thanks. I'll talk to my partner and we'll call you back. Thanks."

"What?" Debbie Sue asked as Edwina placed the receiver back in its cradle. "Who was it?"

Edwina fanned the piece of notepaper in the air. "Wow, partner. I think we just hit the big time."

Debbie Sue made an attempt to grab the note, but Edwina pulled it close to her chest. "I'll read it out loud."

"Fine." Debbie Sue returned to her chair in front of the computer and crossed her arms over her chest.

Edwina cleared her throat. "Paul Scurlock, 212–555–2431."

Debbie Sue waited for more, but nothing else came.

"That's it? A name and a phone number? Who the hell is Paul Scurlock?"

"He just so happens to be the current president of NAPI. National Association of Pri—"

"Private Investigators," Debbie Sue finished, starting to feel an ominous anxiety. She was familiar with the professional organization. At her insistence she and Edwina had joined it soon after establishing the Domestic Equalizers. "The president of the National Association of Private Investigators is calling *us*? Oh, hell. What have we done wrong? We're in trouble, aren't we?"

"We are not in trouble. He called about their annual conference in two weeks. He—"

"The one in New York City? Ed, I visited the site online. I even went so far as filling in the registration form, but I never hit the ENTER button. I swear I didn't."

Edwina looked earnestly at the note in her hand. "Maybe you should have."

"Nope. Number one, we can't afford it. Number two, we'd have to close the shop for five days. Number three, Vic wouldn't like it. Number four, Buddy would divorce me again if I even mentioned it. And number five, we can't afford it. No, ma'am. I didn't hit that ENTER button."

Edwina planted a fist on one skinny hip, her attention still focused on the note. "This Scurlock dude said one of the speakers dropped out at the last minute. He's wondering if the Equalizers would fill in. He says NAPI will pay our way up there and back. They'll pay for our hotel and our meals, and they're offering a small honorarium." Edwina leveled a look at Debbie Sue. "I didn't want to show him my ignorant side on the phone, but what's an honorarium?"

"Are you serious?"

"Of course I'm serious. How would I know what an honorarium is? I never heard that word in my life." She leaned back and leveled a smug look at Debbie Sue. "Unlike some people I know, I didn't go to college for a year."

"It's a fee, Ed. It's a fee. What I meant is, are they serious about the invitation?"

"Sounded serious to me. But if you want my opinion, I'd say they're nuttier than squirrel poop. What would *we* say to professional investigators?"

"Why, what do you mean? Didn't we get written up in *Texas Monthly*? Didn't we investigate two murders? Didn't we find the bad guys? We've hardly had a case go unsolved. We're good at what we do, Ed."

"Debbie Sue, that sheriff in Haskell called us clowns. It's a wonder he didn't lock us up and lose the key. That whole thing with Quint Matthews and Monica Whoever was a mess. I haven't seen Buddy so pissed off since back when he divorced you."

Debbie Sue frowned at hearing the truth. Her husband, Buddy, was a trooper in the Texas Department of Public Safety, on a mission to become a member of one of the most revered law-enforcement organizations in the country—the Texas Rangers. It was true he had divorced her once because of her hard head, but she had reformed and they had remarried a few years back.

She had slightly slipped off the track with the Haskell fiasco and Buddy had taken a very narrow view of the chaotic episode. He had called it an unnecessary risk, an embarrassment and just all-around dumb.

Debbie Sue's eyes misted over. Validation of her and Edwina as private investigators meant more to her than anything had in a long time. She had always needed something to show for her efforts. Years ago that same need, and the mile-wide competitive streak she'd had since infancy, had driven her to become a champion barrel racer in ProRodeo.

"My God, Ed, it just hit me. I can't believe it. Us, the Domestic Equalizers. Invited to New York City to speak to a bunch of people. I've always wanted to go to New York City."

"Yeah, but—" Edwina stopped and pursed her mouth. "I, uh, I . . . well, I just can't imagine getting up in front of a crowd and talking." She got to her feet, moved to her station and began rearranging her curlers, clippies and combs and brushes in her work tray, getting ready for the day. The beauty salon would open in fifteen minutes.

Debbie Sue stared wistfully into space. "I wish we could go. It would be great marketing for us. We've talked about going to one of these conferences and . . ." A new thought brought her back to reality. "Wait a minute. You're acting funny. I know speaking in front of an audience does *not* bother you. I've seen you do an impromptu five minutes in the grocery store checkout line. What's going on?"

"If you have to know, I don't appreciate being invited at the last minute, only because somebody else backed out.

That's just rude. You know I don't tolerate bad behavior."
Edwina continued to move items in her tray.

"What do you mean, 'bad behavior'? You married your
third husband when he got stood up at the altar."

"Don't rub that in. I was young and stupid. Besides, I already had on that damn bridesmaid dress that had cost me a
month's pay and I was holding a bouquet. It seemed like the
most logical thing to do."

"You didn't even have a marriage license."

Edwina's jaw dropped. Her eyes widened in an aggrieved
expression. "Well, we got one . . . eventually."

"I know, I know. What's really wrong, Ed? You know I
won't give up 'til you tell me."

"How long would it take to drive to New York City?"

"From here? Are you out of your mind? It's so far I can't
even imagine it. It's practically in another country. Why
would you even wonder that? Mr. Scurlock didn't say we
had to drive, did he?"

Edwina plopped into her hydraulic chair, picked up a
comb and began teasing the flurry of bangs on the front of
her beehive hairdo. "He said they'd fly us up there and back.
I might think about going if we didn't have to fly. I don't like
flying. There, I said it. Happy?"

"But Ed, you've flown before. I've even flown with you,
that time when we went to the National Finals in Vegas."

"Yeah, but that flight ended before I got out of the bathroom. Less than forty-five minutes. I've had yawns that
lasted forty-five minutes." She laid her comb on her station
counter, picked up a can of hair spray and clouded the air

with lacquer. "It would take, like, two thousand hours to fly to New York City. I don't think stewardesses are allowed to serve that much liquor to one passenger."

Debbie Sue looked at her old friend with a frown. "Why, Edwina Perkins-Martin, I never knew this about you. I didn't think you were afraid of anything."

"Hell, I'm not afraid. But I can't stand the thought of losing my lunch on some bald guy's head. I get airsick. I've had motion sickness my whole life."

"There's medication for that, Ed."

"Oh, really? Why hasn't someone told me this before? I'm over forty fuckin' years old and I'm just hearing about this? Medication, what a breakthrough."

"Oh, hush. Have you ever tried it?"

"Of course I have. But I have to take a lot and it makes me drunk for hours. I'm talking really drunk, without the fun."

Debbie Sue shook her head and laughed. "But you seemed fine when we flew to Vegas and back."

"That flight was so short I decided to risk it with no drugs. Just booze. Worked fine."

Laughing, Debbie Sue rose, walked over and put her arm around the shoulders of her partner and friend. "But you do want to go, don't you? You think it would be fun, don't you?"

"Maybe. But I'm not kidding. You'd have to put up with me medicated all to hell."

"Ed, I've broken horses and ridden a wild bronc. I think I can put up with you medicated."

"You're acting like the only obstacle is taken care of. You seem ready to go home and pack."

Debbie Sue returned to her chair in front of the computer. "Not entirely. I've got to finish up with this blankety-blank bookkeeping before my nine-o'clock appointment comes in. I don't know why they call this QuickBooks. There's not one damn thing about it that's quick." She began to slowly type numbers onto the spreadsheet. "And we still have to call this guy Paul Scurlock tomorrow and get more details."

"Don't forget Buddy Overstreet tonight," Edwina said. "He's the one you've got to talk to. Compared to Buddy, this NAPI dude's bound to be a lightweight."

"No, I haven't forgotten. But I suppose if you can be in denial about your problem of barfing on strangers, I can be in denial about how loud Buddy's gonna yell. For the time being anyway."

Debbie Sue's voice trailed off as she typed more information into the computer, tapped ENTER and watched the flurry of numbers turn into thousands instead of hundreds. "Sonofabitch! Dirty no-good, lousy, rotten, worthless piece of microchip shit!" She followed the outburst with a slap against the side of the monitor.

"My, my," Edwina said. "And here you promised Buddy you'd quit cussing. You'd better be careful, hon. You'll chip a nail. Or nail a chip. Or some damned thing."

chapter three

Dime Box, Texas, July 2006

Celina Phillips lifted two teaspoons of sugar from the porcelain, rose-patterned sugar bowl and stirred them into her black coffee. As she sipped, she stood at the kitchen sink looking outside through the window at nothing in particular, thinking of everything in general. She felt twitchy. Unsettled. Not at all her usual self. Her usual self was levelheaded and prone to being too serious.

Her restless state of mind puzzled her. She had worked hard and succeeded at reaching her goals. Why couldn't she just be happy with her accomplishments? Why was she now, a short year later, standing here looking out the window, thinking, *Okay, now what?*

She moved the flimsy ruffled curtain that veiled her view of the big outside world. Rubbing the fabric between her fingers, she thought back on a dozen different pairs of ruffled curtains that had covered this window over the twenty-three years she had shared this home with her grandmother, Darlene Phillips. Polka dots, gingham, pastels and plaids. Her grandmother's first choice in home décor fit her cute, small home. And Darlene's preference in dress—ruffles and bows—suited her.

Celina couldn't imagine dressing in frills and frou-frou. A bow on Celina Phillips would look as out of place as hair on a frog.

Her father, now deceased, was her grandmother's only child, and like him, Celina was tall and slim with an athletic build. Most of the time she wore her shoulder-length, straight black hair twisted on top of her head, a banana clip holding it off her face and out of her eyes. She used little makeup—only a hint of blush and lip gloss. Her clothing was simple and relaxed. Jeans and T-shirts in spring and summer; jeans and sweatshirts in fall and winter. In spite of her dull attire and her less-than-stylish hairdo and makeup, she had been told often she was the prettiest girl in town.

But exactly how pretty *was* that, in Dime Box, Texas, population 381?

She poured the last of her coffee down the drain, rinsed the cup and placed it on the drain board exactly where she would find it tomorrow morning. Her life was predictable, free of stress.

And dull as a toothache.

"Granny Dee," she called out in the direction of the hallway, "I'm leaving."

Darlene "Granny Dee" Phillips appeared in the kitchen doorway. A pink silk scarf, wrapped around her head like a turban, held her silver hair in place. In front it was tied in a perfect bow. She was rubbing cream onto her hands and diligently massaging each perfectly manicured cuticle. "Sweetheart, you be careful, now, and watch out for traffic."

She said the same thing every morning.

Celina was always careful. And in Dime Box any prospect of traffic had long ago relocated to the larger cities of Houston and Austin. She mumbled under her breath as she let the screen door slam behind her. "Traffic? Heck, I'll be lucky if I don't die of boredom or if the phlegm of tedium doesn't stop my breathing."

A bit melodramatic, but she didn't care. She loved melodrama. It was better than being dull and easier than comedy.

She fished her car keys from her jeans pocket and yanked open the rusted door of her ancient Volkswagen bug. As she cranked the engine, she looked through the kitchen window and watched her grandmother, the only true parent figure Celina had ever known. Her own mother had run off soon after Celina's birth, never to be heard from again. Not ready for "this motherhood gig," she had said in her note.

Celina's dad had left too, but returned for brief stints to fill the house with delight. Then he would pack up and leave again. Celina had learned to live with the highs and lows of his comings and goings, sort of like the circus arriving in the still of the night, setting up tents, entertaining with clowns and animals, then disappearing in the morning light. Ten years back, after a bout with too much booze and too much speed, a late-night collision with a highway road sign had ended his visits. After that, Celina's grandparents became her family, her world.

The words of wisdom Granny Dee had tried to pound into her head or whispered into her ear as sleep overtook her on more nights than she could count came back to her again: *Don't waste your life being ordinary.* Celina realized now with some measure of despair that she hadn't heard her grandmother say those words in a while. Had she given up on her only grandchild? Had she settled on the notion that *ordinary* was what Celina was?

Five dull and uninterrupted miles later, Celina parked in front of Mansfield's Grain and Feed. Beneath the feed store's sign hung a smaller, newer sign that read DIME BOX PUBLIC LIBRARY.

The library was Celina's contribution to the town. For four years she had driven the beat-up VW the round trip of sixty-six miles to and from the town of Brenham, getting her degree in library science from Blinn College.

Sheepskin in hand, she had somehow talked Dime Box's three-member city council into not only purchasing three hundred books and a used computer for a town library, but into hiring her as the librarian as well. When Dewey Mansfield stepped forward and announced that Celina could use the entire east wall of his feed store at no charge, she was in business. Now, customers buying horse liniment, bird feed or pet supplies could stop and check out a book or two.

With a great sense of pride, she had brought the most beloved thing in her life, *books*, to her community family. She dutifully logged the precious books—paperback and hardcover alike—into the computer and organized them on the shelves using the Dewey decimal system. When she told patrons the name of the system and how to find a book by looking at the numbers on the spines, of course they thought she referred to Dewey Mansfield and remarked that they had always known Dewey was smart. She didn't bother to try and explain.

Celina had been raised with a book in her hand. Before she could read for herself, she pestered anyone older than she to read the magic words to her. When she was old enough to read on her own, she escaped to her choice of worlds every night.

As a girl, she had especially loved the Nancy Drew and Robin Kane mysteries, had even dreamed of being a private investigator. But that wasn't what nice girls in Texas did. Nice girls made their families proud, nice girls followed the rules of etiquette, nice girls died a long, agonizing death by boredom. She was a nice girl and rigor mortis was setting in.

"Mornin' Dew," she said when she saw Dewey—it was the same greeting she gave him every morning.

She heard his deep chuckle. The play on words seemed to please him. He, too, thought the Dewey decimal system referred to him.

She didn't have the heart to tell him the difference, either.

"Mornin', little miss. Sam was in earlier. He was on his way out of town, said he'd call you later."

Mental sigh. And Sam Crenshaw was perfectly safe in assuming that she would be here. Another reminder of the mind-numbing predictability of her life.

"Okay, thanks," she said to Dewey, her mind now on Sam Crenshaw.

He was an engineer with a computer hardware manufacturing company in Austin. She had known him forever. They had dated off and on since high school. Well, it couldn't really be called dating. It was more like just going somewhere together because there was no one else to go with. Because Sam and she were seen together often, most people in town had concluded that someday she and Sam would marry.

Not once had Celina ever considered that happy ending. Sam was like her life in Dime Box—comfortable and predictable. And boring. He saw everything in black-and-white and had the imagination of a pancake. She didn't doubt that he felt some sort of affection for her. She felt something for him, too, but it wasn't that white-hot passion she had read about in romance novels. Something could be said for loyalty and dependability, but Lord, what wouldn't she give for a connection across a crowded room. Desire and wild abandon. A part of her refused to give up hope.

She walked past the store's front counter, then the length of the building, to her desk. Well, it wasn't a real desk. It was actually a folding card table on which her computer and a phone sat.

"How's that pretty grandma of yours?" Dewey called after her.

Celina smiled. She knew of the romance growing between Dewey and her grandmother. That was just fine. She was glad her grandmother had found someone. It was cute that both of them thought their big secret was safe. Celina had suspected from the beginning that Dewey had donated the use of his feed-store wall to establish a link to Granny Dee. "Okay, Dew."

As soon as she had taken care of her morning chores, Celina sat down to surf the Internet, as she always did when the library traffic was slow. *And let's face it*, she told herself. *When was traffic not slow?*

She scanned two news Web sites, catching up on national news, stopped off at a few shopping sites and ended up on the site of the National Association of Private Investigators. The real-life cases, posted for viewers to read, held her as captivated as the Nancy Drew stories had. But the NAPI cases were better. They were true.

It was here, on this day of extreme restiveness, that Celina was hit with an epiphany. In the bottom left-hand corner of her monitor screen was a link inviting her to see more details on the upcoming NAPI convention being held in New York City. Among all the tempting topics were seminars explaining how to start your own investigation service.

Celina shot upright in the chair and squealed. New York City. Her entire life, Granny Dee had spoken about her first great love, the place of her upbringing, New York City. She had been a performer with the Radio City Rockettes when she fell for a handsome Texas cowboy competing in a rodeo in Madison Square Garden. When the cowboy left New York, returning to the Lone Star State, a leggy Rockette was on his arm.

Still, as much as she loved the Texas cowboy, Granny Dee never lost her love for the Big Apple. She talked of it so often Celina felt as if it were her second home. The opportunity to learn how to be a detective, in the city to which she felt a kinship, had to be kismet.

Dewey leaned over the counter, craning his neck. "You all right back there?"

"I'm fine," she answered. "Dewey, have you ever been to New York City?"

The storeowner ambled toward her, his hands stuffed into his pockets. "I've never been out of Texas. I joined the Air Force when I was a kid. Intended to see the world. But I never got farther than Dyess Air Force Base in Abilene. Always regretted that, too."

Celina looked at him with renewed interest. "Really? You do regret it?"

"You bet. I plan on doing some traveling one day, before I get too old." His face took on a plaintive expression. "If I was your age, I wouldn't let anything stop me. I'd like to see New York. I've wished many a time that I had seen them two towers before they came down."

Celina looked at Dewey a few seconds more, a plan of action taking root. "How'd you like to come to supper at the house this evening, Dewey?"

His mouth tipped into a shy grin. "Why, that'd be just fine, Celina."

"Good. You know what a good cook Granny Dee is. Come at seven o'clock."

He grinned bigger. "Okay. I'll be there."

Celina couldn't wait to call Granny Dee and tell her. As Dewey ambled up to the front of the store whistling, she picked up the phone receiver and keyed in her home number.

"Celina, honey," her grandmother said when Celina told her about their guest, "you know I don't mind you asking Mr. Mansfield for supper. Or any of your friends. It's just that you should have given me more time."

Granny Dee sounded anxious and out of breath. Celina pictured her scurrying about, wiping imaginary dust from the mantel. She knew the invitation posed no imposition on her grandmother, who had recently lost her job of thirty years as teller in the town's only bank. The bank had closed its doors forever. Now Granny Dee cleaned her home, cooked and gardened.

"Granny Dee, it's only eleven o'clock. He isn't coming over until seven. That's eight hours. What in the world do you need to do that would take more than eight hours?"

"I don't have anything laid out of the freezer, my hair is a mess and the house needs a good cleaning."

Celina lowered her voice. "Granny, Dewey lives in a trailer with two old dogs. He eats pork and beans with Fritos every day for lunch. I'll bet he's lucky to get one home-cooked meal a year, on Christmas. But if you want me to tell him it's not a good time—"

"No, no. That isn't necessary. I'll just throw something together."

Celina relaxed into a big smile. Granny Dee never "threw" anything together. By seven o'clock, the dining table would be loaded with delicious home cooking that she would serve with the flair of a four-star restaurant. The house would be spotless and Granny Dee would be beautiful. Celina had figured out long ago that for her grandmother, the protestation was almost as much fun as the preparation and the presentation.

"When I get home, I'll help," Celina promised.

"Is Sam coming, too?"

"No, not this evening." The last thing Celina wanted was Sam's voice of reason and good sense interfering with her conversation with her grandmother.

The remainder of Celina's day passed briskly. Dime Box's only beauty salon had started a book club. Each member was to read and report on a different book every Saturday evening. Half a dozen women had been in and out of the library picking up books—except that in Dime Box no one ever simply came in and went out. Gossip was exchanged, weather was discussed and family photos were shown.

Someone usually had a son, nephew or grandson he or she wanted Celina to meet. In the past, she had accepted a few of those "fix-ups," but nowadays, she politely declined. The men had never lived up to their loved ones' hype, and it was too awkward explaining later why she and the fix-up weren't becoming a couple.

Finding heroes in books had always been less complicated. Living vicariously through the pages had been enough. But no longer. She needed a life, she needed an adventure. Dear God, she needed something.

At five o'clock, she logged off her computer, grabbed her purse and started for the door. She had walked only a couple of steps when her cell phone rang. A glance at caller ID brought an involuntary sigh. Sam. She didn't know if she was ready for a conversation with him. She was excited about a trip to New York, but if anyone could throw cold water on her enthusiasm, it would be Sam.

They almost always had a weekend outing together, so she couldn't just disappear for a week. She wished she could, but she wasn't brought up that way. She had to tell him her plans. She returned to her chair and flipped open the phone. "Hi, Sam."

"Hey. Have you got dinner plans?"

"Granny Dee and I are entertaining Dewey this evening at the house."

"Dewey. You mean the old guy who owns the feed store?"

A ripple of annoyance brought a frown to her brow. "He isn't old," she whispered, lest Dewey hear her. "He's Granny Dee's age."

"Whatever you say," Sam said in an appeasing tone. "Don't you think your grandmother would rather be alone with him? Why would you want to be underfoot?"

Celina tried not to be irritable, but Sam and his condescending attitude were leaning on her last patience nerve.

"I'm sure she would, but dinner was my idea. I want to talk to Granny Dee and Dewey together."

Sam chuckled and spoke to her again in his "tolerant" voice. "Is this a birds-and-bees conversation? Did you catch them making out?"

Celina gasped. "Honestly, Sam."

"You're the one being all secretive. Why do you have to talk to them together?"

Celina wanted to shout, *"It's none of your business!"* If she wanted to perform a striptease for the two of them, she would, and it still wouldn't be any of Sam's concern. But knowing him as she did, the truth might be more shocking than the idea of her doing a striptease. "I'm going to New York City to a private investigators convention," she said in a rush, "and I want Dewey to help me persuade Granny Dee to go with me or convince her she doesn't have to worry about me going alone."

Long silence. For a minute she wondered if they had lost their connection. Then she heard his laughter. She could also hear the creaking of his expensive leather chair and she secretly hoped it would topple and land him on his butt.

"I swear, Celina, for an intelligent woman, you come up with the most ridiculous ideas."

"It isn't ridiculous. It's something worth doing. And furthermore, Sam Crenshaw, I don't remember a single time in my life when I've done something ridiculous."

"You don't call working hard for four years at getting a

degree, then using it to open a library in Dime Box a ridiculous idea?"

Now it was Celina's turn to be silent as she attempted to tamp down the anger his attitude had spurred.

He broke the silence. "Oh, come on, now. I've made you mad. You know I didn't mean to. But you have to admit, Celina, there were many places you could have gone and gotten a job and made something of yourself."

She made a mental gasp. "I'm sorry I've disappointed you, Sam," she said in an even tone. "It's been my lifelong desire to make *you* proud of me. And as for making something of myself, I think I'll make myself absent from your life."

You elitist, pompous, chauvinistic, over-educated frat rat!

She snapped the phone shut, threw it into her purse and headed for the feed store's front door, passing the open doorway to Dewey's office. "See you at the house, Dewey."

"I sure hope I'm not putting you and your grandmother out," Dewey said, rising from his desk chair. "I haven't had a home-cooked meal since Christmas. My sister over in Austin always puts on a big spread."

Celina mentally patted herself on her back for her astute observation. She would be a great detective. "Our evenings are pretty uneventful. Granny Dee loves company. Having someone over for supper will be nice for her and me both."

"Lord, I know how that is. My nights are less busy than my days, and well"—he looked down and grinned—"you've seen my days."

He was leaning against the doorway, his legs crossed at the ankle, thumbs hooked casually in his belt loops. Though he was in his sixties, he was a handsome man in a rugged way. She could see how her grandmother might feel an attraction.

Bidding him one final good-bye, she strode to the rusty VW and tossed her purse on the passenger seat. Inside it, she had stuffed printouts detailing the NAPI conference in New York. Celina was hoping her grandmother would want to go, too, but whether she did or not, Celina was determined to attend.

It wasn't that she needed her grandmother's permission. She wasn't a child. But it would be hard to leave without her blessing. She was hoping Dewey could help. She didn't win a lot of debates with her grandmother, and using Dewey to help tip the scale in her favor wasn't unsportsmanlike. It was more like leveling the playing field.

She wouldn't mind if Granny Dee went, either. She had a niggling fear in the back of her mind about going alone and being alone in such a huge city. Being in the company of a former New Yorker would definitely make the whole experience more interesting and more fun.

Less than fifteen minutes later she parked at the side of Granny Dee's brick home.

"I'm home," Celina called as she went through the back door into the kitchen. The strong aroma of pot roast and Pine-Sol greeted her.

"Something sure smells good." She noted that the dining table had been set with the best linen, silverware and crystal glasses. Usually, when she and her grandmother dined, they ate in the kitchen with the TV on.

"It's just a roast with some vegetables thrown in. I made a salad and those individual little loaves of bread you like so much." Granny Dee's face was flushed, her voice filled with excitement. "Oh, and I made a chocolate layer cake and a cobbler from those peaches we canned last summer. I really didn't go to a lot of trouble."

"Well, it looks beautiful and so do you. Now, I'm going to change clothes. What can I do to help you before I shower?"

"Not a thing. I've got everything under control."

As Celina left the room, something struck her. Her grandmother always had everything under control, while she, Celina, just sort of floated along like a leaf in a ditch after a rainstorm. It was time to take control, and tonight, she thought as she raised her head high and hugged her purse closer to her chest, was the night.

chapter four

*L*ate in the day, after all of the Styling Station's customers had departed—and the salon had been cleaned and Debbie Sue and Edwina had said their good nights—Debbie Sue sat down with the conference information she had printed out. She felt a thrill just reading the details.

New York City. Just the words teemed with excitement in her mind. She had traveled in the west and the Midwest back in the days when she rodeoed, but that wasn't the same as a trip to New York. As a barrel-racing star, she had dreamed of riding in Madison Square Garden.

She had to call her mom and tell her the news. She picked up the phone receiver and keyed in her mom's number.

Debbie Sue's mom, Virginia, was a composer of country-western songs and had had several successes. After living for years in Salt Lick as a divorcée, she had remarried recently and now lived in Nashville. She answered the phone on the third *burrr.*

"Hi, Mom. It's me.

"Well, hi, sweetheart. How's your day been?"

"Mom, guess where we're going."

"Um, California."

Debbie Sue could scarcely contain her excitement. "New York City. Mom, we got invited to speak at the NAPI conference."

"'We' . . . ? And what's NAPI?"

"The National Association of Private Investigators. Ed and I are going to be guest speakers. Ain't that a kick?"

Now her mother's excitement equaled her own. "Oh, Debbie Sue. I'm so thrilled."

"You just don't know how great this is, Mom. It means huge publicity for the Domestic Equalizers. And it means that people at the top of the game know who we are and are taking us seriously. It means Ed and I are not a joke."

Of course, she didn't intend to tell her mother that the Domestic Equalizers had been the second choice. Considering that Mr. Scurlock could have called thousands of other people before he called them, she thought second wasn't such a bad place.

"Sweetheart, I've never thought you and Edwina were a joke. I'll bet Buddy is so proud."

Debbie Sue wasn't so sure of that. She had supported and cheered his rise through the ranks of the Department of

Public Safety, and most of the time he had applauded her success as well. Sometimes, though, he was a little overprotective of her and needed some assurance she wasn't doing something crazy that would put her in harm's way. "I haven't told him yet."

Her mother made a little gasp. "Well, why not?"

"I haven't seen him since this morning. I'll tell him tonight."

"So what are you going to speak about?"

"We're supposed to just tell how we go about spying on cheating spouses. You know, give tips."

Virginia Miller laughed. "I'm sure you and Edwina are very capable of doing that. Just stay away from murder."

"We will, Mom. After that craziness in Haskell, I had to promise Buddy I would never go near another dead body. He's getting ready to take the Ranger test, you know. I can't be doing things that distract him. Or worse yet, embarrass him."

Debbie Sue and her mother always had plenty to talk about. They moved on to other things and an hour later, they hung up. She folded the pages filled with information she had printed about the conference, slid them inside her purse, turned off the lights and headed home.

Driving across the cattle-guard at the entrance to her and Buddy's rural home, Debbie Sue spotted Rocket Man grazing in the pasture off to her left. Rocket Man, her brown paint gelding, was now twenty and retired. Years back, he had galloped her to barrel-racing championships. These days he grazed and lazed in the West Texas sunshine, and occasionally, she treated him to his favorite. Twinkies and beer.

Buddy's black-and-white DPS car was parked under the shed attached to one end of the house. Damn, he had reached home before her. She had hoped to have supper on the table by the time he arrived.

She thought again of the conference. Perhaps Buddy would like to go. They hadn't had a vacation in a long time. Not a real vacation anyway. Each year they drove four hundred miles to the Fort Worth Stock Show and Rodeo. They saw old friends, watched the rodeo and strolled the exhibit barns. They dined at Joe T. Garcia's, danced at Billy Bob's and walked hand in hand around Sundance Square in downtown Fort Worth. It was wonderful, but a long weekend in Fort Worth wasn't a substitute for a real vacation.

Circling the house to park in the rear, she thought about what Buddy's response to her going to New York might be. It would all depend on the kind of day he'd had patrolling the Texas highways. She would test the water first. "No point putting on your bathing suit if you ain't going swimming," she mumbled.

As she scooted out of the Silverado, three dogs yelping and dancing in frenzied excitement greeted her. That was what she loved about her dogs. Whether she had been gone all day or just stepped out of the house for five minutes, they always showed the same enthusiasm.

What she saw when she entered the back door was the payoff for a long day on her feet. All six feet and two inches of Buddy Overstreet standing at the kitchen counter, Crock-Pot lid in hand, his cop suit protected by a red ruffled apron.

In all her thirty-five years she had never loved another man the way she loved Buddy. They had literally grown up together. Married young, in love and pregnant, they had made mistakes attributed to youth. After the baby they made hadn't survived, she had gone off the deep end for a while and Buddy had divorced her. But that was the past. This was the present and the future.

"Hey, babe," he said, looking up and grinning. "Thanks for putting this stew in the Crock-Pot. You must have done it after I left this morning."

He took a spoon from the drawer, dipped out a spoonful of stew, blew on it and tasted. "Oh, man, that's good. I made some corn bread and—"

His words were cut off by Debbie Sue's mouth covering his. He pulled her close and returned her kiss, the exchange growing more urgent. They pushed apart and she looked up into his chocolate-colored eyes. She and he both burst into laughter.

"Damn, woman, it's good to see you, too," he said. "If I'd known you had a thing for a man in a dress, I would've put one on sooner."

Debbie Sue giggled and flipped the apron skirt. "This isn't a dress, but even if it was, I'd think you looked sexy. I have to admit, though, I liked you better the way you looked this morning in the shower."

"Oh, yeah?" He bobbed his eyebrows and fingered one corner of his black mustache. "Want to see it again?"

She giggled again and stepped away from him. "Later, stud."

She would love to drag him into the bedroom and have her way with him, but in light of what she had on her mind, she didn't want a display of passion to appear to be insincere. She pulled plates and bowls down from the cabinet. "Did anything fun happen to you today?"

Buddy was now dropping ice cubes into tall glasses. "Just the usual. Speed demons and drug smugglers. Nothing really worth repeating. You?"

Debbie Sue swallowed hard, recognizing the opening that had jumped up in front of her. "Edwina and I had a big surprise."

"Lemme guess. Ray McCowan finally paid his bill?"

Debbie Sue laughed. "No, nothing as miraculous as that. He still thinks he doesn't owe us since we never did find proof that his wife was having an affair with Mike Ditka. The best we ever came up with was a flirtation with a priest."

"I don't think anyone would ever mistake Ditka for a priest. Did you ever find out why he was so convinced it was Coach Ditka?"

"She told him it was. Poor thing. Her mind and her body are in two different zip codes."

Buddy chuckled. "If it's not money from Ray, I give up. What's the big surprise?"

Debbie Sue drew a deep breath, cleared her throat and took the plunge. "The Equalizers have been asked to speak at a conference for the National Association of Private Investigators in New York City."

There, it was out. And all in one breath, too. She carried the dishes to the table without looking back for Buddy's reaction. She wasn't sure what to expect. She waited for words, but none came.

She returned to the stove, acting casual, as if she and Edwina received such a prestigious invitation every day. He was stuffing his hand into an oven mitt and looking at her. "Why, Flash, that's great. That's a huge compliment to you and Edwina."

She couldn't control the grin that crawled across her mouth. "It is, isn't it?"

Barely pausing for a breath, she filled him in on all the details. "And," she concluded, "there will be detectives from the New York City police department there, too. I know they're not as cool as the Texas Rangers, but it would be a great time for you to meet and talk to your New York peers."

"When did you say it is?" He bent over and pulled the pan of corn bread from the oven.

"I didn't, but it's in two weeks."

He set the hot corn bread on top of the stove and yanked off the oven mitt. "That's the week before the test. I'll be studying like crazy that week. I can't possibly go anywhere."

Buddy's path toward becoming a Texas Ranger had included four years as the sheriff of Salt Lick, two years working as a Texas DPS trooper and years of college courses. In three weeks he would be taking the test.

Debbie Sue frowned. "Damn, it is, isn't it?" She chewed on her bottom lip, thinking. Suddenly an idea hit her. "You could stay in the room and study while I'm at the conference. I wouldn't bother you." She wrapped her arms around his waist. "Except at night."

"Babe, I can't take off two weeks in a row. I'm using the only week of vacation time I have left to go to Austin for the test."

Debbie Sue nestled her face into his chest. "Then maybe I shouldn't go——"

"Now, that's just plain foolish." Buddy set her away and held her at arm's length. "You and Edwina have worked hard for something like this. This might work out good for both of us. I can use that week alone to study without being distracted by you." He nuzzled her neck. "Besides, didn't you say the place will be crawling with cops? At least I'll know you're safe."

After a long, luxurious shower and a shampoo, Celina dried her hair, gathered it and wrapped it into a French twist. She pinned it and turned from side to side to examine the change. With her black hair and blue eyes, she had been told she resembled the actress Courtney Cox. She was a foot taller than Courtney Cox, but that was beside the point.

New York City. Me, Celina Phillips, in New York City.

Finally aware that she had lost track of time in her woolgathering, she finished dressing and went out to the living room. Dewey was sitting on the sofa and her grandmother was serving him a glass of iced tea.

He rose and nodded to her as she entered. "Good evening, Celina."

She spotted a bouquet of yellow roses in the middle of the table and wondered where in the world Dewey had gotten roses at the end of the day. Of the many things Dime Box didn't have, one was a florist. He had to have driven somewhere out of town. It was fun to see him wooing her grandmother and striving for his most courtly behavior. She forced herself not to chuckle. "Hi, Dewey. Did Granny Dee tell you what's on the menu tonight? I'm starving."

"She sure did. I was hungry when I came through that door, and now that I've smelled that roast, I have to agree with you. I'm starving, too. If it's half as good as your grandma is pretty, we're gonna have a meal fit for a king."

"Oh, stop that." Granny Dee gave him a simpering smile. She might have been born in New York, but tonight, dressed in a frilly blue dress with tiny bows at the sleeves and matching blue bows in her hair, she looked every bit the Southern belle.

She ushered them into the dining area, her hand lingering just a second longer than necessary on Dewey's forearm. "You sit here, at the head of the table, Dewey. I believe a man belongs at the head of the table."

Celina could almost see Dewey's chest swell. She would give anything to possess half the charm Granny Dee doled out. But then, perhaps she did. She had been able to convince the city to back her on something that wasn't exactly a financial windfall for anyone.

Midway through the meal Celina found the opportunity she had been waiting for, a brief silence in the otherwise lively conversation. "Guess what I ran across online today?"

Dewey and Granny Dee both looked in her direction, waiting.

Celina continued. "An announcement of a conference for private investigators. It's for detectives or aspiring detectives and invited guests from the New York police department. They have classes and workshops telling how to start a detective agency."

Granny Dee put down her fork and smiled. "Why, sweetheart, I haven't heard you talk about that since you were a teenager."

"But I didn't quit thinking about it. I never felt it was something I could really do, but those women in Salt Lick have done it, and going to this conference will help me decide if I want to do it, too."

Dewey leaned toward Granny Dee. "Did she say 'detective'? Like a private eye? James Bond and all that?"

Granny Dee smiled sweetly. "Not quite, Dewey. James Bond is a spy. When is the conference, Celina?"

"In two weeks."

"My goodness, that's not very long off. Where is it?"

Taking a deep breath, Celina straightened in her chair and held her head a little higher. "It's in New York City. Would you like to go with me?"

Celina watched and waited. Her grandmother neither moved nor spoke. It was worse than she had imagined. She had thrown the most important person in her life into a catatonic state. She looked to Dewey for the support, but his gaze only volleyed back and forth between her and her grandmother.

Finally, Granny Dee smiled at Dewey, then Celina. "No, sweetheart. The only thing I have left from there are memories, and they're better off resting. This is my home now."

Celina felt her nervousness return and for an instant she wondered if she should make the trip.

Granny Dee's hand covered hers. "But angel, you're going to need a better wardrobe than jeans and T-shirts for New York City."

chapter five

"Thank you, Mr. Scurlock. . . . Yes. Yes, I understand. . . . Nope, no questions. I think you've told me everything I need to know. See you in two weeks."

Debbie Sue returned the receiver to its cradle and spun around in her chair. "That's it. We're going to New York City. Am I the only one who finds it funny that Scurlock rhymes with Sherlock?"

"Yes," Edwina answered, "apparently you are."

"As in Sherlock Holmes, Ed. He was a detective."

Edwina returned a "humph."

Ignoring her friend's sarcasm, Debbie Sue forged ahead. "I still can't believe Buddy and Vic were so sweet about us going out of town together. Vic didn't put up a fight at all, huh?"

Edwina was adding another layer of hair spray to Lloydena

Blanton's helmet hairdo. "It wasn't exactly a fight. He did say something like 'I might as well be pissin' in the wind.' But no, no fight."

Stepping back and fanning the hair spray fog with her hand, Edwina grinned. "I'm just kidding. He's tickled to death. You forget, he's been all over the world and seen everything. He wants me to see things, too. Before we got married, I'd never been anywhere but Vegas, you know."

"Listen, girls," Lloydena said through the veil of lacquer, "if y'all are serious about going up there, y'all be real careful. That's the meanest place on the face o' the earth. Carry your purses real close to your body. Don't be looking around like some damn-fool out-of-towner. Try to blend in."

She looked from Edwina to Debbie Sue, as if she wanted to make sure she had their attention before continuing. "Don't get on one o' them subways, whatever you do. And never, I mean *never*, make eye contact with anybody. Keep your head down, eyes on the ground. There's rapists, murderers, robbers and terrorists everywhere."

Debbie Sue and Edwina exchanged looks and burst into laughter.

"Hell, Lloydena, you just described my last family reunion," Edwina said.

"And my high-school reunion," Debbie Sue added. "Lloydena, when were you ever in New York City? Where did you get this information?"

"Well, I've never actually *been* there. But I watch the news and something terrible's always happening in that place." She gave a knowing single nod.

"You're not confusing the evening news with *Law and Order* again, are you?" Edwina asked, winking in Debbie Sue's direction. "Remember *24*? We almost never convinced you that Kiefer Sutherland wasn't really a serial killer."

"I might be confused, but what if I am? Just where do you think those writers get their ideas? They get 'em from things that happen there." Lloydena began pawing through her purse.

"Actually," Debbie Sue said with a contemplative frown, "Dallas and Houston, statistically speaking, have higher crime rates than New York City. I heard that on TV news."

"Nooo," Lloydena said, wide-eyed. "Why, I don't believe that."

"It's a fact. I also read it in some of the stuff Buddy brought home."

"Humph. That's because that Yankee riffraff keeps moving down here and bringing their criminal ways with them," Lloydena said with smug finality. "I thought a long time ago they should have built a fence without a gate clear from Texarkana to New Mexico. As for me, myself, I wouldn't go to New York. Not for all the tea in China. But if y'all decide to, just remember what I said."

She hefted her bulk out of the chair, waddled over to the payout counter and laid out two twenty-dollar bills. "Now, I'm fixin' to get some supper on the table and make some time for my sweetie. He and I are having playtime tonight, if you know what I mean." She wiggled her eyebrows and grinned. She sent a glance over her shoulder as she left through the front door. "Y'all be careful, now, you hear?"

Edwina waited until Lloydena was out the door. "I'd rather hand out ice water and free fans in hell than spend an evening with her sweetie. I might be in danger of losing my life in New York City, but I guaran-dam-tee you, somebody would be dead if I had to put up with Butch Blanton. And it wouldn't be me."

Debbie Sue laughed. "There's proof right there that God made someone for everyone. It's the Noah's Ark theory. Everything comes in twos."

"Well, I'm here to tell you that I'd come in two if ol' Butch even acted like he was gonna touch me. It's not so much his looks. It's his fear of soap and water that puts me off."

"You're a hard woman to please, Edwina Martin. Now, let's talk about what we're taking to New York. We might need to find time for some shopping."

"Shopping? For what? I've got a closet full of clothes."

Debbie Sue fidgeted in her chair. Clothing—the sort of, or lack of—was never an easy subject to broach with Ed. The woman had her own idea of fashion. Unconventional, unapologetic and unlike anything most people had ever seen. "I'm just saying, Ed, we've got to be sure we look professional. Sharp. We want to show those folks in New York that we're not small-town hicks."

Edwina removed a shoulder-length earring and tugged on her left earlobe. "But we *are* small-town hicks."

"But we don't have to look like it," Debbie Sue said. "We should go to the mall in Midland and let Allison Freeman fix us up."

"I don't see anything wrong with the way we look."

Debbie Sue slowly looked her friend up, down and up again. Edwina's leggy five-foot-ten frame was made even taller by the three-inch stacked heels on her mustard-yellow cowboy boots. Today she had on skin-tight turquoise jeans, a white T-shirt decorated with a rhinestone eagle and a bright yellow sash tied just below her waistline.

"Hell, I'm not talking about the way I'm dressed now," she said, shifting her weight from one foot to the other. "Don't you think I've got any sense at all? I'd never wear these boots if I had to do a lot of walking. They're made for looking, not walking."

Celina pushed away from her computer and rubbed her eyes while she waited for the printer to spit out more pages. She'd been to every Internet site that offered discounted travel fares and hotel rates. Everything was out of her budget, that is, if she actually had a budget. The only things skimpier than her budget were her viable choices.

The conference was being held at one of the newer hotels in Manhattan, the Anson, with an address that made her pulse quicken—1500 Broadway. The block of rooms set aside for attendees was booked to the max and the undiscounted cost of a room for five days was unthinkable.

She had to spend as little as possible because she had so little to work with. She wouldn't even consider asking her grandmother for a loan, though she knew Granny Dee wouldn't hesitate in handing it over.

Granny Dee would move heaven and earth to help, Celina knew, but she still hadn't regained her footing from the loss of her job. She had only a small pension from the bank and an even smaller Social Security check each month. The insurance money she had received after the passing of her husband sat in the bank untouched, gathering interest and waiting for an unexpected emergency. Her cowboy hero had done his best to take care of her, even after his death.

When Granny Dee had mentioned the money, Celina gently reminded her that this was not an emergency. She would pay for the trip herself. Celina knew this was something she needed to do on her own. It was a matter of pride.

Her data printed, she rolled back to the keyboard and minimized the Excel spreadsheet she had built so she could scan her choices with one sweep of the eye.

The numbers glaring back at her made her sigh. It was amazing, the cost of pride these days.

Her preference was to fly nonstop from Houston to La Guardia. The fare would have fallen within the boundaries of her funds had she known about the conference weeks earlier. But purchasing a round-trip ticket for use in less than two weeks meant paying through the nose. And the pocketbook.

Traveling by train sounded romantic and full of intrigue, but it was no cheaper than flying and took days instead of hours.

Her choices dwindled to two: Driving her VW, which would ultimately put her to hitchhiking, or taking the bus. She was weighing the likelihood of her VW making the trip when common sense tapped her on the shoulder and whispered that the bus was the only way.

She looked again at the information in the "Bus" column. One day, eighteen hours and five minutes, one way. She covered her face with her hands and moaned.

She had never traveled by bus, but she had heard horror stories from those who had. *Forty-two hours and five minutes.* Dear God, she would just have to find the bright side of the situation.

She decided to look at the bus ride as an adventure. The bus route would take her through parts of the country she had never seen. She would wipe the dust from her camera lens and snap a picture or two. She would also lug a sack full of snack food, carry her crossword-puzzle book and the newest Nancy Martin mystery she had been saving for a rainy weekend.

On an online search engine she found other hotels in the New York area. Unfortunately, there was only one available during that particular week, but at least it was one she could afford—the YWCA. It was five miles from the conference site and cost only twenty dollars a night.

Arriving on the bus, staying at the Y. Yee-haw. How much more country mouse could she get? The only thing that would make it more evident would be if she showed up with her hair in pigtails, lugging a suitcase held together by a rope and cradling a squealing pig in one arm.

She was concentrating to returning her breathing to normal when she spotted Dewey watching her.

"How'd it go?" Dewey said from behind the counter. He had been unloading sacks of chicken feed all day and had paid little attention to her. "Did you find what you needed?"

Celina beamed. "Sure did, Dew. In two weeks I'll be in New York City. Isn't that incredible?"

"Yup. You must be danged excited."

"Excited, scared, anxious, you name it. I'm all of that." She laughed. "I've had my credit card since college and have barely used it. It's a wonder they don't call to check on who's making these charges."

Dewey began to count the money in the till, closing the register for the day. "What airline you flying on?"

"I'm not. It costs too much. I'm taking Greyhound. But I don't mind," she added quickly. "I'll see lots of scenery. I'll catch up on some reading and things."

"That sounds like a real fine trip, Miss Celina. An adventure you can tell your kids about." His voice was soft and soothing. The reassurance made her feel like a child waking from a nightmare, as if he were trying to convince her that everything would be all right.

"You want me to keep an eye on your books and stuff while you're gone? I won't be able to answer questions for folks like you do or operate the computer, but I sure don't mind helping out."

"Thanks, but that won't be necessary. Granny Dee and I talked about it last night. She's going to work here while I'm gone."

That bit of news startled him so, he dropped the loose change in his hands. Coins hit the floor and rolled in every direction.

"Oh, no! Let me help you." Celina dropped to her knees and began gathering the coins that had scattered.

"My goodness," Dewey said, kneeling to help her. "What made me do that? Tell you what, whatever you find, you keep."

Celina grinned. Super. Her money woes were over. There was a solution to every problem if you just looked in the right place.

chapter six

Debbie Sue rolled over and plumped her pillow for the umpteenth time. The Worthington Hotel in downtown Fort Worth might be a nice place to bunk, but she didn't like sleeping with strange pillows, in strange beds, in strange cities. Even Buddy lying next to her, breathing in rhythmic slumber, didn't lessen her anxiety.

She, Buddy, Edwina and Vic had driven earlier in the day to Fort Worth. All flights from Midland to New York started with the first leg on a small plane routed to DFW Airport, between Fort Worth and Dallas. Edwina had made it clear that she would not fly anywhere in a "souped-up maxi pad." The drive from Salt Lick to the city was less trouble than

Edwina would have been if she had been forced to fly on a small plane from Midland to Dallas.

They'd had a wonderful dinner, then walked to la Madeleine's for dessert before retiring to their rooms. She and Buddy had shared a long bath in the hotel bathroom's oversize tub. Of course, they had ended up making love. Normally, she would have slept like a baby following all of that, but not tonight.

She reached out, turned the clock radio toward her and groaned. The illuminated display screen glowed in vivid red numbers in the pitch-black room: 2:15. She had to be up in four hours and she hadn't been asleep at all. Pushing the clock back to its original position on the bedside table, she accidentally touched the button on the side panel. Suddenly loud Tejano music erupted from the radio and vibrated her eardrums.

Buddy's upper body sprang straight up. "What the fuck . . . ?"

Debbie Sue began frantically punching buttons in the dark. The music stopped, replaced by an enthusiastic announcer's loud voice. *"Saludo y oyen la música fantástica de pequeno Joe!"*

Trumpets and accordions blared in a loud and frenzied musical blend.

Cussing a blue streak, Debbie Sue leaped from the bed, switched on the bedside lamp and grabbed the radio's electrical cord with both hands. She yanked and the music abruptly stopped again.

"The music of Little Joe?" Buddy growled. "Who the hell is that? What the hell's going on, Flash?"

Debbie Sue dropped to the edge of the mattress, her heart pounding. "Oh, my God. I was just trying to find out what time it is. I couldn't sleep."

Buddy scowled. "And you thought a Tejano band would improve your chances?"

"No. I accidentally turned it on." She stifled a giggle. "I'm so sorry I woke you up."

The words were no sooner out of her mouth than the phone rang.

"Oh, that's okay," Buddy grumbled. "I needed to answer the phone anyway." He picked up the receiver. "Overstreet," he snapped.

Debbie Sue could hear a voice broadcasting through the handset. Edwina. "What the hell's going on over there? You two having a party?"

"Debbie Sue couldn't sleep," Buddy said. "Here, I'll let you talk to her." He passed the receiver to Debbie Sue, flopped back onto the mattress and covered his head with the pillow. Debbie Sue pressed the phone to her ear. "Hey, Ed."

"I can't sleep, either. Been awake all damn night. Case of the nerves, I guess. Did Buddy go back to sleep?"

"He's fixin' to. I'll see you in the morning, Ed."

"Don't hang up. Listen, I've been laying here thinking about the plane getting hijacked."

"Good Lord, Ed, why would you worry about something like that?"

"Same damn reason I worry about anything. In case it happens, I want to be prepared."

"You mean like getting yourself right with God?"

"Hell, no. I always stay on His good side. There's just some folks you don't want to piss off. . . . I'm talking about the guys that try to take over the plane. Let's agree to fight like hell. Nothing's off limits. Eyes, balls and dicks go first."

"Eyes, balls and dicks?" Debbie Sue repeated. "In that order?"

"Promise me, Debbie Sue."

"Okay, I promise. Eyes, balls and dicks. Now, let's hang up and get some sleep."

"Okay, shug. I feel better with that out of the way. 'Night."

Debbie Sue shook her head and replaced the receiver in its cradle.

"Eyes, balls and dicks?" Buddy muttered into his pillow. "What was that all about?"

"Don't ask. But the whole world can rest easier now."

Morning came. Following a gourmet breakfast in the hotel dining room, the foursome started for the airport. With the skill of a local cab driver, Buddy maneuvered their crew-cab pickup from the downtown Fort Worth hotel through the snarl of rush hour traffic and multistory overpasses.

Debbie Sue sat in awe of the crush of cars and people and the bustling activity. "Every time we come here, they've built a bunch of new freeways and a bunch of new buildings."

Half an hour later they reached the airport entrance. Not having been to DFW Airport in several years, she had forgotten that it looked more like a small city than an air terminal. She might have thought she had reached another one of those bedroom communities that lay between Fort Worth and Dallas if another snarl of traffic hadn't given the airport entrance away. "How in God's name do people drive in this friggin' nightmare every day? I'd lose my ever-lovin' mind."

"You'd get used to it after a while," Buddy said.

"That's what they said about leprosy," Vic added with a laugh from the backseat.

Debbie Sue turned to join in on the joke, but stopped short. "What's wrong with Ed?"

Edwina's head lay against the back of the seat, her mouth loosely hanging open.

Vic reached over and gently swept her bangs from her forehead. "She didn't sleep worth a damn last night. Not to mention she took medication to keep her from being airsick."

"Good Lord, how much did she take?" Debbie Sue asked.

"I'll wake her up." Vic gently shook her shoulder. "Mama Doll. Baby, wake up."

Edwina raised her head and blinked. "I'm fine. I'm fine. I was just catching a little beauty sleep. I'm okay, really. Are we taking off yet?"

Debbie Sue eyed her anxiously, the hand of dread closing around her stomach. She hadn't forgotten Edwina telling her how the airsickness medication affected her. "We're just now getting to the airport, Ed. We should be at our gate soon. Buddy, are you going to park close to the terminal?"

"There's no point in me parking at all. Vic and I aren't allowed to go to the gate. We'll let you off at the curbside check-in."

"What? Drop us off? You can't come to the gate and wait with us? Why?"

"Because, darlin'," Buddy said. "After nine-eleven, the airport stopped letting all but passengers past the security check-in."

"Tell them you're a state trooper, practically a Texas Ranger," Debbie Sue begged. "They'll let you in. I don't want to tell you good-bye at the curb."

"I'm not going to ask them to break their security protocol," Buddy said. "Besides, by the time they cleared my credentials, it would be time for you to board."

"Dammit to hell," Edwina said as she removed the top from a small plastic bottle. She bumped two pills into the palm of her hand and tossed them into her mouth. "Damn terrorists. They've screwed up everything."

"Now, Mama Doll," Vic said, "promise me you won't make any wisecracks or do and say anything that isn't PC."

"PC. Humph. That's all BS as far as I'm concerned. They can all FO, if you want my opinion."

Dear God, Debbie Sue prayed silently, *please don't let us end up on the ten-o'clock news, or worse yet, in Guantanamo Bay.*

Buddy took an exit, made a left turn and parked at the curb. Turning halfway around in his seat, he pulled Debbie Sue closer to him. "I'll call you on your cell. We'll talk until boarding time. It'll be just like I'm there."

"Not exactly," she said, nuzzling his neck. "I love you, Buddy. Will you miss me?"

"Only every other minute. I love you, too, Flash." They kissed tenderly, and for a fleeting moment, Debbie Sue thought of staying home. How could she survive for nearly a whole week without Buddy, even in New York City?

Buddy climbed out of the Silverado, reached into the bed of the pickup and heaved pieces of luggage to the ground.

Vic opened his door in the rear compartment of the extended-cab vehicle and took Edwina's hand. She scooted from the leather seat, missed the side step and fell to the ground in a heap.

Vic and Buddy rushed to her aide, but she waved them away.

Ignoring her protest, Vic lifted her to her feet and dusted off her bottom.

"I'm fine. I'm fine," Edwina said. "I just missed the step. It's these damned shoes." She bent over and started collecting the contents of her purse, which were scattered about her.

"Mama Doll, promise me you won't take any more of those pills," Vic said in a low voice.

"What pills?" Edwina asked, swaying slightly.

"The motion-sickness stuff."

"Oh, hell, my motion-sickness pills. I need to take them now if they're going to work." She stuck her hand into her cavernous purse opening.

"Shit. Edwina, listen to me." Vic's deep voice of authority would have gotten anyone's attention, but to Debbie Sue's horror, it had no effect on Edwina. She leaned into him and smiled seductively.

"Hey, sailor. You finished brushing dirt off my ass? Or do you want to give it another go-round?"

Debbie Sue eyed her dubiously. "Vic, is she going to be all right?"

"She'll be fine once she gets on the plane. She just needs to sit down and she'll go to sleep." Vic took her by the elbow and walked her to the baggage check-in stand. Debbie Sue and Buddy followed.

The skycap was a rotund black man with a broad smile that lit up as the foursome approached. "Good morning, folks. Please have your tickets and picture ID where I can see them. It's a wonderful day for a trip. Yessir, wonderful."

His smile was contagious and Debbie Sue couldn't help but feel bolstered. She stepped forward and handed over her driver's license and ticket.

"Miss Debbie Sue from Salt Lick," he said looking at her ID. "You flying with us this morning all the way to New York City? You got any luggage you want to check?"

Before she could answer Edwina stepped forward. "Eyes, balls and dicks!" Her voice echoed through the underground area.

Everyone within hearing distance froze. Debbie Sue's left eye began to twitch. She managed a halfhearted smile.

"What'd she say?" the skycap asked, his smile now gone.

"Please. Don't mind her," Debbie Sue said quickly. "She gets airsick and she's taken maybe one or two too many pills. She's fine really." Buddy shoved her suitcases forward. "Here, I have two pieces of luggage."

"Why'd you look at me like that?" Edwina said, glaring at her. "You promised me. You promised me last night that if there was any trouble—"

"Miss," the skycap said, "may I see your ticket and some ID?"

"You bet." She leaned forward and put her mouth close to his ear. "But don't look at my picture," she whispered loud enough for all to hear. "I hate that picture. I don't photograph well. Not well at all." She laid both items on the counter in front of him. Tilting her head in Debbie Sue's direction, she said, "My friend here's afraid I'm going to embarrass her or say something wrong. I haven't done anything wrong, have I, officer?"

"No, ma'am. You're doing just fine, but I'm not an officer."

She gave him a frown and a glare. "Then why'd you pull me over?"

Vic quickly stepped forward, gently nudging Edwina aside. "She has two pieces of luggage and a carry-on."

The skycap grinned as he stamped the ticket, placed it and the boarding pass into a folded envelope and handed it back to Vic.

"You ladies will be boarding in one hour from gate Twenty-seven C. Right through those doors, up the escalator. Once through security, that is *if* you get through security, it's two gates to your right. Have a nice trip."

Debbie Sue clutched Buddy's arm. "Oh, my God. What if she's not okay?"

Buddy patted her hand. "She's all right. If she wasn't, Vic would take charge."

Debbie Sue chewed on her bottom lip as Edwina tottered back to the skycap and leaned across his narrow counter. "You've been a perfect gennelman. We all 'preciate what you boys are doing in the war." Giving him a salute that fell three inches below her eye, she joined Debbie Sue.

Debbie Sue looked up at Buddy. "Go on, now," he said. "It's gonna be all right."

As she took Edwina's arm, Debbie Sue glanced nervously at Vic. The look on his face didn't reassure her at all.

Debbie Sue guided Edwina to the escalator and turned to look back at Buddy one last time. He and Vic stood shoulder to shoulder on the sidewalk wearing grim expressions on their faces. Before Debbie Sue could fall into an even deeper pit of worry, the sudden movement beneath their feet caught Edwina off balance and she pitched forward. Debbie Sue grabbed her and propped her back on her feet as the moving staircase took them away from Buddy and Vic. Edwina declared loudly to no one in particular, "I'm fine. I'm fine. It's these damned shoes."

To Debbie Sue's great relief the dismount from the escalator went without challenge. But the next hurdle loomed directly in front of them. Security. She stopped and moved in front of Edwina, grasping her shoulders with both hands. "Ed, I want you to listen to me like you've never listened before. We're about to go through airport security. These people take their job real serious. They won't put up with any bullshit. Do exactly as they say. Do you understand?"

"You sound like Vic." Her voice took on a tremor. "God, I miss him."

"Fuck, Ed. We just walked away from him. Did you hear what I just said?"

"I *heard* you, Dippity-do."

"Ed, don't call me Dippity-do. People will think you're weird."

Edwina hoisted her chin. "Why, whatever do you mean? I'll have you know, I am not a country pumpkin that can't be trusted in civil libation." Her indignation collapsed and she grinned. "God, I'm thirsty. Are you thirsty, hon?" She staggered away. "Let's go find a Dr. Pecker."

Debbie Sue scurried after her. "Ed, stop here. Remember, it's Debbie Sue, *not* Dippity-do, and we've got to get in this line. Don't forget what I said." Debbie Sue grasped her friend's elbow and steered her toward the uniformed inspector sitting behind a table.

"I need to see your boarding pass and your picture ID," the woman said in a monotone.

"The officer downstairs already did that." Edwina started to walk past her.

The woman rose from her stool and blocked her from moving farther. "Ma'am, I'm going to need to see your boarding pass and your picture ID."

Debbie Sue thrust both her and Edwina's IDs forward. "Here they are. She's just confused."

The inspector eyed Edwina studiously. "Has your friend been drinking?"

"No, ma'am. No, not at all. She gets airsick and has to take medication. It makes her a little loopy, but she's not drunk. Once she gets on the plane, she'll go right to sleep. Promise." Debbie Sue didn't even try to disguise the plea in her voice.

"She's right," Edwina piped up. "I have not been drinking. Well, not yet. I take Dama . . . Diama . . . Dammit, I take drugs to keep from blowing chunks. Say, do you know where can I get a Dr. Pecker?"

"What kind of doctor did she say she needed?" the woman said, handing the documents back to Debbie Sue as she continued to look Edwina up and down.

"Dr. Pepper. Apparently her pills make her thirsty, too. Thank you, ma'am. You've been very kind."

Two down, two to go. Ahead of them, a long-faced older man awaited their approach. He stood straight, arms folded in front of his body, no expression on his face. Apparently one of the requirements for these security jobs was to have no personality. Debbie Sue let out a deep breath and urged Edwina forward.

"Please remove your shoes," the uniformed man ordered. "Place them with your purse in the basket, then step through the metal detector."

Debbie Sue turned to Edwina. "Do you want me to help you with your shoes?"

"No thanks. I'll just wear them. They're not heavy."

"Dammit, I wasn't offering to carry them. You have to take them off. So they can x-ray them."

Giving the older man the squint-eye, Edwina leaned down and whispered to Debbie Sue, "Do I have to?"

"Yes, dammit. Let me help." Debbie Sue knelt, unbuckled one of Edwina's platform sandals and slipped it off her foot, then moved on to the other one. She plopped the shoes into a basket with her own and nudged Edwina toward an arch-way in front of them. "Walk through that little gate. I'll be right behind you."

As she turned and placed her own purse into the basket alongside Edwina's large cowhide satchel, Edwina obediently walked through the doorway without incident. A woman wearing a uniform like the other employees they had en-countered met her on the other side. "May I see your board-ing pass, please?"

"We already showed it to that man back there," Edwina replied.

"I need to see your boarding pass, please," the woman said firmly.

"Dammit, you people need to get together and figure out who's gonna do what," Edwina said. "I can tell you right now it's not very efficient having half a dozen people doing the same job."

"Step aside, please," the woman ordered.

Debbie Sue walked through and spoke to the inspector, "I'm sorry. I didn't know we needed to show them again. We're traveling together and I put both of them in my purse."

"Step aside. We'll get them after your belongings clear X-ray."

"Thank you. Thank you, so much." Debbie Sue expelled a deep breath of relief and moved through to the clearing area. Once both boarding passes were checked, they were free to move on. Debbie Sue was exhausted, but she grabbed Edwina's shoes and purse. "Well, Ed, we're almost done," she said.

Spotting a plastic chair, she plopped her load onto the floor, sat down and bent over to put her shoes on. "Now we just need to get to our gate. Look, keep an eye on our purses, okay?" When she heard no response, she straightened and looked around. "Ed? . . . Ed, where are you?"

Panic zinged through Debbie Sue's chest. Only seconds had passed. How could Edwina have disappeared from her sight? And without her shoes?

Just then she heard a beeping sound and a voice from her left. She turned to see an oversize golf cart inching through a throng of people. "Please step aside," the driver called out. "Courtesy cart coming through. Please step aside."

As the cart passed, Debbie Sue saw Edwina, sitting on the backseat facing outward, smiling and waving like some damn beauty queen.

"Hey, Dippity-do," she yelled. "Let's go take a bite out of the Big Orange."

"Apple, Edwina, apple," Debbie Sue mumbled as the cart steadily moved away.

Letting out a string of cuss words, Debbie Sue dashed after it, two purses on one arm, two pieces of carry-on luggage on the other. And Edwina's platform shoes dangling from her hand.

Debbie Sue didn't know yet what the price would be, but she intended to make Edwina Perkins-Martin pay dearly.

chapter seven

Celina adjusted her pillow and sighed. She had been on the road eleven hours, which equated to eighteen stops in as many whistle stops, towns or cities.

The bus ride hadn't been as bad as she had anticipated. She had passed through some wonderful scenery she wouldn't have been able to notice if she had been driving. Letting someone else battle the traffic snarls was a definite plus. Still, she was anxious to get to her destination. Unfortunately, time wasn't flying by as quickly as her view from the window.

She hadn't been able to sleep much. It had nothing to do with the fact she was on a bus or that she wasn't exhausted. Physically, she was comfortable. What bothered her was the overweight man sitting in the seat beside her, the one who kept nodding off, his greasy head falling onto her shoulder.

She had gently pushed him back to his side twice. After that, she had resorted to shoving him. Before she pushed him again, she had a flashback of the past six hours, before he had fallen asleep. "Bob" had talked nonstop about his wife. What a joy she was in his life, what a wonderful cook, an angel on earth.

Normally Celina would think this sweet and romantic, but in the hours that had passed since he sat down, he had shown her three pictures that he lovingly described as "my wife." Each picture was of a different woman. Celina couldn't tell if he couldn't keep his stories straight or if he was lying through his teeth, but because every seat was taken, she hadn't been able to move.

Reaching overhead, she clicked on the privacy light and groaned. Two fifteen in the morning. They should be pulling into Nashville soon for a fifteen-minute stop. Enough time to visit the ladies' room and stretch her legs.

She reached under the seat for her purse and placed it on her lap. She slipped her hand inside and touched an envelope. She brought it up so she again could read her name scrawled across the envelope in masculine script. She opened it and peeked inside, just to make sure the money was still there, then tucked it back into her purse.

As she had boarded the bus in Dime Box, Dewey had waited until the last possible second before handing her the envelope. "This is a little present. Don't open it until you get to where you're going," he had ordered as he pushed it into her hands.

Of course she had figured he had given her some money. He knew what the county paid her and he had probably heard from Granny Dee what little money she had in her savings. Celina guessed he had given her a hundred-dollar bill to be used as "mad money." She waited until she lost sight of him and Granny Dee before tearing open the envelope. Inside, on a piece of three-hole notebook paper, was a simple message: *Have a good trip.*

That, and not one, but three one-hundred-dollar bills.

The gesture had brought tears to her eyes.

Now, thinking back on it, she heaved a sigh. She might not have a huge family, but she was blessed with many good friends. Her life was good, even if the past few hours of it had been shared with a sweaty person of questionable background.

Resting her wrists on her purse, she did a mental inventory of her money. Granny Dee had given her two hundred dollars, calling it "birthday money." Celina had used most of her meager savings and bought a matching amount in traveler's checks at the grocery store. The additional money Dewey had given her made her feel more secure. She might even have a little extra. This was going to be a great trip.

A nudge against her shoulder alerted her that Bob had awakened. Hadn't he said his destination was Nashville? He had told her so many stories she was confused, but she hoped Nashville would be the end of the line for her and Bob.

He shifted in his seat and pulled his wallet from his hip pocket again and began sorting through his little stack of photographs. All at once, they slipped to the floor, under her feet. Not wanting him to come any closer to her than he already was, she said, "I'll get them." She tucked her purse at her side and bent forward, retrieving Bob's wallet photos.

"Oh, thank you," he said when she handed them to him. "You're so kind."

"You're welcome." Celina resettled in her seat and returned her purse to her lap.

At last she heard the hiss of the bus's air brakes. Nashville. Thank God. Bob stood and stretched, then gathered his belongings from overhead. He offered his right hand. "It's been nice getting to know you. You have a good time in New York City."

He exited the bus a few passengers ahead of her. She watched as he crossed in front of the coach and met three women. All three embraced him. They bore a striking resemblance to the photos he had shown her earlier. The three of them disappeared into the crowd.

You just never know, she thought.

She made her way to the ladies' room. Fortunately, she didn't have to stand in line. After washing her hands and straightening her hair and clothing, she searched out the concessions area. Hours had passed since she had eaten a sandwich for supper in a town she didn't even know the name of. A bottle of juice and a candy bar sounded good.

She found a candy vending machine and opened her purse

to reach for her wallet. Suddenly her heart plummeted. The envelope with her name on it was gone. Had she accidentally pulled it out of her purse and dropped it? . . . No. She had tucked it back into her purse securely just an hour or two ago. Who had been near her purse? The realization hit her like a hammer.

Bob.

Heart pounding, she looked around, knowing as she did that he was long gone.

The jerk! The crooked jerk! He had distracted her by dropping his pictures on the floor, then stolen her money. She was such an idiot. A naïve idiot. She fought back tears, the idea of juice and a candy bar no longer appealing. Dejected, she trudged back to the bus and reclaimed her seat.

She pawed through her purse one more time, hoping to find the envelope crumpled in the bottom, but to no avail. All she found was a wadded up Kleenex. She pulled it out and dabbed her eyes.

"Is this seat taken?"

The question startled her and she looked up. Looming over her was a skinny young guy she guessed to be about eighteen. His hair was bright green. His neck and arms were inked with colorful tattoos. Jewelry protruded from various piercings on his face. A tiny silver arrow looked to have been driven through one eyebrow, and each earlobe had a large hole into which a copper penny had been inserted.

Ouch.

She had to force herself not to stare. She had seen people

with multiple tattoos and body piercings when she had been in college, and she saw them when she went to Austin. But she couldn't think of a one who lived in Dime Box, Texas. She had never sat within one foot of someone whose face sported more metal than a hardware store.

She managed a smile and said, "Uh, no."

Earphones hung around the young man's neck and an MP3 player filled his hand. He plopped into the seat beside her, plugged in his earphones and closed his eyes. Something made her feel confident that he wouldn't disturb her, though she didn't know why. Hadn't she already proved her judgment wasn't worth spit? She zipped up her purse, placed the handle over her wrist and tucked it tightly under her arm. She closed her own eyes and slept straight through two states.

"Edwina," Debbie Sue said louder than she wanted to. She jostled Edwina's shoulder. "Try to wake up. We're getting ready to land."

To her relief the flight had gone without incident. Edwina had fallen asleep the moment she was seated and had slept the entire trip. She had snored, mumbled incoherently and passed gas, but she had not thrown up. Debbie Sue's biggest fear had not happened.

"Ed, are you awake?"

Edwina opened one eye. "Why did you wake me when we're still in the air? Why didn't you wait 'til we landed?"

"I want to be sure you're awake enough to walk off the damn plane."

Edwina raised her head from the tiny pillow the flight attendant had given her and patted her hair with both hands. "How did I get on the damn plane?"

"I got a wheelchair. When they called early boarding for anyone traveling with children or physical limitations, I rolled you on."

Edwina's head turned toward her slowly and she looked at Debbie Sue through one half-closed eye. "You're kidding, right?"

"Hell, no, I'm not kidding. You have no idea what a pain in the ass you were before we boarded."

"I warned you. You can't say I didn't. I told you outright that I'd be drunk."

"Look, let's not fuss. C'mon, look out the window and try to see the city skyline."

"You look out the window. I'd just as soon wait and see it from the ground."

Debbie Sue was peering out the window when the plane suddenly dropped like a roller coaster, rose, then dropped again. A collective "whoa" chorused from the passengers.

Edwina smiled triumphantly. "See? It's crap like that that makes me sick if I don't take something. It's not the flying that bothers me, it's those sudden dips and . . . Debbie Sue? . . . What's wrong?"

Debbie Sue only half heard Edwina's words. She felt extremely warm. She broke into a cold, clammy sweat as nausea overcame her. She licked her lips and reached up to adjust the direction of the air. "It's hot in here."

"Uh-oh. Lord, I know that look. You're whiter than

a marshmallow. Do you need a barf bag?" Edwina rifled through the magazines in the pocket on the back of the chair in front of her.

"I don't think so. I'm just feeling yucky all of a sudden." Debbie Sue held her head with her left hand as she rocked back and forth in her seat.

"Irony's a bitch, ain't it? Here I was worried about getting sick and now *you* are. I never felt better in my life. That little swoop up and down and then up—"

Debbie Sue's stomach made another roll. "Ed, please. Could you just be quiet for a second? If I can make it 'til the plane lands, I'll be okay."

A deep male voice announced their approach to La Guardia and reminded all passengers to return to their seats and fasten their seat belts.

Edwina reached under her feet and began to dig. Debbie Sue cast a dubious eye in her direction. "Ed, you're making things worse. Can't you just sit still? What in the hell are you looking for?"

"I've got perfume in my bag. I'm gonna dab a little on. So I'll smell good for New York."

"What kind of perfume?"

"Jungle Gardenia."

Debbie Sue rolled her eyes and wiped her damp brow with her sleeve. "Oh, my God. I'll throw up for sure."

Edwina began to chuckle.

"What's so damn funny?"

"You know what? You just can't buy good times like this, kiddo. Nosiree, you just can't."

"Well, you probably could," Debbie Sue grumbled, "but I don't know who'd be dumb enough to think they could sell 'em."

With the plane safely on the ground, passengers jostled one another to retrieve their overhead luggage. Debbie Sue remained seated and continued to fan herself with her magazine. She still felt shaky and didn't trust her legs to carry her up the aisle. Edwina, on the other hand, greeted each person who passed.

"Y'all have a good time," she told a stodgy couple, reaching across Debbie Sue's face to pat the husband on the arm and smothering Debbie Sue with a cloud of gardenia scent. "Hey, now, y'all don't get into any trouble," she called to a young couple.

"Ed, just let them get off," Debbie Sue said through clenched teeth.

Edwina gasped and flopped back in her seat. "Fine, grumpy. I'll just sit here and not say a word."

"Fine."

"Fine."

Everyone had disembarked before Debbie Sue finally felt able to make a move. "I think I'm feeling better. Let's go. But I want to stop off at a ladies' room."

"I'll go to baggage claim," Edwina volunteered.

Panic seized Debbie Sue again. "No. Oh, no, you don't," she said firmly. "We stay together. You come into the restroom with me."

Inside the ladies' room, Debbie Sue found an empty stall

and pulled her phone from her purse. She keyed in a number and waited for Buddy's voice.

"Hey, Flash," he said enthusiastically. "Are you in New York?"

"We're here. We just got off the plane."

"So how was the trip? Did Ed get sick?" He laughed. "Man, she wasn't kidding about getting drunk on those pills, was she?"

"No, she wasn't kidding. She did just fine. I'm the one who got sick."

"You? Why, darlin'? Did you eat something you shouldn't have?"

"I don't think so. I guess it was the excitement of the trip. And I've been so worried about Ed. Then the plane did one of those extreme hoopty-doos, kind of like the roller coaster at Six Flags. Maybe the worse thing that could happen on this trip already has. Maybe the rest of the week will be a piece of cake."

"God, I hope so. Wherever you two go, trouble seems to follow."

"There won't be any trouble," Debbie Sue said quickly. The last thing she wanted was for Buddy to be distracted from studying for his test. "I promise. We'll be fine. I love you."

"I love you too, Flash."

Debbie Sue disconnected. Buddy was wrong. Trouble didn't always follow her and Ed. Not always. Sometimes they just flat-out went out and found it.

But she hadn't come to the NAPI conference to do that.

She was here as a professional and she was determined to present herself as such. She intended to make Texas proud of the Domestic Equalizers.

Just then she heard Ed's cackling laughter echo off the tiled walls. No telling what had prompted that. Her mom's latest award-winning country-western song passed through Debbie Sue's mind: "Anything Worth Doing Ain't Easy."

chapter eight

ood Lord, Debbie Sue, that's the Empire State Building." Edwina pressed her face close to the cab's side
window. "It looks just like it did in *Sleepless in Seattle*.
Remember the scene where Meg Ryan met Tom Hanks at
the top?"

"I didn't see it," Debbie Sue said, "but I saw King Kong
hang off the side and fight off airplanes."

"And what about that old one where Cary Grant waited for
this woman and she got run over. . . . Hey, I know. Let's look
for celebrities. I've heard they're butt-high to a giraffe in New
York. Oh, my God, what if we spot somebody famous?"

Debbie Sue wasn't bowled over by spotting celebrities.
She had seen her share. Even knew a few. Not movie stars,

but you couldn't be a ProRodeo champion and not see and know other ProRodeo-ers or country-western singers and the like. Lord, during the years when she wasn't married to Buddy, she'd had a fling with a three-time world champion bullrider. For that matter, at one time, she had been a minor celebrity herself.

"Wow," Edwina said, "just look at all the dogs. Did you ever think there would be so many dogs?"

Edwina was acting like a kid in a candy store, but she was right about the dogs. There were dogs on leashes everywhere. All sizes, all breeds. They appeared to be unaffected by the surrounding crowds and traffic. Definitely not something one would see in downtown Dallas or Houston.

Debbie Sue spotted signs pointing to Fifth Avenue and Madison Avenue. "Look! I've heard those street names my entire life. I feel like I'm in an episode of *CSI: New York*."

A red light halted the cab's progress. Debbie Sue could see the cab driver cut his eyes to the rearview mirror. So? Maybe she and Edwina were a little carried away, but surely he had seen excited tourists before.

"So do I." Edwina tugged on Debbie Sue's sleeve. "Look out my window. There's a body under that sheet, where those three cops are standing."

"Oh, my God, Ed. Is that a real body?"

"I can't think of a reason for it to be a fake one."

"Maybe they're filming for a TV show." Debbie Sue leaned forward and spoke to the cabbie. "Hey, do you think that's a real body on the ground? Could they be filming a movie?"

"I no see," the driver said, without turning his head.

"Right there." Debbie Sue pointed to the right. "Look out your right window. It's on the ground, twenty feet away."

"I no see," the driver repeated, staring straight ahead and honking his horn as the light changed.

Debbie Sue leaned back against her seat. "Well, if that doesn't beat all," she whispered. "Why do you suppose he wouldn't even look?"

"Maybe he didn't understand you. Or maybe he doesn't want to get involved."

"Hell, I didn't ask him to *identify* it. I just asked him to look in that direction."

Edwina shook her head. "It's different here, Debbie Sue. It's just different."

"You're telling me. A body on the ground back home, covered up by a sheet? Everyone in the county would be on the phone, checking up on who's missing or dead. And if this many people drove around in Dallas, all honking at each other, somebody would get his ass kicked."

In less than fifteen minutes, the driver delivered them to the front entrance of their hotel, heaved their suitcases onto the sidewalk and sped away. Edwina hooked her carry-on's long leather strap over her shoulder and hoisted another bag to her hip. She bent and picked up two additional bags, one in each hand.

But Debbie Sue wasn't ready to stop looking at her surroundings. "Wait a minute, Ed."

"What's wrong? This is the right hotel, isn't it?"

"Yeah, yeah, this is where we're supposed to be."

Edwina started forward. "Well, I think it's a pretty fair bet nobody's coming out here to get us. Let's go in. I'm carrying over a hundred pounds of crap."

She limped another two steps under her load, then stopped and set her bags and suitcases on the sidewalk. "Okay, what's up? What's going on? You look like a six-year-old that just heard Christmas was canceled."

"I don't know, Ed. It's just that all of a sudden I don't feel like we belong here."

"You mean in New York City? Hon, I'm not sure if anyone *belongs* here, but the fact is, this is where we are."

"I mean at this conference. Good Lord, Ed, just look around us. What in the hell can we tell people who live here about anything, much less about conducting a criminal investigation? They see more shit walking down the street than we run up against in Salt Lick in a lifetime."

"Oh, no, you don't. You're the one that talked me into coming. You don't get to have second thoughts. Besides, we're not here to reinvent the wheel, Debbie Sue. They have their way of doing things and we have ours. All we're going to do is tell them what works for the Equalizers. It's a chance to share methods, that's all. Just a chance to share methods."

Debbie Sue dredged up a smile. "You're right. We can all learn something from each other."

"That's my girl." Edwina repositioned her bags with a series of grunts.

"You're right. I'll be fine." Debbie Sue fell in step with her friend and they entered the hotel lobby.

A bellhop met Edwina with a cart and relieved her of her burden. "Debbie Sue, give him your stuff."

But Debbie Sue was stopped in her tracks, staring at a display board of activities in the hotel. The display spelled out NATIONAL ASSOCIATION OF PRIVATE INVESTIGATORS in bold letters, and listed the speakers in smaller type. Debbie Sue's jaw dropped. "I can't believe this."

"What?" Edwina said from behind her.

"Look at this." Debbie Sue stared at the notice, which read, "Investigating for Dummies, presented by the Domestic Equalizers of Dallas, Texas."

Edwina came to her side, frowning at the display board. "We're not from Dallas."

"I can't believe this," Debbie Sue said again, tears springing to her eyes. "I've never been so embarrassed."

"A dummy's a step down from a clown, right?"

"Shut up, Ed. It's bad enough *they're* making fun of us. You don't have to do it, too." The hot flames of anger had finally reached Debbie Sue's cheeks and tongue. She sliced a hand through the air. "Fuck 'em. Get your shit off that cart, Ed. We're leaving. They can find somebody else to make fun of."

"Now, Debbie Sue, don't get your titties in a twist. We've already taken these people's airplane tickets and I sure as hell don't want to have to pay for this hotel myself. This joint looks like it costs a little more than Motel Six."

Debbie Sue's disillusionment stuck like a huge burr in her

throat. She had been so wrong to think the Domestic Equalizers had gained some stature in the world of professional private investigators. She should have known they wouldn't expect to learn something from country bumpkins. Why, whoever made the display didn't even show the town she and Edwina came from. All they wanted the Domestic Equalizers for was comic relief. Tears brimmed her eyelids and one trailed down her cheek.

Edwina's long arm looped around her shoulder and she began to pat. "Now, now, Debbie Sue, c'mon. We're here, so let's make the most of it. We'll get even. We'll invite 'em all down to Texas and take 'em to a working ranch or a rodeo. Then *we'll* make fun of *them*. C'mon, now."

Debbie Sue shook her head. "I don't think I can, Ed. I don't think I can face a roomful of people, knowing—"

"What are you talking about? You rode a damn horse around three barrels in *coliseums* full of people. And for a few years you did it better than anybody else. Listen, girlfriend, I'll bet, in this whole convention, we don't run across another human being that's done that. Or *can* do it."

"But that was different, Ed. Those were my people and they weren't making fun of me."

"You know what? If these folks want clowns, the Domestic Equalizers will give 'em a circus. Now, let's go find the bar."

Edwina's tone had an ominous ring to it. Somehow, Debbie Sue didn't feel reassured.

So this is New York City, Celina thought. The Greyhound inched its way through a snarl of traffic like she had never seen, not even in Austin. Horns honked. Yellow cabs changed lanes at random. Bike riders took risks that made her want to hide her eyes. Pedestrians jaywalked with abandon. The whole scene was mesmerizing and exciting.

On the sidewalks, throngs of people, mostly wearing athletic shoes, scurried along and crossed intersections. She had expected to see a fashion show. High heels and super models. Beautiful people strolling the streets of the most exciting city in the world. But the crowd she could see from her bus window looked no different from her. Except that they obviously knew where they were going.

At last the bus came to a stop. Passengers got to their feet and started gathering belongings. A wave of panic hit Celina.

Dear God, after forty-two hours and five minutes, she was leaving her cocoon of security. Like a baby bird, she was being pushed from the nest into the noisy, busy, hurrying world. Was she ready? Hardly.

Outside the bus, time passed at a snail's pace while she waited for her one large suitcase to be unloaded. Once it was in front of her, she didn't quite know what to do. She could barely lift it and she certainly was unable to carry it. Dewey had carried it to the bus stop in front of the drugstore in Dime Box. She sighed. Well, she could drag it. What choice did she have?

She was relieved to see a taxi stand at the entrance to the terminal, but she wasn't happy to see such a long line of people waiting. Cabs were also lined up in a long queue, as each one picked up passengers. Apparently, they went by strict rules, because she saw a sign saying that no more than four fares could ride in a cab.

A party of five stood in line ahead of her, talking nervously. A swarthy cab driver was speaking to them in broken English and pointing to the sign. After several minutes of pleading and explaining that they were afraid of being separated and possibly losing each other, the driver relented and threw up his hands. He stalked to the driver's seat, muttering in a language Celina wouldn't attempt to guess.

Just as the five started to board the cab, a caftan-wearing driver of the cab behind it darted forward, waving his arms and yelling at the first cab driver in yet a different language. Celina cringed and stepped back, lest he trample her. The driver who had agreed to take the five passengers shouted back. All of the party of five, wide-eyed and slack-jawed, stared helplessly at the two men.

Shouts between the cab drivers turned into pushing and shoving. The two cabbies fell to the ground, rolling and slinging punches, the caftan wearer's robe a tangled mess. The five passengers moved furtively to yet another cab, where yet another driver quickly loaded their bags into his trunk, slid behind the wheel and sped away, barely giving them enough time to climb in.

When the two cab drivers engaged in fisticuffs on the ground paused and saw the cab speed away, each jumped to his feet, climbed into his respective cab and tore after the cab with the five fares.

"Wow," Celina muttered under her breath.

As she stood there weighing her few options, another

brown-skinned man wearing a turban and a chest-length gray beard approached her. "You need ride?" he asked in broken English.

Celina hesitated. "I, uh, I'm not sure."

"You in line, you need ride. Where you go?"

Before she could answer he heaved her suitcase into the trunk of his cab.

Left with little desirable choice, she hesitantly opened the back door. The driver had already scooted behind the steering wheel and motioned for her to get in. She drew a deep breath and crawled into the backseat, leaving one foot on the sidewalk.

"Where you go?" The driver asked as he scribbled something on a clipboard.

"How much to take me to Fifty-two Broadway?"

"That Y?"

Celina squinted, uncertain what he had asked her. "Uh, yes." *I think so.* "How much?"

He set his clipboard aside. "Two fifty in the front, a buck and fifty for the mile. Fifteen bucks." He held up ten fingers. "You got that? I do not have all day."

Confused and still smarting from the theft of her money, Celina tried to do a quick mental calculation of jaunts between the YWCA and the conference hotel. At this rate and with her cushion gone, she would have to keep her trips to a minimum. "Do the subways run there? That fight was a little unsettling and—"

"Do not let those foreigners scare you." He rolled his dark eyes. "Foreigners!" He made a spitting motion toward the seat. "They ruin the city. You want ride or no? I try to make the living here. What are you, some ball and screw?"

Ball and screw? . . . Oh, screwball! "Yes! . . . I mean no! . . . Yes, I have the money. Let's go."

The bearded driver looked at her squint-eyed in the rear-view mirror. "Put in foot. Close door."

"Foot?"

He made a gesture with his hand.

In the challenge of trying to communicate with the driver, she had forgotten her right foot was still planted on the side-walk. "Oh, foot. Yes."

She jerked her leg into the cab. She barely had time to close the door before they raced away.

chapter nine

The cab's backseat was covered with a plastic protective barrier. Celina soon found that while it might keep the upholstery pristine, its slick surface made sitting in the moving vehicle and casually observing the city impossible.

She slid from one side of the seat to the other as the cab careened through the city streets, squeezed between cars, pushed traffic lights and dodged pedestrians. She secured herself in the middle of the seat with arms extended, palms out. She was still jostled, but not as much. At least now she had some control. At least she could remain upright.

Just when she thought she had mastered the ride, the cab lurched to a stop so abruptly she was pitched halfway into the front seat.

She gathered herself, stumbled out of the cab, straightened her clothing and checked her moving parts. The driver was already quickstepping to the trunk. A small man, he struggled to heave her suitcase out and onto the street, mumbling in whatever language he spoke. As she pressed eighteen dollars into his hand, he neither looked her in the face nor counted the money. In an instant he was back in the cab and on the phone. He pulled away from the curb, leaving her struggling with her heavy bag.

With a tight grip, she attempted to tug it by its strap off the street and onto the sidewalk. In mid-tug, the leather strap broke. She staggered backward, lost her balance and landed on her back on the sidewalk with the suitcase on top of her. So far, her view of New York City as a sidewalk pedestrian was straight up. Before she could move she heard males voices and laughter.

"Ten Eighty-four all units, Ten Eighty-four."

"You sure that's not a Ten Fifty?"

Celina looked up into three grinning, extremely good-looking male faces. Further inspection revealed that one wore a huge coat and . . . *Oh, my goodness. Firefighters.*

She moved her eyes from side to side, then straight up, looking for smoke. She saw none, nor did she smell any.

One of the men leaned down and offered her his hand. "Can I help you up, miss? You hurt?"

He spoke with an accent Celina had heard most recently on TV during an episode of *The Sopranos.* She took his hand and was instantly lifted to a standing position.

She began to brush at her clothing. "Is there a fire? I don't see any smoke."

"No, ma'am," the man, who had an American flag embroidered above his shirt pocket, said. "Not here. But if there was, we'd know what to do about it." They all laughed.

A few times in her life, a good-looking man had singled her out. She had found that unnerving enough, but being surrounded by three turned her brain mushy. She hooked a sheaf of hair behind her ear and reached for the strap on her suitcase. "Y'all don't have to worry. I'm just fine. I was trying to get my suitcase off the street when that driver just took off. He just about pulled me along with him. I don't know why he's in such a hurry."

She sensed that the men weren't moving and looked around. All of them were staring at her. "Where *are* you from?" the one with the flag said. "Wait, don't tell me. I got it. You're a Georgia peach if I ever heard one."

She laughed. "Georgia? I'm not from Georgia." She couldn't believe it, but even she heard how her speech had taken on an exaggerated drawl. She sounded like Scarlett O'Hara.

A different man, his smile slow and seductive, picked up her suitcase as if it weighed nothing. "I know you're from the South. The South's got the prettiest women in the world." He handed her the suitcase.

Awestruck and forgetting the weight of the bag, Celina took it from him. And immediately dropped it on his foot.

His eyes bugged and he grunted.

"Oh. Oh, my gosh!" She slapped her palms against her cheeks. "I'm so sorry. That suitcase is so heavy—"

"No problem," he said, and smiled faintly as he lifted it off his foot.

Celina felt as if she were watching a bad play. If the actress playing her had dug her toes into the pavement and said, "Aw, shucks, I bet you say that to all the girls," she wouldn't have even been surprised. "I'm from Texas," she said, striving for composure. Only it came out, "I'm frum Taxes."

The trio broke into laughter again. The one with the flag said, "Texas. I should have known. I went to Amarillo once to help my brothers fight some range fires. I think they call that the Panhandle. You know where that is?"

Celina brightened. It was good to be talking about home, hearing familiar names of locations.

"Oh, yes. Of course I do. You must come from a large family. How many brothers do you have in Amarillo?"

The men laughed again and she realized that their impression of her as a rube had become cemented. She felt the heat of a flush crawling up her neck.

"Don't be embarrassed," the youngest-looking of the three said. "Brothers are what we call other firefighters. We're all brothers to each other."

"Oh, yes," she said. "Now that you mention it, I remember hearing that somewhere."

"Just where in Texas do you live? If all the women look like you, I need to go there sometime."

Though embarrassed at her lack of sophistication, Celina still thoroughly enjoyed the attention of these men.

They definitely weren't Sam. She gave them her best smile. "Dime Box."

The men looked at each other, then laughed again. "Is that a town?" one of them asked.

She was still enjoying the moment when an ear-splitting alarm sounded. A huge panel door in the wall beside her opened and one of the men said, "That's it. Gotta go, guys." And they were gone.

Celina stood there, eye-to-headlight with a huge fire truck. She hadn't realized she was in front of a fire station. At home, a fire station was a freestanding structure, easily recognized. Here, it was part of a wall. The full panel door was the only thing distinguishing it from the other buildings with storefront windows or doorways. She grabbed her suitcase and heaved and shoved it out of the fire truck's path.

She hadn't noticed it before, but now she saw the huge "no parking" zone painted in bright white across the front of the station. No wonder that cab driver had driven away so quickly. And no wonder those men were having such a good time flirting with her and making fun of her. She squeezed her eyes shut and clenched her teeth in total embarrassment.

In lieu of a hole to fall into, she looked for a door and saw one right beside the fire station, with a sign affixed over it: New York City YWCA, Est. 1932.

"Well, duh," she mumbled, and gripped her suitcase handle tightly.

Half an hour later, she was shown to her room, or "the closet," as it would have been referred to back home. It had a twin bed only and a highback chair pressed against the wall near the head of the bed, just to the right of the small window that looked out on a brick wall. She supposed the chair served as a nightstand as well. Celina scanned the walls for crosses or other religious symbols, for surely this was a nunnery.

Tossing her purse on the bed, she sank to the chair seat and looked out the window. *This isn't so bad*, she told herself. It's clean, it's safe. Practically an entire army of heroes was just next door. "It's only for a few days," she mumbled.

Tomorrow the seminars would start and hopefully, her new life.

"First things first," Debbie Sue said, taking Edwina by the arm and pulling her toward the registration desk. "I'm not letting you near a bar 'til we get checked in."

Registration went without a hitch and soon they were standing in the middle of a luxurious hotel room on the sixth floor. The bellhop put their bags down and hurried over to a set of drapes that covered the entire wall.

"I think you ladies will enjoy this view," he said, pulling the cord and revealing floor-to-ceiling windows and a priceless view of Times Square. "A few of the rooms on this floor have a balcony. You can't actually use it because the windows have these little bars that keep them from being opened, but still, isn't it to die for?"

"I don't know if I'd go that far," Debbie Sue said, taking in the view, "but it's pretty cool, all right."

Edwina slipped some money into the young man's hand.

"You ladies enjoy your stay in New York City," he said on his way out the door. Before closing the door, he stopped. "What part of Texas are you from?"

"It's a tiny place you've never heard . . ." Debbie Sue stopped in mid-sentence. "Wait just a minute. How did you know we're from Texas?"

The young man laughed. "That's a good one. You ladies have fun." With that, he closed the door.

Debbie Sue glanced at Edwina. "I suppose he thinks we have an accent."

"You do, but I don't," Edwina said between gum smacks.

"You're kidding, right? Because, Edwina Perkins-Martin, you sound like reruns of *Hee Haw*, *Green Acres* and *Dallas*, all rolled into one."

"Maybe I do, but I'll tell you one thing. Men love that Texas twang. *That*, I am certain of, Miss Priss." She crossed the room, plopped onto one of the queen-size beds and gave a low whistle. "Man-oh-man. These NAPI folks might think what we do is for dummies, but they shelled out some bucks for this room."

"I'll say," Debbie Sue said, still in awe at the quality of the furnishings. "This makes even those fancy hotels in Fort Worth look low-rent."

Edwina arranged her pillows, lay back and crossed her ankles. "I think I'll call up Lloydena and tell her 'Lloydena, honey, you gotta see this.'"

Fooling with the TV remote, Debbie Sue nodded her agreement.

Edwina sat upright. "Where's the john? I'm fixin' to pee

my pants." She got to her feet and began to rummage in her suitcase. "And I'm going to change my clothes." She headed for the bathroom.

Twenty minutes later she emerged. She had changed into her size-eight Wranglers, tucked into the tops of pink knee-high, full-quill ostrich boots, with turquoise eagles across the shafts. She had on a pink satin western shirt, the yokes piped with black satin. A black belt encrusted with glittering pink stones encircled her waist. Chandelier earrings of turquoise cabochons, accented with pink crystals, hung three inches from her earlobes. "I'm ready," she announced. "Let's go downstairs."

Debbie Sue looked up from where she'd been patiently lounging in an oversize chair and leafing through some literature left in the room. "Whoa! Look at you, rodeo queen. Is that belt a B.B. Simon?"

Edwina strutted around the room flashing the buckle proudly, "It sure is. Gen-u-ine Swarovski crystals. Vic bought it for me when he was in Fort Worth a few weeks ago."

"I'm not even gonna ask what he paid for it. Can I borrow it sometime?"

"If you ever get it off me you can. With what my honey paid for this thing, I'll be holding my britches up with it for a long time. C'mon, let's go."

"Just wait, dammit. I haven't even been in the bathroom yet. My hair hasn't been brushed all day. I gotta clean up, I gotta change clothes and I gotta call Buddy."

"Hell, that's too many gotta's for me," Edwina said. "I need a drink. I'll go ahead and leave the room to you. I'm headed for the bar." Edwina picked up one of the key cards and waved it over her head. "*Hasta luego*, girlfriend."

"Yep, see you later."

Then a tiny fear slithered through Debbie Sue. Edwina, running loose in New York City, even if it was just to the bar downstairs, was enough to propel her from her chair. Indeed, she wanted to see where "Good Morning America" was taped, but she sure didn't want to be on it. "Don't go anywhere but the bar, Ed. I'll be right behind you."

Edwina stood in the dark hotel bar's open doorway, allowing her eyes time to adjust. Too many times she had dashed into a bar without that forethought and too many times her butt had met the carpet. Today, she wanted to make an impression, not leave one.

When she could see, she sauntered in and made her way to a tall stool at the bar. She loved sitting at the bar. There was something about being perched on the tall stools that was cool and sophisticated. Here she was, the aloof woman alone, sitting at the bar drinking. Men might have most of the advantages in life, but it was more fun being a female.

"Margarita. Straight up with salt," she said to the bartender.

"Would you like that with our top-shelf tequila?" the young woman asked.

"Naw, I don't see the point in covering up good tequila. Just use the cheap stuff. If I get to the sipping stage, I'll order the good stuff."

The young woman grinned. "A woman who knows how

to drink. My name's Mary. I'll be taking care of you this evening."

Edwina cocked her head and grinned. "Well, now. Do yourself proud, Mary. And make that a double." She chortled at her own joke.

She turned her head and noticed for the first time that she was being stared at by a woman sitting on the stool next to hers. The neighbor was about the same age as Debbie Sue, Edwina guessed. She even had hair down to her butt like Debbie Sue. It fell down her back in layers. Unlike her partner, Edwina saw that the neighbor wore heavy makeup—but it was artfully applied. She had on a slinky fire-engine-red dress, low cut and curve hugging, leaving nothing to the imagination. And it must be split all the way to kingdom come, Edwina figured, because she sat there with her legs crossed, exposing an ample amount of thigh. And her shoes. Black stiletto heels with a rhinestone strap around the ankle.

Hard-looking, Edwina thought. But maybe that's what living in this big city did to an otherwise pretty woman. She did have good taste in shoes, though, which made her worth knowing. Edwina gave her a huge friendly grin. "How ya doin' this evenin'? My name's Edwina and I'm from Texas."

Unsmiling, the woman scanned her up and down. "Gee. I would have never guessed."

"I come from a little town called Salt Lick, where—"

"Can I ask you something?"

Edwina kept grinning. "Sure."

A frown creased the woman's brow. "Does that Annie Oakley getup work for you?"

Edwina's grin fell. *The nerve!* She hated getting into a tussle before Debbie Sue arrived, but this broad was asking for it. Edwina squared her shoulders and looked down her nose. "Oh, I don't know. Does that 'I'm a ho' getup work for *you*?"

The woman didn't bat an eye. "Pretty much all the time, though I'm thinking about trying something new."

Edwina's bluster collapsed and her eyes bugged with shock. "You're a pro? I mean, a real pro?" She clapped a palm against her chest. "And you think *I'm* a pro?"

"Well, aren't you?"

"Oh, hell no. Though I think all women prostitute themselves on some level. Some do it to make a living, some do for a four-carat ring or a new SUV." Edwina conjured up a laugh. "Or a membership in a country club."

For the first time, her drinking neighbor smiled and her face grew animated. "I've never heard it put better." Extending her right hand, she said, "I'm Cherubino Annunziata San Giacomo. My friends call me Cher."

Edwina looked into her face and blinked. "Well, I'll be damned. I'll just bet they do." Laughing again, she shook Cher's hand. "I'm Edwina Faye Perkins-Martin. My friends call me on the phone asking for money."

Just then, a computer version of a pop song Edwina didn't readily recognize started up. "What's that?"

"'Strangers in the Night,'" Cher said. "It's my cell phone. Cute, huh?" Without waiting for a reply, she turned away and plucked the phone from her purse.

"Yeah, cute," Edwina answered anyway, liking her new-found friend more all the time.

Two drinks later, Debbie Sue walked up. "I see you've made friends already."

"Debbie Sue. Cher and I were just talking about business."

"Cher?" Debbie Sue asked.

"Oops, sorry. Debbie Sue, this is Cher the Prostitute. Cher, this is Debbie Sue Overstreet, my friend and partner. She's a hairdresser, but she used to be a barrel racer."

"How do you do," Cher said to Debbie Sue. "A barrel racer?"

"Yep," Debbie Sue said. "It was a long time ago."

"So how does that work? I can't get a visual."

"Well, you see, there's three barrels in this big arena, set up in a triangle. They're usually painted in bright colors. You ride a horse around them as fast as you can. And the one who does it the fastest wins."

"Uh-huh," Cher replied. "I still can't get a visual. How fast is the fastest?"

"My best time was fifteen point seven seconds."

"And where did you do this?"

"Rodeos," Edwina said. "She used to be a ProRodeo performer."

"Well, whaddaya know," Cher said, eyeing Debbie Sue and smiling. "You're a real cowgirl."

Debbie Sue smiled. "Yep, that's me. I even own a horse. You ever been to a rodeo?"

"Can't say that I have."

"You should go. They have one every year right here in New York City. Madison Square Garden. I always wanted to be in it, but never was that good."

"I've heard about it. Maybe now that I've met some"—she leaned back and gave Edwina a head-to-toe again—*cowgirls*, I'll do that."

"Oh, I'm not a cowgirl," Edwina said. "The most I know about a cow is when a steak appears on my plate."

"This is true," Debbie Sue said with a laugh. "And there's a horse in Texas that'll vouch for that."

She took a seat on a stool beside Edwina and called to the bartender. "Ma'am? I'll have whatever they're having."

Several margaritas later, Edwina said, "I'm still starving. Let's go get something to eat."

"Sounds good to me," Debbie Sue said. "I haven't eaten since breakfast. Cher, would you like to join us?"

"No, you girls go without me. I'm working. I'll see you later."

"Mary," Edwina said to the bartender, "we need to settle our tab."

The bartender placed a tray holding a receipt in front of her and Edwina grabbed it. "I've got it, girls. Drinking makes me feel generous."

"Better you than me," Cher said. "Being generous could put me out of business. And speaking of business, here, let me give you one of my cards."

Debbie Sue took the card and read aloud, "Cher Giacomo, sex therapist. Have mouth, will travel." She looked up at Cher and grinned. "Well, it's original."

Cher gave her a thumbs-up.

From the corner of her eye, Debbie Sue saw Edwina studying the bill. "I must have had more to drink than I thought,"

Edwina muttered. "I can't make these numbers out. Debbie Sue, what does this look like to you?" She thrust the check toward Debbie Sue.

Debbie Sue took it and turned on her stool to hold the small piece of paper in better light. "Oh, my God, Ed. This says two hundred and forty-three dollars." She waved the bill in the air at the bartender, "Ma'am, can you come here a sec?"

The young woman came to where Debbie Sue sat. "Yes?"

"You must have gotten our tab mixed up with someone else's. We didn't order drinks for the house. This bill is over two hundred dollars."

"Yes, ma'am. Nine house margaritas. Twenty-seven dollars each."

Debbie Sue's eyes bugged. "Holy cow!"

"What?" Edwina gasped.

"For that price," Debbie Sue said, "I could fly to Mexico for a margarita."

Edwina tried to make a calculation in her head, but tequila had made her mind fuzzy. "You know, if you caught a plane in Midland, I think you could." She plucked the bill from Debbie Sue's hand. "We'll just put it on the room."

Cher reached across, took the check and handed it back to the bartender, along with three crisp one-hundred-dollar bills. "My treat ladies. It's a tax write-off for me."

Debbie Sue sat back on her stool. "Whoa. You file a tax return?"

Edwina, too, stared at Cher. "You mean income taxes, like with the IRS?"

"Why not?" Cher laughed and swung a look from Edwina to Debbie Sue. "I may make a living on my back, but I don't have my head up my ass."

Just then, "Strangers in the Night" began to play again. Cher put the phone to her ear and strolled toward the bar's doorway, talking.

"What was that song?" Debbie Sue asked, watching her.

"'Strangers in the Night.' That was her cell phone. Cute, huh?"

"Appropriate, I'd say, considering her job."

chapter ten

Celina stretched out on the bed for a while, staring at the dingy ceiling, then decided to move to the chair. She stood with one knee on the chair seat, bracing her hands on the windowsill and peering out like a tragic agoraphobic.

When she had first considered attending the conference, the thought of a few days alone and on her own sounded wonderful, but now she wasn't so sure. The idea of making her first venture onto the busy city streets alone was down-right hair-raising, especially with darkness descending. But her stomach thought fear and trepidation were no excuse. It rumbled and grumbled and reminded her that a Snickers bar and a vending-machine hot dog several hours earlier weren't enough to tide her over until morning.

The young woman who had checked her into the Y told her about a corner eatery, explaining that the family-operated business had been in the same location for more than twenty-five years and served good home-style food. "Cheap food and lots of noise," the desk clerk had said.

That settled it. On Celina's first evening in New York City, she would dine with working people like herself. Besides, with three hundred dollars of her money gone, she had to eat cheap.

The walk to the corner restaurant took only a few minutes. She was met at the diner's entry by a din of voices. A woman about her age with a row of filled plates balanced on her left arm made eye contact. "Seat yourself," she shouted above the clamor. All at once, Celina felt at home. The crowded informal diner was just what she needed on her first evening in the Big Apple.

A vacant seat at the back of the room caught her eye. She moved through the crowd, having the distinct impression that people were staring. The waitress who had greeted her at the door came to the table and handed her a menu. Celina perused it quickly and ordered a bacon cheeseburger with a side of fries, a chocolate milkshake and a slice of cheesecake for dessert.

The waitress wrote the order without a word, but before she turned to leave, she smiled and leaned down. "I thought you guys ate like rabbits. I mean, this is enough food for an army. What's your secret?"

"Excuse me?"

"You're a model, right? One of those runway babes?"

Celina couldn't control the smile that traveled all the way across her face. She grabbed the girl's hand and squeezed it between her own. "Oh, my gosh, that's the nicest thing anyone's ever said to me. Thank you so much."

The waitress tucked back her chin and frowned. "You're not a model?"

"Heavens, no. I'm a librarian."

"I gotta read more books," the waitress muttered as she walked away.

Celina sat in the booth relishing the confetti of dialects all around her. Soon she was served a burger the size of a dinner plate, a separate plate heaped with french fries and a slice of cheesecake as big as her size-ten shoe. Even after she had scarfed down as much as she could eat, she still had enough left for both tomorrow's breakfast and lunch. This bounty was an unexpected blessing. She asked for a doggie bag. The waitress gave her a look, but then grinned when she figured out that Celina wanted to take the leftovers with her.

The restaurant's crowd was thinning out. Celina glanced at her watch and saw that it was nine o'clock in Texas, which meant it was ten o'clock in New York City. She left the diner and strolled back to the Y, fascinated. At ten o'clock, there had to be more people out on the sidewalks all around her than there were citizens in Dime Box.

Back in her room, she prepared for bed, her body acutely aware she had slept sitting upright for almost two days. She picked up her overnight bag and headed for the bathroom at the end of the hall. Sharing a bathroom with who knew how many others hadn't exactly been a part of her plan.

She returned and settled into the narrow bed. Just extending her long legs should have brought relaxation, but now she felt as if she had swallowed a potent dose of caffeine. Combined with the newness of her surroundings and the unfamiliar bed, the sounds of the city seemed amplified.

She had set the food she had brought from the restaurant on the chair beside the bed. The aroma teased her. Frustrated, she clicked on the reading light clipped to the headboard, threw back the covers and sat up. She reached for the sack of food and, sitting cross-legged in the middle of the bed, indulged herself with cheesecake.

Between bites she reached for her purse. One of the benefits of a really small room, she concluded, was that she could reach almost all four corners and not leave the bed. She pulled the conference information from her purse and read it for the umpteenth time.

Registration and picking up material began at 11 A.M. Odd that things didn't start earlier, she thought. A luncheon and a welcoming speech by the esteemed forensic pathologist, Dr. William Wray, were scheduled at noon. She couldn't believe she was actually going to see him in person. She had listened to his commentary on highly publicized murder cases on the TV news for years.

Two breakout sessions presented by two detectives from the NYPD were scheduled in the afternoon, then a happy hour at the hotel lounge. In a sudden surge of giddiness she wrapped her arms around her body and grinned. *Happy hour in the hotel lounge.* She had never been to happy hour *anywhere.* Tomorrow would be a great day and she intended to make the most of it.

"You asleep?" Debbie Sue whispered in the dark.

"Yes," Edwina mumbled.

"No you're not. Listen, since we're both awake, let's go over our presentation. We've got time to put a shine on it. You know, really dazzle 'em."

"If you want me to dazzle an audience, you'd better let me sleep. I need all the rest I can get. I'm fighting a battle with Mother Nature and she's winning. Have you looked at the skin around my eyes lately? It looks like the Mohave Desert."

Debbie Sue sat up and switched on the lamp. "No, it doesn't. C'mon. Get the speeches we worked on out of your bag and let's read them again. Or if you don't want to, tell me where they are and I'll go over them by myself."

Edwina pushed a black satin sleep mask edged with red lace to her forehead and squinted against the light. "They aren't in *my* bag. I thought *you* had them."

"Don't tease like that, Ed. Look, you don't have to get up. Just tell me where they are and I'll get them."

Now Edwina sat up, the spaghetti strap of a red-and-black teddy falling off one shoulder. "Honest, I don't have them. Don't you remember the last night we worked on them at the shop? You said you'd take them because I, and I quote you here, 'can be such a dumbass I'd probably forget them.' End of quote."

The memory and her own words came back to Debbie Sue. Edwina was right. "Holy shit, Ed, what are we gonna do?"

In a panic, Debbie Sue left the bed and began to pace, shaking her hands as if she were drying a fresh coat of nail polish. "We worked for hours on those speeches. We can't get up in front of all those people without some notes or something."

Edwina yawned. "Hell, let's just wing it."

"Wing a ninety-minute program? Ed, your hair curlers are wound too tight." Debbie Sue sank to the edge of the mattress in despair. "I had slides, I had handouts, forgodsakes." Tears welled in her eyes. After seeing the insult on the sandwich board in the lobby, she had intended to knock their socks off with their presentation.

Edwina dragged herself out of bed, took a seat beside her on the bed and looped an arm around her shoulder. "Now, now, don't cry. I'm awake now. We'll work on it. I remember pretty much what we were gonna say."

Debbie Sue sniffled and looked at her best friend, "But Ed, it'll take all night."

"Yeah, I know." Edwina picked up a jar from the nightstand and began to slather gooey pink stuff on her face. "Just give me a sec to slap on another layer of this miracle cream. My face might look like Mother Nature tromped across it in golf shoes, but it damn sure won't be because I didn't put up a fight."

Spurred by a tiny stab of hope, Debbie Sue glanced at the digital clock. "Fuck, Ed. It's twelve fourteen."

"Piece o' cake," Edwina said.

"We need paper." Debbie sprang to her feet and began opening and closing drawers, finding a notepad featuring the hotel's logo. "Yay!"

And they began.

At three thirty, they looked at each other and declared their second effort complete.

"I don't know if this is as good as the first one," Debbie Sue said, "but it's better than nothing. I saw a business center in the lobby. Their sign said they open at six. I'll go down and type up these notes and use their copier." Debbie Sue plumped the pile of more than thirty note pages into a neat stack.

"What's a business center?" Edwina said, stretching.

"I read about it in the hotel brochures. It's a complete office for guests only. You can use computers, copiers, printers—"

"Fax machines?" Edwina asked.

"Yeah, fax machines." Suddenly Debbie Sue stopped and looked at her friend, "Good God almighty, Ed. We wasted the whole night. I could have called Buddy and had him fax our stuff to us. He could have gone to the sheriff's office last night and sent it. We could have picked it up at six."

"Shit," Edwina growled, climbing back into bed and plumping her pillow. "Like I said earlier, I'm in a race with that bitch Mother Nature and she's taken the lead again. I've only got four hours of sleep time left."

Debbie Sue sprawled in one of the swivel chairs located in the business center as she read to herself. She had awakened at five, showered and dressed; then she had called Buddy and asked him to fax the draft of their speech to her. Thank God he was an early riser, and thank God again, he was on vacation this week. She couldn't help but laugh. The speech Buddy had sent was longer than what she and Edwina had thrown together in the wee hours. But, in truth, she thought the second speech was better.

Now she pondered just how many great speeches or literary works throughout time had been authored in the midst of turmoil and haste. She had discovered something profound. "Wow," she muttered.

She pulled her cell phone from her pocket and pressed the single button that connected her to Buddy.

"Did you get them?" he asked without a hello. "Did they all come across okay?"

Debbie Sue cradled the phone against her cheek. "I can't thank you enough for getting up and doing this. Was Billy Don at the office yet?"

Billy Don Roberts was the sitting sheriff of Salt Lick. A few years back, when Buddy was sheriff, Billy Don had been his deputy. When Buddy chose not to run for reelection so he could dedicate his time and energy to becoming a Texas state trooper, Billy Don got the sheriff's job sort of by default. He ran with no opposition. Up until then his only ambition had been to perfect his calf roping skills by practicing on the fire hydrant in front of the sheriff's office.

Debbie Sue heard Buddy's soft chuckle and wished she were home. "No. I called him and he said he'd meet me, but he locked himself out of the county unit. I had to go by his house for the keys. Luckily, the office keys weren't on that ring."

"Nothing ever changes with Billy Don," Debbie Sue said.

"Yep, he's still Billy Don."

After a few more minutes of small talk, she said a reluctant good-bye and gathered up the pages he had faxed to her. There was no point in telling him she and Edwina probably wouldn't use them after all. She wasn't about to let him think he wasn't her knight in shining armor coming to her rescue.

Exiting the elevator Debbie Sue checked her watch. Just two hours before the NAPI-sponsored welcoming breakfast for the conference speakers and special guests. Edwina required a minimum of two hours to get gussied up. Debbie Sue hated to do it, but she had to wake her.

To her relief, when she swiped the key card and opened the door, she could hear Edwina talking and laughing.

"No, no. That's all right, you didn't call too early. . . . Yes, you're right. It is an hour later here. It's time I got up. . . . Yes, ma'am, it's pretty exciting for us, too. Okay, you take care, now, and don't do anything I wouldn't do."

Debbie Sue sat on the edge of the bed. "Who was that?"

"Maudeen. She wants us to bring them a memento of our trip."

Maudeen Wiley, a resident of the Peaceful Oasis home for senior citizens, was Debbie Sue's favorite octogenarian customer at the Styling Station. "Well, how nice of her to call."

"She and her roommate have been sitting by the phone for an hour, waiting to call us. They're so excited they can't think straight."

"A memento, huh? I don't know anyone but Maudeen Wiley who would use that word. What kind of memento do they want?"

"They want some pictures of John Wayne's hand and boot imprints from Grauman's Chinese Theatre," Edwina said, stretching and scratching her head.

"But isn't that in California?"

"Yeah, Hollywood. But I didn't tell her any different. If I've learned anything from working in beauty shops all these years, it's to not argue with old women. Just agree and go along."

"But how will we explain coming home without the pictures?"

"Just take her some little something from one of these souvenir shops and it'll tickle her to death. She won't even remember asking for the pictures. Did you get the speech from Buddy?"

Debbie Sue explained that the newer version they had worked on all night was the better of the two.

"Ah, a happy ending," Edwina said. "I love happy endings. Now, we've got breakfast in less than two hours. I better get started."

Debbie Sue stretched on the bed and congratulated herself for getting dressed ahead of time. While her friend primped and preened, she would catch a nap. She wanted to be bright eyed and bushy tailed for her introduction to Dr. William Wray. She planned on sitting near him and hanging on his every word. Though they hadn't met, he was no stranger.

He had performed autopsies in her living room, courtesy of HBO. He was practically family.

She drifted away and the next thing she heard and felt was Edwina calling her name and tugging on the toe of her boot. "Hey, sleeping beauty, let's get going. I'm starved. If I don't get something that came out of a chicken, sitting between two slices of what used to be a pig, I'm gonna faint."

Debbie Sue sat up and blinked herself awake. "You have a unique way with words, Ed."

"A waitress in Denny's told me the same thing, but I thought she was just trying to get a good tip."

"Okay, just let me brush my hair." She pawed through her bag, looking for a brush. "One of these days I'm gonna cut this horse blanket clear up to my ears."

"Yeah, uh-huh. And the day you do, Buddy'll divorce you again." Edwina picked up a long sheaf of Debbie Sue's long hair and let it fall. "He loooves these chestnut tresses."

The special breakfast in one of the banquet rooms was abuzz with activity. As Debbie Sue and Edwina stopped for a moment in the doorway, a middle-aged man in an expensive-looking suit approached them. "Excuse me, but would you ladies happen to be the Domestic Equalizers?"

"The Domestic Equalizers from *Salt Lick, Texas*, which is in West Texas, which is a heck of a long way from Dallas." Debbie Sue made the statement with a smile, but she had intended to make the point. Salt Lick was her hometown. No way was she going to allow it to be slighted.

The man laughed and extended his hand. "Sorry about that. I've had it corrected on the sign. I'm Paul Scurlock."

"No harm, no foul," Debbie Sue said, still smiling as she shook his hand. "I'm Debbie Sue Overstreet and this is my partner, Edwina Perkins-Martin."

"Pleased to meet you, Paul," Edwina said. "Would you mind if I hit the buffet? I'm so—"

"I just need to talk to you briefly. I have to tell you, this speakers' schedule has been a nightmare from the beginning—"

"Real snakebite, is it?" Edwina asked.

Debbie Sue sent her a scowl.

"Snakebite?" He gave them a quizzical look. "Um, yes, you might say that. I had you ladies on the schedule for today. But one of the Friday speakers has to leave early. I've rescheduled you for Friday and canceled your presentation for today."

With a plastic smile, Debbie Sue hid the video clip playing in her head of their all-night session of speech writing. It had been for nothing.

"Why, that's just fine with us, Paul." Edwina slugged him on the arm. Hard. "We're planning on staying right up to the end of this rain dance, so we'll be here."

"That's wonderful. I can't thank you enough. Excuse me, would you? I see some other guests I need to greet."

He floated away, leaving Debbie Sue glaring at Edwina. She knew Edwina. The woman had done that cowboy-talk routine on purpose. "Snakebite? Rain dance?"

Edwina opened her palms and looked wide-eyed. "What?"

Debbie Sue ignored her and sighed. "Okay. So we pulled an all-nighter for nothing."

Edwina came back with a wide grin. "But, hey, girlfriend. Like you said. No harm, no foul."

Debbie Sue grinned back. "Fuck you, Ed. Let's go eat something that came out of a chicken."

"Sitting between two slices of what used to be a pig. Now you're talking my language."

chapter eleven

The banquet room was packed. Sitting even remotely near Dr. Wray was impossible. Debbie Sue could see the captivated expressions on the faces of those fortunate enough to get seats close to him.

"Damn," Debbie Sue said. "We got here too late."

"Wait 'til after we've eaten," Edwina advised. "He's not going anywhere and neither are we. Let's just enjoy breakfast."

"You're right. There'll be other opportunities."

The hours after breakfast were taken up with miscellaneous announcements, introductions and speeches. Afterward, the Equalizers loitered in the hotel gift shop, which was filled with every possible interpretation of the New York City skyline.

"This crap's all made in China," Edwina complained.

"Everything's made in China," Debbie Sue replied. "Most of my truck's probably made in China."

Lunch, too, was crowded. Debbie Sue and Edwina had spent too long in the gift shop and were forced to take seats at the back of the huge room. They could barely see Dr. Wray. The sound system in the room was poor and they scarcely heard him, either.

They hadn't finished dessert before Debbie Sue was on her feet and striding out the door. Edwina trotted up behind her. "Where you going? What's the rush? I wanted to eat that piece of chocolate—"

"I intend to get a good seat at the afternoon sessions," Debbie Sue said. "I want to hear about reading body language during interrogation."

"Hmm, well, the one on blood spatter's the one I'm waiting for, especially so soon after lunch."

Suddenly, right in front of them, alone, looking at a magazine at the newsstand, stood the esteemed pathologist Dr. Wray. Debbie Sue gasped. "Oh, my God, Ed. There he is. I'm gonna talk to him."

She was within a few feet of her target when a stunning brunette at least as tall as Edwina tapped his shoulder and offered her hand to him.

Debbie Sue stopped and waited. With the black-haired woman, who had a definite big-city look about her, the doctor was more animated than he had been with the group who shared his table at breakfast. To Debbie Sue, he seemed to be flirting. Twice, the young woman excused herself and tried to walk away, but both times he took her arm possessively and pulled her back to him.

Debbie Sue hadn't yet attended the body-language workshop, but she didn't need a two-hour lesson to discern that the young woman was no longer enjoying the conversation with Dr. Wray. Stepping forward, she said in a loud voice meant to startle him, "Hey, doc, how about an autograph?"

Maintaining his viselike grip on the brunette's arm, Dr. Wray turned in Debbie Sue's direction and gave her the head-to-toe. "My, my. I didn't expect to see so many beautiful women attending this conference."

Debbie Sue wanted to shiver under his gaze. She felt as if he were looking through her clothes. "I'm not only attending, I'm a speaker." She flashed her best rodeo-champion smile and offered her right hand to the young woman in distress. "I'm Debbie Sue Overstreet. My partner and I are—"

"The Domestic Equalizers." The brunette stranger enthusiastically pumped Debbie Sue's hand.

Keeping a grip on the stranger's hand, Debbie Sue turned her own attention back to Dr. Wray. "Would you excuse us, doctor?" She pulled the stranger away from the newsstand and the doctor.

"Oh, my gosh," the brunette gushed. "You and Edwina are my heroes. I'm Celina Phillips, from Dime Box, Texas."

Lord, this girl had an even more pronounced Texas twang than Edwina.

"Hope you didn't mind my dragging you away," Debbie Sue said. "That creep was hitting on you. I've seen him on

TV about a thousand times. I thought he was something special, but turns out he's just another creep."

"I know," the newfound friend said. "I thought he was special, too. I watch him on TV all the time, too."

In no time Debbie Sue spotted Edwina standing outside a meeting room's doorway, reading a flyer. "Hey, Ed," she shouted. She motioned for Edwina to join her and Celina. "C'mere. I found another Texan." She turned back to Celina. "I don't know why it feels so good to run into someone from home, but it does. So, you're from Dime Box?"

"Yes, ma'am," Celina said, beaming. "You've heard of it?"

"Sure have. I've even been in a rodeo not far from there."

Edwina joined them. "Did I hear you say you're from Dime Box? I used to date the best-looking sucker from Dime Box. I can't remember his name, but he had the cutest butt in a pair of Wranglers."

Celina pressed her hand to her heart, "Edwina Perkins-Martin. I can't believe it. Ma'am, may I just say what an honor it is to meet you and Mrs. Overstreet?"

"Mrs. Overstreet?" Debbie Sue said. "Please don't call me that. Ever. Mrs. Overstreet's my mother-in-law. I'm Debbie Sue. How do you know about us?"

"You're kidding, right? Everybody in Texas knows about y'all. How you solved the murder of Pearl Ann Carruthers? The way you caught that horse thief in the middle of the night? Why, you're practically Texas legends. Just like Willie Nelson."

Debbie Sue shot a glance at Edwina. "Willie Nelson? Well, I wouldn't go *that* far."

"Well, *I* would," Edwina said. "In fact, I've been thinking about getting a tattoo while I'm here, and that might just be it. 'A Texas Legend.' Whatcha think?"

Celina squealed. "What a great idea. Where are you going to get it?"

"Just hold everything, Ed," Debbie Sue said. "We've got a session to attend and I'm trying to get a good seat. Celina, which breakout are you going to?"

"The two of you aren't speaking now?" Celina asked, thumbing through the program.

"Nope. We got moved to Friday. We're headed to hear a couple of NYPD detectives talk about body language and what it discloses in an interrogation."

"I already know everything there is to know about body language," Edwina said, her hip canted to one side. "You girls want me to show you some?"

"No, we do not." Debbie Sue took Edwina's arm with one hand and their new acquaintance's with the other. She herded both in the same direction. "We're going to hear some big-city boys give us *their* version."

"I'll bet they didn't have as much fun learning their method as I did learning mine," Edwina grumbled.

Celina leaned around Debbie Sue and grinned at Edwina. "Y'all are funny. This is going to be so great."

The three women gathered handouts at the door of the Big Apple Room and made their way to chairs at the center of the front row.

Two men sat on the stage, one significantly older than the other. Debbie Sue read their biographies. Frank Rogenstein, thirty-five years as a detective for NYPD. His curriculum vitae read like a police "Who's Who." He had served on specially formed mayoral committees, had earned just about every award and commendation NYPD bestowed.

"Did y'all read this guy Rogenstein's biography?" Debbie Sue asked.

"Yep," Edwina answered. "He looks like the real deal all right, a real New York City slicker'n-shit detective."

Debbie Sue grew misty eyed. "If only Buddy was here."

"I'm more impressed with the younger one," Edwina said. "Read about him."

Debbie Sue read on. The second man, Matthew "Matt" McDermott's bio was indeed impressive in a different way. He didn't have years of experience behind him as a NYPD cop, but, man-oh-man, did he have the foundation laid for a stellar career in law enforcement.

He had earned his college degree while serving in the U.S. Army Rangers. After completing his military tour he continued his education, graduating at the top of his class at NYU, then obtaining a master's degree in criminal justice. After only three years as a police officer, he catapulted to detective third grade and was clearly on a fast track to whatever sights he set for himself.

"I'll bet you could tell what Rogenstein had for lunch by looking at his tie," Edwina said.

Debbie Sue gazed at the older detective, who looked overweight and almost slovenly. The contrast between him and the sharply dressed, well-groomed young detective was so stark, Debbie Sue couldn't help but wonder why they were on the same bill. Ten minutes into their program, the reason became obvious. The younger man provided the animation and comedic relief for his somber co-presenter.

The audience, primarily male, laughed at the banter, but the women in the audience were clearly drawn to the handsome young detective. All but Celina Phillips. She was scribbling notes at a furious pace, smiling occasionally, but intently focused on the content rather than the speakers. She appeared to be oblivious to the young detective's charm, as well as to the fact that he had spent the better part of the first half hour of the program trying to catch her eye.

"What's that all about?" Debbie Sue asked her, glancing down at the copious notes she had taken.

"I'm going to be a private detective someday, just like you and Edwina."

Suddenly the senior detective announced it was time for a demonstration using an audience member. Detective McDermott left the stage and headed for Celina like a heat-seeking missile. As he came closer, Debbie Sue could see that his eyes were almost as dark as Buddy's and they showed a mischievous glint. He was tall, at least six three. He had on a blazer, but it was still obvious that he was well built. It might be a tired old cliché, but dammit, he *was* tall, dark and handsome.

He stopped in front of Celina. "Miss? Would you please help us?"

On top of all of that, his voice was soft and husky and sexy as hell. Debbie Sue laughed at the astonished expression on their new friend's face.

Celina turned red and stammered and resisted. "Oh, my gosh, I can't. No—"

"Go, girl!" Debbie Sue pushed her to a standing position.

The minute Celina had walked into the room and spotted the younger of the two detectives, she felt an unfamiliar sensation. It wasn't a bad feeling, just different. Now, as he led her up onto the stage, it seemed as if all of her blood had rushed to her face. Knowing he was well-versed in reading body language made what was happening all the more unnerving. Was he reading her body language now? Could he see that she was bowled over by him and doing everything possible not to show it?

The young detective thrust the microphone in front of her mouth. "Would you please share with the group your name and where you're from?"

Celina looked out over the sea of faces. There could be more people in this meeting room than there were residents of Dime Box. "Uh," she said in a tiny voice.

"And?" The detective prompted with his hand.

"Well . . . I'm Celina Phillips . . . And I'm from Dime Box, Texas."

Titters rippled through the audience. What was so funny?

The detective chuckled, too. "Well, Miss Phillips, I'm going to ask you to have a seat here, in our interrogation room." He took her by the arm and gently moved her toward a small table flanked by two metal chairs. He pulled one chair back for her to take a seat, then turned to the audience. "You folks in the audience who have pen and paper, would you please number a sheet of paper from one to six? I'm going to ask our volunteer a series of questions. After each question, mark if you think she is lying or telling the truth. We'll see how much you've learned from our presentation."

He moved to the chair opposite her. "Celina, I want you to answer yes to every one of my questions. No matter what the truthful answer is, just always say yes. Okay?"

Celina squirmed in her seat. She was a terrible liar. She had never been able to tell a lie and get away with it, which was why she always just stuck to the truth. This audience, any audience, would read her like a large-print book.

"We already know your name is Celina," the detective said, "and that you reside in Texas. Is that correct?"

"Yes." Celina chewed on her lip. "Have we started yet?"

Her interrogator grinned and patted her hand. "Yes, we've started."

Celina looked down at her hand to check for blistering, because his touch felt like a hot iron. "Okay."

"Are you married?"

She hesitated, realizing all of a sudden that she was required to tell a lie. "Uh . . . yes."

"Do you have children?"

"Uh, yes." At least that lie came easier.

"Are you staying in this hotel?"

"Yes." That one required no effort at all. Maybe lying wasn't as hard as she had always thought. Maybe it just took a little practice.

"Do you find me attractive?"

Celina blinked and swallowed hard. These questions seemed to be very personal. But then, perhaps they had to be for the game to work. She looked out to the audience for help, but everyone seemed to be sitting on the edge of his seat.

"Please answer the question."

Heat crept up Celina's neck. "Y—Yes."

"Would you meet me tonight around seven o'clock by the fountain and have dinner with me?"

The room gasped. Celina shot a help-save-me look at Debbie Sue and Edwina. Edwina slapped her knee and gave her a thumbs-up. Celina was confused to speechlessness.

"We're waiting for your answer," the detective said softly.

Celina looked into the deep brown eyes across the table from her. Was he serious? Or was this still a game? And was he making fun of her because he thought she was a hick from a small town? She cleared her throat. "Would . . . would you please repeat the question?"

"Certainly. Will you meet me tonight by the fountain and have dinner with me?"

"Yeah, I guess so. Or, uh, I think I mean yes."

The young detective grinned like the Cheshire cat. "Thank you, Miss Phillips. You did great." He turned to the audience again. "Let's give her a big hand for her participation."

As soon as the applause died, Celina rose and started toward the steps, leaving the stage. She was confused and strangely disoriented. Had she just made a date, or was it all a joke? She felt a hand on her elbow and looked up.

"See you at seven," the detective said softly.

She walked back to her seat dismayed. It had been disclosed to all present that she was single, had no children and was not staying at the hotel. She had fooled no one. Everyone in the room had read her clearly.

At the end of the session, members of the audience surrounded the two presenters, asking questions. Celina followed Debbie Sue and Edwina out into the hallway.

Edwina's hand came to her forearm. "Heavens to Betsy, girl. That piece of Yankee eye candy asked you out."

"I don't think so, not really."

"Oh, yes he did," Debbie Sue said. "And you should *not* go alone."

"I wasn't planning on going at all," Celina said. "Why, I'd look like an idiot showing up at that fountain. Especially if he didn't."

"No, you won't, because we're going with you." Debbie Sue gestured at herself and then Edwina.

"That's right," Edwina added. "We might have just met you, but hon, you're a fellow Texan. And you have no business going off with a man you barely know. Especially in New York City."

"Ed, you sound like her mother," Debbie Sue said.

"Don't get all teary-eyed," Edwina said. "I've got selfish motives. I'd like another chance to look at him myself. He's like my Vic. He's the kind of man that makes you forget your thighs are too skinny and your boobs are too flat. He just makes you feel like a woman, like you're the center of his universe."

"Wow," Celina said, still dazed. She hadn't thought of all of that. "I think I can't wait for seven o'clock."

The next presentation, conducted by the older detective, was "Blood Spatter at the Crime Scene and What It Reveals." The accompanying slides were gross enough to entertain a group of preteen boys. Celina found herself shocked at the graphic nature of real homicides. She had never seen such pictures on the NAPI Web site. A tiny doubt crept into her ambition. Did she really have the stomach for detective work?

During happy hour, as they sipped margaritas, Celina confessed to Debbie Sue and Edwina that she was staying at the YWCA because that was what she could afford, but new money concerns had cropped up. She didn't think she could attend all of the sessions, taking expensive taxi rides back and forth between the Y and the hotel. She was still trying to decide if she dared walk or take mass transit. She was too embarrassed to mention the theft of her extra money on the bus.

"That's just nuts," Debbie Sue said. "You're not going to commute back and forth from the Y. We've got a room upstairs bigger than most Salt Lick houses and it's not costing us a dime. You can bunk with us."

"She's right," Edwina added. "No point in you staying in that tiny room when we've got all that space. It's the least we can do. Hell, we Texans have to stick together in Yankeeland."

Debbie Sue grunted. "Dammit, Ed, people can hear you. Would you please stop talking about Yankees? The Civil War is over."

Celina's eyes grew moist. This trip was better than she could have imagined. Here she was, sitting with women she admired and could now call friends. And she had caught the eye of a man she could only dream about in her other life in Dime Box, Texas.

She had always believed there came an opportunity in everyone's life when all the pieces fell together for a memorable moment. The hard part was recognizing it and not letting it slip past. Was this the time, the moment? If so, she had to get a Velcro grip on the situation. She was *not* going to waste her life being ordinary.

Not for the next four days, anyway.

chapter twelve

At the end of happy hour, Celina excused herself and took a cab back to the YWCA to collect her belongings. Before leaving her tiny room, she called Granny Dee and gave her the big news.

"Well, sweetheart, it was awfully nice of those ladies to ask you to stay with them," her grandmother said, a slight hesitation in her voice. "Are you sure you won't be putting them out?"

"I guess not," Celina replied, "I haven't seen the size of their room, but they said it's big enough for all three of us. It was their idea."

"And it won't cost you anything?"

"It isn't costing *them* anything. It's one of their perks for being invited speakers. I'll save me a lot on carfare alone."

"Bless their hearts, this is just a godsend, isn't it?"

"Yes, ma'am, a godsend."

Celina and her grandmother talked a few more minutes before saying good-bye, but Celina made no mention of the Detective McDermott and the dinner plans for the evening. The date was still an uncertainty. Fantasies like the one in which she was presently suspended just didn't happen to girls from Dime Box, Texas. If they did, she would know about it. Following knowing about it, she would have read about it and studied what her reaction should be, which would have resulted in her feeling far more confident than she did now.

In the process of refolding and packing her clothing, she slipped her high heels off and wiggled her toes. She rarely wore high heels, but believing she needed them for her trip, she had bought them. In fact, she had a suitcase full of new clothes she and Granny Dee had gone to Austin and bought. She had maxed out her only credit card.

Still, what she wouldn't give to be wearing her boots, her tried and true Tony Lamas. She found herself wondering if Detective McDermott ever wore boots, or if he even owned a pair. She had always worn cowboy boots. And living a country life in a country setting, she had always imagined a cowboy in her future. The idea of anyone else had never crossed her mind, so why was she thinking about it now?

The answer was basic. Primal, in fact. Detective McDermott had turned her on like she'd never been turned on before. Sam might be comfortable, but he didn't give her a giddy feeling all the way to her toes. He didn't make her so nervous she couldn't talk. And until the detective had drawn her up onto that stage and she had looked into his deep brown eyes, she didn't even know those feelings were absent from her life.

She stopped at the registration desk and checked out, dragging her heavy suitcase or sometimes pushing it with her foot. Her run of good luck was apparently holding up, because just outside the Y's door, right in front of her, a man was climbing out of the backseat of a cab. She walked to the cab driver's window. "Excuse me, but could you please take me to Times Square?"

"I ain't doing this for my health," the driver said, without looking at her. "Get in."

Just a day ago, this sharp reply would have brought her near to tears, but today, she laughed. It just goes to show you, she thought. You can take the girl out of the country, but you can't take the best day this country girl has ever had and diminish it.

Edwina surveyed the hors d'oeuvres spread before her. She hadn't expected this much food on a complimentary buffet in the bar. A bag of Doritos and some hot sauce would have been just fine, but this was a banquet fit for a king.

Taking a seat and a table for two, she scanned the room for Debbie Sue. They had left the Big Apple Room together, but an overcrowded elevator forced them to separate. She didn't spot her, but she did notice several men sitting at a table together. Frank Rogenstein, the detective who had been partnered with Detective McDermott onstage earlier, was among the group. He caught her eye and raised his glass to her.

Edwina smiled and returned the gesture. It seemed like a harmless-enough response, but apparently he thought it was an invitation. He pushed his chair back and said something to his companions that caused raucous laughter. Then he headed in her direction. As far as Edwina was concerned, a man approached a strange woman with a drink in his hand and a stagger in his step for only one reason. *Shit. Where the hell is Debbie Sue?*

"Mind if I join you?" he asked.

Okay, she told herself, there was no reason to make a cynical assumption. She was a visitor in his city and, compared to him, a novice detective. No point in being rude. She smiled up at him. "Suit yourself, cowboy." She pushed the chair across from her away from the table with her foot.

He moved the chair around until it was adjacent to her and sat down, only inches away. "You're a cowgirl, eh?"

Edwina looked down at her clothing. Today she had on a hot-pink broomskirt and a glitzy white western shirt. "Naw. I'm a Broadway star. I'm in costume."

He chuckled and threw back a gulp of his drink. "Smart mouth."

She gave him a mouth-only grin.

He put his face close to hers. "You and your friend staying at the hotel?"

His whiskey breath almost singed her eyebrows. She leaned away from him. "Yes, we're in . . ." She caught herself. Good God, she had almost given him their room number. "Uh, we're on the eighth floor," she lied. "Great view."

Of course, somebody with his background and skills

would have no problem with a small challenge like getting a hotel room number if that was what he wanted. *Damn*.

"I'm on six. Haven't checked out the view. When you've lived in this city as long as I have, you've seen every view there is. Good and bad."

"Oh, I'm surprised you're staying here at the hotel. I mean you actually live in the city, right?"

"The rooms were part of the speaking offer, so McDermott and I decided to take them. It's convenient and we both got nobody to rush home to. Where's your partner?" He leaned back and adjusted his tie.

"Oh, she's got to be around here somewhere. We got split up on separate elevators. Where's yours?"

"Oh, he's around somewhere, upholding the law and defending the defenseless." He settled a look on her that she was positive was a leer. "You know how these young pups are, full of piss and vinegar. He's on a quest to make the city a better place."

"That doesn't sound like such a bad thing," Edwina said. "At least he's not robbing banks."

"It's an exercise in futility." He tilted up his glass and drained it, then motioned the waitress over. "How'd you and your partner get to be private eyes?"

Edwina spent ten non-stop minutes explaining how The Domestic Equalizers came to be. She figured she would bore him with an overload of detail and he would find something else to do. It appeared she was right. His eyes darted about the room. It didn't take a body-language expert to figure out that he wasn't listening.

To her surprise, he suddenly focused on her and leaned toward her. "You two were pretty smart, using a tracking device on that horse. Be sure to check out the vendor show while you're here. McDermott and I do some demonstrations on equipment that will blow your mind. Pure state of the art. You won't find anything like it in Texas."

Before Edwina could reply, Debbie Sue walked up. Taking a seat, she extended her hand to Rogenstein. "Hi. I'm Debbie Sue Overstreet. I enjoyed your speech this morning."

"Thanks. I was just telling your friend about some communications equipment you need to look at while you're here. It's a couple of steps up from the two tin cans and a string you country girls most likely use." He tilted his head back and guffawed.

Uh-oh. Edwina had seen Debbie Sue react to being laughed at before. Glancing her way, Edwina could almost see her hackles rise.

Debbie Sue glared, her chin thrust forward. "Tell you what, Slick—"

"Hi," Celina said. "I've checked out of the Y. Got my suitcase with me. Hope y'all weren't kidding about me staying with you." Their leggy new friend struggled to the table, dragging a suitcase the size of Dallas.

Debbie Sue shifted her attention to Celina. "No, we weren't kidding. The more, the merrier."

"It'll be like a slumber party," Edwina said, relieved at the interruption. "Let's go upstairs and get you settled in."

As they stood to leave, a beefy hand reached out and

grabbed Debbie Sue's wrist, pulling her down until her hair fell forward and brushed the surface of the table.

"If you girls want somebody to crash your little party, just let me know."

Debbie Sue pushed her hair back and gave him a sweet smile. "Tell you what we'll do if you're willing."

"You name it, babe. I guarantee I'm willing."

"We'll take off our clothes and get a couple of cans and some string, and when we're ready for you, we'll call you."

After a struggle to get her suitcase into the elevator, the doors closed on Celina and her two new friends.

Debbie Sue turned to her. "What's in that suitcase, bricks?"

Celina smiled sheepishly. "Everything I own, practically."

"Are you excited?"

"About what?"

"Your date this evening. It's only an hour from now. C'mon, tell me you just can't wait."

"You've got to be excited," Edwina put in. "Christ, that dude's so hot he probably wears flame-retardant shorts."

Celina laughed. It felt as if she had known these two forever. The new friendship reminded her of high-school years. Until this moment, she hadn't realized she missed female friends in her life. She made a mental note to remedy that situation when she returned home.

"Debbie Sue," she asked, "isn't your husband in law enforcement?"

A prideful grin spread across Debbie Sue's mouth. "He's a DPS trooper, working out of Midland. He's home now, studying for the state exam. He's trying for an appointment to the Texas Rangers."

"Texas Rangers! Are you serious? I've never even seen a Texas Ranger. You must be so proud."

"Proud?" Edwina said. "Look at her face. She's grinning like a virgin on prom night."

All of them laughed.

"Don't get off the subject, Celina," Debbie Sue said. "Seriously, aren't you excited about tonight?"

"I would be if I thought he'd really be waiting for me."

"I tell you what," Edwina said. "If he doesn't show up, it's his loss and our gain. One way or the other, we're gonna see the city tonight."

"Oh, gosh, if that's true, I've got to change shoes."

"You and me both," Debbie Sue and Edwina said in unison.

They reached their door, Debbie Sue swiped the key card and lifted Celina's suitcase. "Ugh," she said and set it back on the floor. "Damn, I'm used to lifting sacks of oats and bales of hay, but that sucker's heavy as lead."

"Let me help you," Celina said, and with one of them pushing and the other pulling, they slid the suitcase into the room.

"Make yourself comfortable," Edwina said.

Celina walked in, slowly looking around. The room was cavernous compared to the one she'd just left at the Y. "Oh, my Lord. This is fantastic. I mean, it's so, so, fancy. My grandmother said y'all were a godsend for asking me to stay with you and she was right. Thank you so much."

"Go on, now, it's our privilege." Edwina gestured toward the dresser. "Half those drawers are empty and there's plenty of room in the closet." She opened the door on the small refrigerator near the room's entrance. "Check out this courtesy bar, shug. I don't know what you do for a living, but I'll bet you could blow a month's pay on a Snickers bar."

Debbie Sue giggled. "Ed and I learned that the hard way. We checked out of a room in Fort Worth once and the tab for the"—she crimped the air with two fingers of each hand—"'courtesy bar' was higher than what we paid for the room. It took us three credit cards, getting out of there."

"Well, hell's bells," Edwina said indignantly. "How was I supposed to know? Who ever heard of paying five bucks for an undersized candy bar? Christ, I give away candy bars bigger than that at Halloween." She slammed the refrigerator door. "And all those cute little bottles of liquor were just there for the taking. I thought they were souvenirs. They shouldn't call it courtesy when it ain't free."

"Listen," Debbie Sue said, looking up at Celina, "all Ed and I need to do is slip on some comfortable shoes. You probably want the room to yourself while you freshen up, so we'll just grab our shoes and get out of your hair."

Edwina chuckled. "Hair. Get it?"

Celina blinked at the skinny brunette.

"Hair. We're *hair*dressers. Get it?"

"Oh, yes," Celina said, laughing. "I do get it. But you don't have to leave. I'll just change my shoes, too. Really. I don't need to do anything else."

Looks volleyed between Edwina and Debbie Sue, then settled on Celina. She suddenly felt uncomfortable. "What? What is it?"

"Your Granny Dee was right, sweet cheeks," Edwina said. "We are godsends. You've got a hot date tonight and we're the best damn hairdressers and cosmeticians in Salt Lick, Texas. Debbie Sue, grab your makeup kit and I'll get the hair spray."

"Uh, wait a minute. How many other hairdressers are there in Salt Lick?"

"Two." Edwina pulled a straight-backed chair from the desk and planted it in the center of the room. Then she grasped Celina's shoulders, moved her to the chair seat with a plop and started in on Celina's long hair before she could say another word.

While Edwina styled, Debbie Sue applied fresh makeup to her face. "Hey, you've got great cheekbones," she said as she brushed on blush. "Your eyes are the color of Martina McBride's and I've got this cool frosty lavender eye shadow. It's a perfect color for blue eyes." Debbie Sue dug through her makeup. "I brought this earthy rose color of lipstick—"

"Uh, I usually just wear something light and pinkish," Celina managed to interject.

"But you've got great heart-shaped lips. You need more color. Don't talk while I put this liner on you." Debbie Sue outlined her lips with a rosy brown color, then filled in with swipes of rose.

In a scant twenty minutes the makeover mavens were standing side by side behind Celina and she felt as if she were being scrutinized by artists viewing their masterpiece. "Can I look now?" she asked.

Debbie Sue stepped out of her line of sight, exposing the mirror behind her. "What do you think?"

Celina had never done much to herself with cosmetics, having always been afraid she would look like a clown. When she walked to the dresser mirror and looked, what she saw left her too stunned to reply.

Edwina had parted her hair on the side, leaving only wispy bangs. The ends of her hair had been turned under with a curling iron. Celina picked up a hand mirror and turned her head from side to side, viewed the back of her hair. "Oh, my gosh. This doesn't even look like me."

"Do you like it?" Debbie Sue asked, obviously anxious for approval.

"It's amazing. I love it. I mean, I love me. It's just . . . I don't know what to say."

"Just consider it a mini-makeover, courtesy of the Domestic Equalizers," Edwina said. "And when *we* say courtesy, *we* mean it's free."

"Ed and I are good," Debbie Sue added with a grin. "We can do more in twenty minutes than a lot of those city broads can do in an all-day spa."

"I really do love it." Celina continued to look in the mirror and touch the ends of her hair, feeling almost like it didn't belong to her. "Thank y'all so much. I just hope your work won't go to waste."

"Honey, looking beautiful is never a waste. A blessing, an inheritance and yes, sometimes a curse." Edwina swung her long, manicured finger back and forth. "But never, ever a waste."

On the elevator ride down to the lobby, Debbie Sue and Edwina talked and laughed nonstop, but Celina scarcely listened. Just thinking about Detective McDermott still had her unsettled. He was bound to be so worldly, so streetwise.

And he was so handsome and charming. How in the world had he remained single all this time? Then it struck her. What if he wasn't?

"What if he's married?" she blurted into Debbie Sue and Edwina's banter. "What if he intends to take advantage of me because he thinks I'm such a dumb hick I won't know the difference?"

Edwina gasped as her bony arm looped around Celina's shoulder. "He wouldn't dare. Besides, his partner said he doesn't have anyone to go home to."

"He could lie," Celina said.

"And if he did," Debbie Sue replied, "he'd be a turd. A big-city turd. And Ed and I have a remedy for turds."

"Yeah, we flush 'em." Edwina's tilted her head back and filled the elevator with her raucous laugh.

"Right," Celina said. "And I'll help you."

The elevator's chime sounded and the door glided open. Squaring her shoulders and lifting her chin, Celina made her exit. She might be overreacting and playing the role of drama queen, but she didn't care. Marriage was a sacred trust and she would never be a part of breaking one up. If this big shot showed up, she intended to let him know that she might be just a librarian from a tiny town in Texas, but she was no one's fool.

As she made her way to the fountain, she saw a throng of people all around it. She didn't see the detective and a small part of her was relieved. But a large part was disappointed. "See, I told y'all he wouldn't be—"

"Celina." Her ear instantly picked up his soft husky voice. "Hey, I'm glad you came."

She turned and right in front of her was the tall, dark and handsome big-city dude she was ready to put in his place. The cad that surely had a pregnant wife cooking his supper and darning his socks while she waited for him to come home.

His eyes moved all over her and came to rest on her face. "You look fantastic."

"Uh, hi," she managed, barely in a civil tone.

"I was afraid you wouldn't come. I thought maybe you didn't think I was serious."

"Why, that never crossed my mind," Celina said, hating herself for sounding like a Southern-fried fool.

"Detective?" Debbie Sue said. "Pardon me, but I want to introduce myself. I'm Debbie Sue Overstreet and this is my friend and partner, Edwina Perkins-Martin. We have an agency in Texas called The Domestic Equalizers."

"Hey," Matt McDermott said, shaking hands with them. "You're private eyes, huh?"

"That we are," Debbie Sue answered and Celina heard

the note of pride in her voice. "We own the only investigative agency in Salt Lick, Texas."

"That's just great," Matt said, and Celina was impressed. If he had figured out that Salt Lick might not have over a thousand residents, he didn't show it. "Are you three ladies traveling together?"

"No, we just met today," Debbie Sue said. "Just before your presentation, in fact. Which, by the way, we enjoyed."

"Thank you. Is this your first trip to New York City?"

Celina stood by as Matt and her new friends made polite chitchat. Suddenly she heard a voice that sounded like her own. "So, is your wife at home darning your socks while your supper gets cold on the table?"

Matt, Debbie Sue and Edwina all three turned and looked at her as if she had said something in an extinct language.

Finally, a slow smile tipped up the corners of Matt's almost perfect mouth. "No, Celina, there's no one at home waiting for me. I'm not married. You?"

"I live with my grandmother." She closed her eyes and cursed herself. So much for sophistication and glamour. So much for mystique and depth.

He leaned closer and looked into her eyes. "Then I envy you, Celina. My grandmother helped raise me and I can't think of a better place to be than at my grandma's house."

His words went straight to Celina's heart.

His attention turned to Debbie Sue and Edwina. "You know, it wouldn't be right for Celina to go out alone with a stranger in this city. Even a cop. Why don't you two ladies join us? I'd love to show you New York."

"Great," Debbie Sue said.

"Lead me to it," Edwina followed up.

Detective McDermott ushered all three out of the hotel lobby and into the bright lights, the strange smells and the din of the Big Apple. "Let's start with Times Square. Ladies, watch your step coming off that curb."

chapter thirteen

*H*aving an escort who had an NYPD badge to flash opened more doors than a run-of-the-mill guided tour could offer, Debbie Sue noticed.

Stage-door entry to a Broadway theater wasn't in any of the brochures she had read. She hadn't counted on an express elevator ride to the top of the Empire State Building, with no waiting in the tourist line, either.

Through all of this, Debbie Sue was busy observing the young detective and her fellow Texan. Detective McDermott was attentive and polite to all three of them, but his eye was unquestionably on Celina.

"You sure know how to make a good impression on the first date," Edwina said to Matt as they exited the Empire State Building carrying bags of souvenirs.

The detective laughed. "It's as much fun for me as it is for you. I was amazed by all the sights when I first came here, but with the job I do now, I tend to forget the great things to see and do."

"You're not from here?" Celina asked.

"Nah. I'm a small-town kid. Born and raised in Osceola. It's about five hours northwest of here. Population two hundred sixty-five, most of whom are related to me."

"But you seem so sophisticated and so . . . well, so citified. No one would ever know you weren't born and raised here. You act as if you've never lived anywhere else."

He laughed again. "One of the first things you learn in Special Forces training is that we each have it within us to be anything we want to be."

Celina was leaning toward him as if she had been hypnotized. Though Debbie Sue hadn't known Celina long, she could see she was truly a small-town girl whose sophistication level was far lower than the detective's. Celina hadn't told them her age, but she couldn't be more than twenty-five or twenty-six, Debbie Sue surmised. No way could she let a fellow Texan be taken advantage of by a city slicker. She frowned and chewed on her bottom lip, looking for a way to change the mood. "Say," she said brightly, "let's go somewhere and have a drink."

"Great idea," Edwina said. "I'd like a martini. New York City style."

"Now you're talking," Matt said. "If it's a martini you want, the Blue Bar in the Algonquin is the only place to go.

They have a martini on their menu that costs ten thousand dollars."

"Christ-on-a-crutch," Edwina exclaimed. "I'm guessing you pay up front when you order that."

"Actually, you have to make a reservation for that drink."

"No shit. That's plumb crazy. And here I thought Texas had everything."

Taking Celina by the elbow, the detective walked to the curb and hailed a cab. While they waited, Debbie Sue felt Edwina's stare. "Why are you looking at me like that?" she whispered.

"You haven't said ten words all evening. What's going on with you? I know you're tumbling something around that head of yours. What is it?"

"I'm trying to decide if I like him."

"Why? What's wrong with him? He's been the perfect gentleman. He's definitely taken with Celina."

"I can't put my finger on it. You know how you get these feelings? There's just something about this guy. He's too good-looking, too smooth. My instincts tell me there's more to him than just good looks and good manners. I think it's what we're not seeing that's bothering me."

"Excuse me, but are these the same instincts that kept you in the company of a womanizing rodeo cowboy when you and Buddy were divorced? A man who most likely holds the record for paternity testing?"

"Okay, okay," Debbie Sue said. "I never said my instincts were perfect."

★ ★ ★

"The Algonquin is the oldest hotel in operation in New York City," Matt told them as they walked through the lobby. Celina's eyes darted everywhere. The surroundings looked like money with a capital M. Very old, very well kept money. The place even smelled like money. Just as in the blue-collar diner where she had eaten supper, Celina again had the impression that people were staring at her. *Oh, my gosh, I'm not dressed right*, she said to herself.

As if he were reading her thoughts, Matt placed a hand on her waist and pulled her closer. "You're the most beautiful woman here. All eyes are on you."

"That's because this is a fancy place and I'm not dressed for it. I don't feel right being here."

"Don't think that. They admire how you look. As for being here, all that's required is that we cover our tab, and unless you or one of your friends orders that high-dollar drink, we'll be all right."

At the bar's entrance, he stopped and spoke to a gentleman who ushered them to a table. Celina didn't see Matt show his badge, but she did notice a transfer of money from his hand to the host.

Once seated, the ritual of getting to know each other continued. The more they drank, the more they revealed. To Celina's surprise, Matt came from a large Irish family and a long line of cops. He was the youngest of seven children. He had six older sisters.

"No wonder you seem so at ease with women," Debbie Sue said.

"Were you their baby?" Edwina teased.

"Their baby, their pupil, their dance partner and eventually their confidante. It was great. They still fuss over me and try to protect me. One thinks I'm too thin, another too heavy. I need to be married, I need to keep looking for the right girl. If I ever bring a wife into my life, she'll have to be tough, to deal with my sisters."

Edwina ordered another round of drinks. The longer the evening wore on, the bolder the stories and jokes got. Celina absorbed every word, laughing at one point in an embarrassing snort. She had never had so much fun. Her life in Dime Box seemed a planet away. Could she return there and be content?

A question came to her. How had Granny Dee left this pulsating place? This glamour? This activity? The answer came just as quickly as the thought. For love. She had done it for love. Celina sneaked a glimpse in Matt's direction. He was so different from what she had first thought. Like her, he was from a small town. He had strong ties to his family. He was ambitious and hardworking. But how could something come of this chance meeting? They lived two thousand miles apart and she was here for only four days.

Debbie Sue asking Matt a question jolted her from her musing. "Detective McDermott, are you working on an interesting case now?"

Matt had loosened his tie and was sitting in a relaxed posture. "All cases in homicide are interesting. Otherwise I wouldn't do it."

"I read an article about some murders the NYPD thinks are linked."

"Oh, you mean the seven prostitutes? There's been a lot of publicity about that."

"The article said they'd been murdered in nice hotels. No sleazy rent-by-the-hour places. And they were all strangled. The article said the police have no leads."

"NYPD might be holding information back. They rarely release everything they know to the press."

"I just figured no one was working on it very hard because the victims were prostitutes and no one really cares," Debbie Sue said.

Matt's jolly demeanor changed. He straightened and drilled Debbie Sue with a direct look. "That's not true. Cops care about clearing cases. And they care about the victims no matter who they are."

Sensing the tension in his reply, Celina asked, "Y'all want to hear my theory?"

"We'd love to," Matt said, relaxing again and turning to her with a smile.

"Okay. Now mind you, I have no experience, but I've read a ton of books about the criminal mind and crime solving. And I wrote a paper on criminal psychology in college."

Edwina stared at her slack-jawed. "You don't say," she said.

Celina laughed. "I'm a librarian, remember? I read everything, including labels on bottles and jars."

"So, give us your theory," Matt said.

"Well, I'm betting he takes them to nice places because he fits into that environment. He probably wears a business suit and a tie. He meets them in the hotel bar or the lobby. I've read that strangulation is the most personal type of killing. A killer is very close to the victim, physically, I mean. Close enough to see her face. To him, it's all about power."

"Not a bad assessment," Matt said, still smiling. "You really have done your homework."

Celina grinned, looking around the table and tapping her temple with her forefinger, "See? I know something about detecting too."

"You sure do," Edwina said. "Now put those skills to work and tell me where the bathroom is. My eyeballs are floating."

By the time Celina and her new friends left the steeped-in-tradition Algonquin Hotel bar, just before 2 A.M., the entire bar staff and most of the customers knew them by name. Edwina had gone to each table and hugged the occupants good-bye. She had invited all of them to Salt Lick for a "big ol' barbeque with all the fixin's" and had offered Debbie Sue and Buddy's home as sleeping quarters.

Stepping into the warm night air Celina was stunned to find the streets still alive with activity. And smells. The brilliantly lit giraffe at Times Square peeked from behind its sign at the streets below. A Styrofoam cup of coffee, four stories tall, steamed and looked so real she could almost taste it. This truly was the city that never slept.

"I can't believe there are so many people up and around this time of the morning," she said to Matt, no longer fearing that she might sound like a country mouse.

"Some are just waking up. And some haven't been to bed

yet. There are clubs, restaurants and bars that don't even open until now. Where I came from, the streets fold up at nine o'clock and most self-respecting people go to bed."

Celina tilted her head back, stretched out her arms and turned in a circle, drinking in the moment and her surroundings. "It's all crazy. And wonderful."

"Could you get used to living in this city?"

The question caught Celina off guard. He surely couldn't mean anything by it. They had only just met. But there was something in his steady gaze that made her wonder. "Gosh, I don't know. I mean, this place is like nothing I've ever seen. But I guess what it would boil down to for me is that it's not home. Good old dull, predictable, sweet, soothing home."

Matt's mouth tipped up in a smile and he gave her an unexpected hug. "I'd have been surprised if you'd said anything else." Releasing her, he gestured toward Edwina and Debbie Sue, who were standing at the curb having a contest over who could stop a cab first. "I need to remind them that your hotel is only two blocks from here."

Before he could reach them, a cab pulled over and they climbed into the backseat, leaving the detective to shake his head and observe.

Celina could see the driver of the cab waving his arms and shouting. He attempted to open his door and crawl out, but Matt stepped forward, showed his badge and held the door shut. He bent to eye level with the driver.

"What's the problem?" His tone spelled no nonsense and demanded a clear answer.

Edwina leaned forward. "Detective McDermott, this guy's refusing to give us a ride back to the hotel."

The eyes of the driver grew wide. "You police? You police? Anson hotel two block. They walk two block. You make them. This my cab."

"We don't want to walk," Debbie Sue said. "You drive."

"No. Get out. You get out now."

"Nosiree-bob," Edwina said. "We got money, you got cab, move it."

"This is not *your* cab," Matt said to the cab driver. "It belongs to the City of New York. You're required to take fares anywhere within the metropolitan boundaries. Do it now, or I'll call for a truck to tow this vehicle back to your garage."

The driver blinked.

"Do you understand me?"

"Yes. Yes, okay, yes. I take them."

Matt looked into the backseat and smiled, his relaxed personality back, "Ladies, have a nice ride."

"Wait a minute," Debbie Sue said and looked at Celina. "Aren't you coming with us? You should come with us."

"We'll walk," Matt answered.

"I don't mind walking," Celina said to Debbie Sue.

Celina stood with him watching the cab pull away. She turned, looked up at him and laughed. "Good grief, you're Clint Eastwood."

Chuckling, he took her arm and urged her along the sidewalk. "Come on. I'll bet we can get to the hotel before they do."

Sure enough, just as Matt said, they reached the hotel first. They waited in the lobby for the arrival of her new friends from Texas.

When Debbie Sue and Edwina appeared, Matt asked Edwina, "Did you give him a tip?"

"I gave him a coupon for a buy-one, get-one-free dinner at Dickey's Barbeque Pit in Fort Worth. I don't usually shaft somebody on a tip, but he was rude. I don't believe in rewarding rude behavior."

Debbie Sue yawned. "Well, I don't know about the rest of you, but I'm beat. Ten o'clock will be here real quick and I'm going to my room. Detective," she said, extending her hand, "thank you so much for a fun evening. I wish my husband Buddy could have been here to hear some of the stories."

"Let me walk you to your room," Matt said. "What floor are you on?"

"We're on six," Celina answered.

"Good. I'm on seven. It's on my way."

Herding the three women in the span if his arms he ushered them to the elevator.

Once they were at their door, Debbie Sue and Edwina said their good nights and hurried into the room, leaving Celina and Matt together outside the door. He touched the gold numbers on the room's door. "Six eighteen. Rogenstein must be on the other side of you. He's in six twenty. I remember it because it's my badge number."

"Who?" Celina asked.

"The detective who was with me in the demonstration earlier. Frank Rogenstein."

"Oh, yes, of course," Celina said, laughing. "My gosh, was that just this afternoon?"

Suddenly Matt moved a step nearer and braced his hand against the wall beside her head. He was so close Celina could see a tiny scar on his upper lip, smell his woodsy cologne. He looked at her for long seconds before brushing her lips with his. It was soft and sweet, barely a kiss but more intimate than she had expected.

"I hope you don't think I'm moving too fast," he said softly, "but you aren't going to be here very long."

Celina surprised herself by placing her hand on his cheek and pulling him back for more.

"Ed," Debbie Sue said, "get away from there. What's the matter with you?"

Edwina had plastered her ear to the door. "Shhh, they'll hear you. I just want to hear how things are going. You know, who makes the first move and all."

"I guarantee it's him making the move," Debbie Sue said, now pressing against Edwina's back and trying to hear also. "He hardly took his eyes off of her all evening."

"I know. It was sweet."

Debbie Sue straightened and planted her hands on her hips. "Sweet? You think it's sweet watching a cobra move in on a helpless mouse?"

Edwina straightened, too. "Hell, Debbie Sue, you've been watching too much *Animal Planet* on TV."

"I'll have you know I worried all the way back to the hotel about leaving her alone with him."

"C'mon. They're two single, good-looking, healthy young people. They look like they were made for each other."

"Humph. Says who?" Debbie picked up her makeup kit and padded to the bathroom.

Edwina followed and leaned a shoulder against the door-jamb. "You don't like him, do you?"

Debbie Sue looked at her reflection in the mirror. "It's not that I don't like him. There's just something about him that makes me nervous and I don't know what it is."

"Cut him some slack. He was in Special Forces. My Vic was one of those guys. They're cut from a different cloth."

"Yeah, you're probably right. But did you see the look on his face when he was talking to that cab driver tonight?

Edwina's eyes widened and her palms lifted. "What's with looks?"

"He looked like if that cab driver had twitched a wrong muscle, he would tear him apart."

"Just think of the job he has, what he deals with every day. He has to be tough. Hell, I've seen Buddy Overstreet give a look that could stop a current in a creek after a gul-lywasher. He gave me that look when I asked him to fix a speeding ticket for me."

Debbie Sue dug a hairbrush from her satchel and began to brush her hair. "You're right. And I remember that I was afraid of Vic when you first introduced him to me. I didn't trust him one little hoot. For a full year I hoped y'all would break up. But that was before I learned to love him too."

"You've never said you were afraid of my Vic? How come?"

Debbie Sue secured her hair in a scrunchie, then slathered soap on her face, mumbling through her washcloth. "Well, there was the whole ex-wife thing. Every time she called I'd think he was going to leave and break your heart."

"That was once a week. Why didn't you tell me that back then?"

"I trusted you." Debbie Sue said, drying her face and digging for her toothbrush. "I knew if he wasn't the real deal, you'd pick up on it and send him packing."

Just then the door opened and Celina floated into the room. Her hair was a little tousled and the perfect makeup job Debbie Sue and Edwina had done on her was more than a little smudged.

She leaned back against the door and sighed. "Don't y'all just love New York City?"

"I was just telling Debbie Sue what a hoot it is," Edwina said.

"Guess where Matt is taking me tomorrow night?"

Debbie Sue came out of the bathroom, exchanged a glance with Edwina and shrugged. "No clue."

"To Madison Square Garden. Isn't that romantic?"

"If you say so," Edwina said.

"Don't you remember me telling you, that's where Granny Dee met my granddad? He was competing in a rodeo and it was love at first sight."

"I do remember now. So he's taking you to a rodeo?"

"No, I think it's a basketball game, but it's still romantic."

Debbie Sue's brow rose in an arch.

Edwina elbowed her in the ribs. "Get that look off your face and smile."

"Ow! What look?"

"The one that looks like you just coughed up a hairball."

"Oh, *that* look."

chapter fourteen

On Thursday morning, Debbie Sue awoke in a less frivolous mood than when she had gone to bed a few hours earlier. All she could think about was aspirin. And food. Then she remembered that Edwina had had the forethought the night before to order coffee, orange juice and pastries to be delivered to the room by nine o'clock.

She threw off the covers and eased to a sitting position. "Please tell me I smell coffee."

"Yes, ma'am," Edwina said. "Hot coffee with sugar and real cream. That and sugar-loaded goodies. Look at this. Cinnamon rolls, strawberry tarts, banana muffins and cheese blintz. A ton of sugar. Just what you need to kill a hangover."

"I'll have a little of all of it," Debbie Sue said. "Take the cup, put the pastries inside, pour the coffee over them and hand it to me."

"I don't have a hangover," Celina announced cheerily. She had come from the bathroom wearing a terry-cloth robe and carrying a towel.

"That's because you're an infant," Edwina said, pouring steaming coffee into three cups. "The young still have strong-enough brain cells to fight off drinking too much."

Debbie Sue took the cup Edwina handed her. "There's that. And the fact that you drank a third of what we did."

Edwina carried her own cup of coffee and a huge cinnamon roll to a chair. "My downfall must have been those chocolate sundae martinis. I lost count at five."

"You ordered six, but I drank three of them," Debbie Sue said. "There oughta be a law against making something that lethal taste so fuckin' good. The surgeon general should look into that."

"Do you remember what was in them? I'd like to make them for Vic. He'd really get a kick out of them."

"I don't remember and if you don't mind, I don't want to talk about it anymore. My head hurts just thinking about it."

"I remember," Celina said triumphantly. "It was vodka, white and dark Godiva chocolate and white cocoa liqueur, topped with whipped cream and chocolate shavings."

Debbie Sue rolled her eyes. "Sweet mother of God. She's got beauty, youth, legs that require their own area code and a memory to boot. I think I hate you."

Celina laughed. "No, you don't. You love me and I love

y'all. And I love New York City and everything about it. I'm going to the health club on the roof for a swim. Anyone want to come along?"

Debbie Sue stared at her. Even if she had been in the mood for physical activity, she wasn't about to admit that she couldn't swim.

Edwina gave her the thumbs-up sign. "Hon, you just go right on ahead. We'll get our swim in later."

"Okay. Byeee!" Celina left the room waving a bagel over-head.

Debbie Sue waved to her back. "Ed, when she comes back to the room, I want you to kill her. Nothing bloody, just quick and to the point. Better yet, follow her up to the roof and push her off."

"Oh, come on, now. She's in love. Don't you remember when you felt the first blush of a new love?"

That statement brought on a deep thought. Debbie Sue took a bite from a muffin, a bagel and then a strawberry tart. "Kind of. But I've been in love with Buddy my whole life, so it's kind of hard to pin down the exact moment."

"Well, as far as I'm concerned, it's the best damn feeling in the world. I've felt it a dozen times and this last one is the best. I think I'm going to take my cell phone in the bath-room and do some dirty talking to my baby back home. You need to get in there first?"

"Naw, go ahead."

"Okay. Byeee!" Edwina entered the bathroom waving her cell phone over her head.

"Don't steam the mirrors up," Debbie Sue yelled back.

★ ★ ★

At ten o'clock the three of them stood at the fountain, each with her list of the day's programs. Debbie Sue scanned the names of presenters. "See anything that strikes your fancy?"

"Oh, pooh. Matt's name isn't listed," Celina said. "This must be the day he's working in the exhibit area."

"Nothing toots my horn until three P.M.," Edwina said. "High-Tech Undetectable Listening Devices. That's the one for me."

"Gee," Celina said, chewing on her bottom lip. "Everything up to then is DNA or weapons. I really don't care about either one. But you're right, that three o'clock sounds cool."

"I'm gonna make a suggestion that will sound really bad," Edwina said. "I mean, we came all this way to attend sessions on improving our detecting skills. But *I* want to go shopping."

"Shopping!" the others chorused.

"Well, think about it. When are we going to go shopping?"

"Do we *have* to go shopping?" Debbie Sue asked. "You know I hate shopping."

"This is New York City. How can we *not* go shopping? The first thing anyone back home is going to ask is, what'd you buy? How can we answer *dinner*?"

"I'll admit," Debbie Sue said, "I've never seen you pass up the chance to hit the stores."

"I want one of those knock-off designer purses," Edwina said.

"Oh, me, too," Celina said. "No one in Dime Box will

ever know the difference. And I'd like to get something special for tonight." A soft hue of pink flushed her cheeks.

"And shoes," Edwina added. "How can I not buy a pair of shoes in New York City?"

Debbie Sue heaved a great sigh, just to make her companions aware of her sacrifice. "Okay. I'm not into fancy clothes unless they're western and I can't imagine giving up my cowboy boots for *shoes*, but I do want some of Tiffany's perfume. I've seen *Breakfast at Tiffany's* a dozen times."

"Then it's settled," Edwina said. "We're going shopping. Are we going together or going our separate ways and meeting back here at three?"

A warning sounded in Debbie Sue's head as a dozen nightmarish scenarios involving Edwina alone on the streets of New York passed through her thoughts. "Together. We started this together. We stick together."

At two thirty the trio returned to the hotel and struggled through the revolving door carrying bags and boxes. They had been to Tiffany's, Bergdorf Goodman and Saks Fifth Avenue. Edwina had haggled with a handful of street vendors on everything from handbags to sunglasses. Not a bad day for a group of out-of-towners with a limited budget, Debbie Sue figured.

Edwina started for the elevators. "Let's go upstairs and dump our stuff and change our shoes. Then come back down for the session and catch happy hour again."

Debbie Sue, carrying her one tiny bag with her bottle

of perfume tagged behind. "I can't believe I'm going to say this, but a drink sounds good right now."

Edwina pushed the elevator call button. "See? What doesn't kill you makes you stronger."

"This walking won't kill me, but the drink after the session will sure make me stronger," Debbie Sue quipped.

"Definitely change the shoes," Celina said. "In fact, I'd like to change my feet. They can say what they want about New York, but it is all about the shoes, isn't it?"

"Spoken like a true Texan," Debbie Sue said as they trooped onto the elevator.

Across the lobby, a man watched the three women board the elevator. He had been following them all afternoon as they chatted and laughed without a care in the world.

At first he had thought they might be different from most women—ambitious and eager to work in a man's world—but they weren't. They weren't interested in their careers. Just like every bitch he had known, they only wanted to shop for expensive perfumes, enticing undergarments and stiletto high heels.

Oh, each one of them would say she did it for a man waiting for her at home, but he knew why they really did it. They did it to fool their men into thinking the shopping spree was a gift from them, their idea. Then they would meet over lunch and laugh at the poor saps. These three were no different from whores. They knew what they wanted and what they had to do to get it.

At least the pros were upfront and honest about it—no

pretense about what *they* wanted. They were dirty but didn't act like they weren't. Not at all like this Texas trio.

They flirted and cooed and batted their eyes. They were the disgusting ones. Liars.

Conniving bitches.

They were a triple threat to men and he was the "Righteous Avenger." He only needed a pair of tights and a cape. Maybe a really cool mask.

He chuckled at this thought. He was still laughing as he stepped onto an elevator and the door closed.

Debbie Sue, along with her two friends, listened to a short, rotund speaker wearing shiny black pants. "This microphone is designed to convert minute vibrations to voice-band audio that can be received by headphones or secondary measurement equipment." He held up an item no bigger than a pack of cigarettes for all to see.

Apparently satisfied his audience had a clear view of his product, he continued, "The Ear-Millennium Edition—or as we call it, the Ear—far surpasses any listening device on the market. Place it against the wall, put in the earphones and you're in business. If desired, a recording device or speakers can be plugged in. To the innocent bystander, you might appear to be listening to your iPod." He laughed as if he had said something funny.

The memory of an incident she and Edwina referred to as "a total FUBAR" popped up in Debbie Sue's mind.

A Salt Lick resident, J. W. Jones, had been convinced his wife, Trixie, was having an affair with Stony Curtis, a local truck driver who also happened to be J. W.'s best friend. J. W. hired the Equalizers to follow Trixie and report their findings.

Indeed, they discovered Trixie entering and exiting Stony's home on several occasions. The ear-to-the-wall technique, or huddling outside the subject's front door, revealed a conversation that Debbie Sue and Edwina agreed was particularly telling. Stony had clearly asked Trixie if she would like to take it doggie style.

What the Equalizers discovered too late was that Trixie had been looking to purchase a motorcycle Stony had for sale. She intended to give it to J. W. on his fortieth birthday. What Stony had really asked was if Trixie would "like to take the hog for a ride." Unfortunately for all involved, the Domestic Equalizers' listening technique had been a dismal failure.

Luckily, in the end J. W. was so relieved that his wife was faithful, that he hadn't lost his drinking buddy Stony and that he was now the owner of a new motorcycle, he dropped the whole matter and didn't take the Equalizers to task. But the debacle would forever haunt them.

Debbie Sue wrote the name of the state-of-the-art listening device on her notepad. *Gotta have this*, she wrote beneath the name, followed by several exclamation points. Beneath that she drew a circle, put a big dollar sign inside and drew a line through it. The shopping escapade had been more expensive than she had planned. Leaning toward Edwina she whispered, "Let's go to the exhibitors' room. I'd like to look at this up close."

"Good idea," Edwina whispered back. "I was just thinking about the time when we really could have used that."

"Yeah, I know, I already thought of it. M.S.U."

"Huh? Oh yeah, major screw up." Edwina eased out of her chair and followed Debbie Sue from the hall.

They had barely walked six feet when they heard Celina call their names. "Debbie Sue, Edwina, where are y'all off to?" She was struggling with some literature in her hands and her purse strap was falling from her shoulder.

"We're headed to the exhibit room. We want to look at the Ear," Debbie Sue said.

"Want to join us?" Edwina asked.

Celina giggled. "No. I just wanted to be sure you weren't going to the bar without me."

"Well, look at you, party girl," Edwina said. "What about your date tonight?"

"Oh, I'm wouldn't miss that for anything. I just wanted to have a drink and eat something before he picks me up. I'm starving. See you at happy hour."

Debbie Sue watched the door close on Celina and turned to Edwina. "Now that I think about it, I'm hungry too."

"After all those hot dogs and pretzels you ate from the street vendors?"

"I didn't eat that much," Debbie Sue said, defending herself.

"Excuse me, but we didn't walk past one, not one cart, that you didn't stop and buy something."

"I couldn't help it, Ed. It was all good. Why does everyone say eating out in New York is so expensive?"

"I guess it's all in how you interpret the word *out*."

"Let's go to the bar, have one drink, eat some of the free-bies they have on their buffet, then go look at the Ear."

"Great. I'll round up Celina."

Five minutes later they were seated in the dark hotel bar.

"May I bring you ladies something?" the cocktail waitress asked.

"Christ, I haven't forgotten the price of margaritas in this joint. I'll have a Coke," Edwina said to the waitress.

"Me too," Celina said. "Something nonalcoholic sounds good."

Debbie Sue added her order to the round of drinks. "Light beer." She rose from her seat. "I'm going to the buffet. You two want anything?"

"No thanks," Edwina said.

"I'll go with you," Celina said, and stood up, too.

While Debbie Sue and Celina filled plates at the buffet, Edwina noticed a woman's silhouette in the doorway. The light behind her prevented immediate identification, but something about her was familiar. Then it hit her. Cher Giacomo.

Edwina strained to make eye contact and waved. Cher, spotting her, waved back and came in her direction. She was dressed for the evening, Edwina noticed, in something that looked to be expensive. It was extremely revealing.

"Have a seat. Debbie Sue and another person who's here from Texas are at the feeding trough."

"I can't stay but a minute," Cher said, casing the room. "I've got a date in half an hour."

"Oh? Is this a regular date or a business date? Or is that question too personal?"

Cher flipped her wrist. "Nah. I don't care if you ask. It's a business date. I'm business all the time. And speaking of that, I'm going to step into the ladies' room and make a call. Order me a scotch and water, will you? And if a guy comes in wearing a pilot's uniform, would you wave him over?"

"Hey, a date with an airline pilot, huh?"

"He's not a pilot. But he gets off dressing like one. Be back in a second." She sailed away on four-inch heels toward the ladies' room.

Debbie Sue and Celina returned with plates of hot wings, shrimp, chips, dip and vegetables.

"Wow, who was that?" Celina asked. "She looks like Rita Hayworth in *Gilda*."

Edwina reached for a stick of celery. "How do you know who Rita Hayworth was? Or for that matter, *Gilda*? Even *I'm* not that old."

"Granny Dee is a movie buff. Any era, any genre, she's got them all. I've seen *Gilda*, oh, probably a dozen times."

"Gives me new hope for the youth of today," Edwina declared.

Celina laughed. "Now, stop it. Who is she? Is she attending the conference, too?"

"She's just a lady we struck up a conversation with the first night we were here," Debbie Sue said. "She's not attending the conference, but I think she works close to here."

Not wanting to reveal Cher's occupation to Celina, Edwina looked for a way to change the subject. "I wish they had a jukebox in here," she said.

"Yeah," Debbie Sue muttered. "Nothing says class and refinement like a lit-up Wurlitzer in the corner."

Edwina was all set for a comeback when a tall, distinguished-looking man wearing a pilot's uniform came into the bar, stopped just inside the entrance and looked around.

"If y'all will excuse me," she said, rising from her chair, "I see someone I know."

The wanna-be pilot was obviously scanning the room. Edwina sidled up to him and gave him a gentle elbow in the ribs. "I can sure see why you'd want to be the pilot. This suit looks great on you."

He smoothed the front of his jacket with his hand. "Well, thanks."

Edwina tapped his sleeve. "Do these stripes mean you're the captain?"

"Uh, yes, I'm a captain. I'm looking for my copilot."

"Oh, I get it. Need someone to help with the takeoff and the landing, do you?" Edwina gave him a knowing grin. "Cher had to go to the ladies' room. She asked me to let you know she'll be out in a minute."

"Cher? Wow. Cher? She's in the ladies' room? And she mentioned me? Wow."

Edwina gave him an even bigger grin and a wink. "She sure did."

A squatty, balding man walked in and stood beside them. Edwina glanced down and saw that he, too, was wearing an airline pilot's uniform, but it was poorly made and unpressed and his pants were too short. White socks showed above dirty athletic shoes.

Oh. My God. Edwina swerved her attention from the obvious phony to the real deal. The handsome pilot was wearing a puzzled expression and still looking over the crowd in the bar. "Listen, I've got to get back to my table," she said to him. "My friends are waiting on me." Without another word, she quickstepped back to Debbie Sue and Celina.

"What was that about?" Debbie Sue asked. "And who is that?"

Edwina shook her head. "Nothing. Sometimes I just can't get my foot in my mouth quick enough."

"I'll drink to that," Debbie Sue said, and took a swig of her beer.

Before Edwina could draw a sip of her Coke, a man's hand touched her shoulder. She looked up and saw the handsome pilot standing there. "You ran away so quickly," he said. "Does this mean I don't get to meet Cher?"

chapter fifteen

Thirty minutes later Celina excused herself to go up to the room and dress for her date with Matt. Debbie Sue and Edwina headed for the exhibitors' room.

Debbie Sue continued to snicker over Edwina mixing up the pilots. "Ed, you just fracture me. Traveling with you is like going with a three-ring circus."

"Just drop it. It was an honest mistake. Let's go find the Lip, or the Butt or whatever that damn thing is."

"The Ear, Ed. It's called the Ear."

"Whatever. Let's check it out."

The location of the booth couldn't be mistaken. Mounted high above all of the other exhibitors' booths was a plastic human ear, easily six feet tall and a good three feet wide.

"I think I see the Ear," Debbie Sue said.

"Yeah, me, too. Hah. I'd like to see the other body parts that go with that sucker."

The short, heavyset man who had given the earlier presentation stood in front of the booth rocking back and forth on his heels. Debbie Sue noticed he had a three-hair comb-over that started just above his left ear and ended above the right one. On a laugh, she pointed it out to Edwina.

"Sheesh," Edwina muttered. "I should do him a favor and volunteer to give him a haircut."

The man's face brightened when Debbie Sue and Edwina approached, and he stood straighter and adjusted his jacket. "Ladies. Beautiful ladies. So nice to see the softer gender attending more of these shows. I couldn't help but notice both of you in my presentation earlier today. I see by your badges you are speakers. Comrades."

He sidled up to Edwina, his head barely reaching her shoulder, and gave her five-ten frame an up-and-down inspection. He arched his brow. "You, in particular, I noticed."

"And you—"

"Excuse me," Debbie Sue said, rushing to avert a disaster. "Excuse me, but we'd like to know more about this product."

The salesman instantly switched to his selling demeanor and gave her a short version of his earlier stage presentation.

"So how much money are we talking here?" Debbie Sue asked.

"This model, with all the accessories, is fifteen hundred."

He gave her the same lascivious inspection he had given Edwina.

"Ouch. That high? Ed, what do you think?"

"It's more than I thought it'd be. Let's go. I'll bet my cousin can find it cheaper on the Internet."

"Tell you what I'll do," the salesman said. "Because you ladies are speakers here, I'll offer you a one-time-only conference special. I'll sell you the product for twenty-five per cent off."

Edwina began to do the math, figuring with her finger on her palm.

"I don't know," Debbie Sue said. "That's a generous offer, and mighty sweet of you, too, but it's still over a thousand dollars." She moved a little closer and lowered her voice. "You see, we did just the silliest thing. We went shopping and spent all our money on frilly things."

"Oh, my." The salesman gave a nervous laugh. Beads of sweat broke out on his bare scalp showing through his comb-over.

"We just couldn't pass them up," Debbie Sue said. "We live in a really small town in Texas and we don't get to see the fancy things they have here. They're not very comfortable, I have to say." She adjusted her bra strap. "But they were so pretty we blew our budget. Isn't that right, Ed?"

"Uh, yeah, they just jumped off the shelf into our hands."

The man's pudgy cheeks had taken on a pinkish hue and his face now glistened with perspiration. "Did you buy any shoes?"

Momentarily thrown off, Debbie Sue hesitated but recovered quickly. "Why, you do know women, don't you? Guilty as charged." She presented her wrist to him. "Lock me up and throw away the key."

The salesman sniggered and she did, too. She moved closer to him. "Listen, Ed bought the most darling high heels. They're three-inch stilettos, little strap around the ankle, to-die-for red patent leather. Just precious."

The salesman all but swooned, and for a fleeting moment, Debbie Sue feared she had pushed him too far.

He reached under the exhibit table and came out with a boxed set emblazoned THE EAR—2006 MILLENNIUM EDITION. "Please, take this tonight and use it. Or try it out for as long as you're going to be here. The product speaks for itself."

"Gosh, I, uh, we couldn't possibly do that. That's just too generous of you. We still can't afford to buy it, even with the discount you offered."

"Here's what I'll do," he said, wiping his head with his handkerchief. "We'll call it a floor sample and I'll offer it at half price. How does that sound?"

"Oh, my goodness. Ed, did you hear that? Half price. Can you believe it?"

"I'm having a hard time believing any of this," Edwina mumbled.

Debbie Sue shot her a murderous look, then swung her attention back to the salesman. "Tell you what, sugar. We'll take it and try it out. If we think we can use it, we'll take you up on that half-price offer. You'll be here all week, won't you?"

"Oh yes, I'll be here."

"We'll come back in a day or two and let you know what we've decided. Second thought, maybe we should just return those shoes Ed bought and we'd have more money."

"No! God, no. Don't do that. You come back to see me whenever you can." He pushed the product into Debbie Sue's hands.

As soon as they had walked out of the salesman's earshot, Edwina whispered, "You should be ashamed of yourself."

The salesman's voice halted their steps. "When you come back, could you please wear those red high heels?"

Edwina shot him a toothpaste smile and yelled back. "Sure thing. Just for you." Turning back to Debbie Sue, she whispered, "I take it back. You're a genius."

"Yeah," Debbie Sue said. "It's a bitch being the weaker sex."

Celina relished having the hotel room all to herself, pretending it was all hers. She had never had the pleasure of luxurious surroundings. She had leisurely showered with fragrant soap and washed her hair with some melon-scented shampoo Debbie Sue had insisted she try. As she dried and styled her long black tresses, she noticed their extra sheen under the bathroom lights. Before leaving the bathroom she slathered silky cream all over her body.

She moved out into the room and after much searching found a static-filled country station on the radio. She danced around the furniture as she sang along with Gretchen Wilson's "Redneck Woman."

Granny Dee had taught her to dance. She had memories from her earliest childhood of Granny Dee pushing the dining-room table against the wall, then using the open space to teach Celina how to count musical beats and how to do dance steps. Dancing seemed to have come to her naturally and so had her love for music. Apparently, she inherited that from her grandmother.

Picking up the plastic bag with BERGDORF GOODMAN stenciled in black, she smiled devilishly. In spite of having lost the three hundred dollars Dewey gave her, the money saved on carfare and having a free room had put a little extra in her pocket. Browsing in such an elegant store and knowing she would never do this again had compelled her to buy something special for the evening. While Debbie Sue and Edwina oohed and aahed over summer sandals and beach thongs, Celina had drifted to the intimates department. She had never owned sexy underwear. Her intimate wardrobe consisted of plain white cotton. Before she left, she had purchased matching bra and panties in lacy black silk.

Her goody-two-shoes side would like to claim innocent motives for the purchase of sexy undergarments instead of perfume or earrings, but the truth was, she wanted to *feel* sexy. She wanted a secret nudge that might push her to seduce Matt. And if that took her to . . .

Well, the very thought of what could happen made her stomach tighten.

Having grown up in Dime Box and having never lived away from Granny Dee's home, she had been a late bloomer to much that her peers took for granted. Sex was almost as foreign as the streets of New York City. Matt had led her to feel comfortable on these strange streets. Perhaps he might lead her to feel comfortable in other areas, too.

She dropped her robe and stepped into the black thong panty, then put on the matching bra. She hooked the front closure, stepped in front of the dresser mirror and caught her breath at the sight of her reflection. She almost didn't recognize her own body. The thong made her long legs look even longer. Strategic padding in the bra pushed up her breasts and gave her cleavage. Her waist appeared to be smaller.

Oh, good grief. How did women walk around and function normally knowing they looked like this under their outer clothing? She drew a deep breath. Could she do this? What she was thinking was so out of character for her. Then she remembered kissing Matt at the door last night in the most carnal of kisses. That had been out of character, too. Instantly she decided there were worse things in life than being out of character.

"Don't waste your life being ordinary," she murmured to the woman in the mirror.

The only voice that came back was Gretchen Wilson's.

Edwina and Debbie Sue had just left the elevator and started up the hallway to their room when they spotted Celina walking in their direction, dressed casually in white cropped pants, black mules and a black ruffled blouse, its low cut showing off enhanced boobs. She had a discernable lightness to her step.

Edwina was stunned at how striking their new friend looked. Why, New York models had nothing on Celina

Phillips. Before Edwina could voice a compliment, Debbie Sue said, "Damn girl, you look hot. What have you done to yourself?"

Celina giggled and bounced to a stop. "I do?"

"Is that a new outfit?" Debbie Sue asked.

"Well, not exactly. I brought it in Austin a while back."

"Well, I don't know what you're proud of," Edwina said, "but you got a strut in your gut, a swing to your gate and there's more fortitude to your attitude."

Celina laughed. "I'm going to miss you guys so much when I go home."

"Our doors are open all the time," Debbie Sue said, "but call ahead. Don't forget that Ed invited the whole bar to come stay with me and Buddy when we get back."

"You're meeting Matt at the fountain?"

"Yes, I am. I'm so excited. I've never seen a professional basketball game. In fact, the last basketball game I saw was the Dime Box High School boys. They went to bi-district my senior year, but had to drop out when one of the players got mono."

"At least y'all had five to play," Edwina said. "Not bad for a town as tiny as Dime Box."

"And now you're off to Madison Square Garden with thousands of other fans to watch a pro game," Debbie Sue said, smiling. "Aren't we lucky to be able to wake up in this world every day?"

"I'm definitely the luckiest girl alive," Celina said. "What are y'all doing this evening?"

"There's karaoke in the hotel bar at eight," Edwina said. "I've been wanting to do that, but I've never wanted to embarrass Vic. After that, we're back here."

"Maybe an in-room movie," Debbie Sue added.

"Sounds fun. Y'all have a good time." Celina waved and started toward the elevator doors.

"You, too, shug," Edwina said. "And if you happen to get your hand on the ball, don't double-dribble."

Debbie Sue gasped. "Ed! Cut it out."

Double dribble? Celina gave her a weak smile, unsure of the meaning of that expression. But given Debbie Sue's scolding, it must be naughty. She waved again as she stepped into the elevator.

Looking up, watching the numbers descend, she was struck with the same fear as last night. What if he wasn't there? What if, after some time to think about it, he decided not to show? It wouldn't be the end of the world if he didn't, but it would be the end of her newfound sense of self. Her fear began to grow and by the time the doors opened, it took all she could muster to leave the car.

Entering the room, Edwina spotted a piece of fluorescent green paper on the floor, a color not easily overlooked. It was too early for the bill and she doubted a place as classy as this would print it on bright green paper anyway. She picked it up and read the message in bold red lettering: KARAOKE TONIGHT AT 8 P.M. IN THE BAR. $250 PRIZE!

Damn, she could use that money. With an additional two

fifty, she could buy those Jimmy Choo shoes she had passed up today.

"What is it?" Debbie Sue asked, glancing at the message. "You weren't serious about karaoke, were you?" She tossed her purse on the bed.

"Yeah, kind of. I've always wanted to know how I sounded with honest-to-God musical accompaniment. Don't you want to?"

"Ed, we give our presentation tomorrow. We need to concentrate on that."

"What's to concentrate on? We've already written it. Twice. All we do is get up and read it."

"We can't just stand there and read from the notes. We can only *refer* to the notes. We can't read them word for word."

"I wasn't planning on doing that. I know my part. I don't need to practice."

"I'm not so confident. Just go over it with me once. We could order room service and turn in early. Doesn't that sound good?"

"Do you want my honest answer, or a responsible, mature, serious-as-all-get-out adult answer?"

Debbie Sue laughed. "The adult, please."

"Fine. Let's practice the speech, order supper, give each other a manicure and turn in early. Happy?"

"Happy."

"I really do think it's kind of sad, though."

"What?"

"Because the opportunity for the fabulous Patsy Cline to be heard again will be silenced."

"The world has lived a long time without Patsy. I guess we'll just have to be satisfied with her voice captured on tapes and CDs."

Debbie Sue dragged out their notes, and Edwina allowed herself to be dragged through the presentation again. It made no difference what the notes said, she figured. When they got onstage, she would do it her way anyway.

When Debbie Sue declared that they had rehearsed enough, she put the notes neatly back into their folder and said, "Let's eat."

Edwina sighed, unable to stop thinking about the karaoke show downstairs. "You bet. Toss me that menu, will you? I feel the need for New York cheesecake with strawberries."

Debbie Sue grinned. "Now you're talking."

Soon room service delivered a cart of food. Two bacon cheeseburgers with fries and two cheesecake slices big enough to warrant a snapshot.

"I'll have to diet for a month when I get back home," Debbie Sue said between bites.

"Maybe not. Think about all the walking we've been doing." Edwina chomped into the thick burger.

"I don't have to think about it. I've got the blisters to prove it."

"Me, too." Edwina lifted a foot to boast and almost fell over backward.

They ate in silence for a few minutes. "We don't have to go over the speech again, right?" Edwina said.

"I think we'll be all right now," Debbie Sue said. "I feel better about it. The question-and-answer part still makes me nervous, but we'll just have to get through it as best we can."

"You and I worry about different things," Edwina said as she spooned into the slice of sumptuous creamy cheesecake.

"You're worried about something? Good Lord, Ed. I don't know that I've ever heard you admit that. What in the world could be bothering you that you'd admit to?"

"Well, people have their choice of the speakers they want to hear. What if no one comes to hear us?"

Debbie Sue sat upright. "Holy shit, Ed. Why would you say something like that? That has never even crossed my mind."

"Good, because it's probably nothing to worry about. There'll be some people there. And Celina will be there. We only need one, right?"

"One? My God, I bet you're right. Why *would* anyone come to hear us? This is New York City, and we're two bumpkins from small-town Texas."

"Now, now, don't go to worrying. It'll be fine. One hundred and one or one, we're ready."

"Right," Debbie Sue said, but Edwina could tell she had started a new worry in Debbie Sue, who had more than a little streak of OC personality. "Now I'm gonna worry about it all night."

"I feel like a heel for upsetting you, but hell, you never leave a stone unturned. I assumed you'd given some thought to the idea that people might not want to hear what we've got to say."

They sat in silence for a few beats. Edwina could almost see gears grinding behind her partner's eyes.

"Well, fuck it," Debbie Sue said finally. "I'm gonna soak

in a hot tub and call Buddy. When I start feeling this inse-
cure, I need Buddy. I'm bailing on you for a while, Ed."

"Hon, you go right ahead and do what will make you feel
better." Edwina picked up the TV remote and plopped into
a chair. She watched very little TV at home, didn't have the
patience for flipping from one channel to another. "You go
on and get your bath. I'll just sit here and watch TV."

Soon she heard water running in the bathroom. Soon after that, she heard the murmur of Debbie Sue's voice. She
couldn't stop the mischievous grin that curved her lips. That
girl would be a good hour or more talking to Buddy. Those
two were so tight they weren't comfortable unless one knew
what the other was doing and thinking.

chapter sixteen

Trying to appear cool and detached while looking around, Celina sat on the upholstered bench that encircled the fountain and crossed her legs. As usual, there was an assembly at the fountain, talking, glancing at watches, placing calls on cell phones. Matt was nowhere to be seen.

By the time fifteen anxious minutes had passed, Celina's heart had sunk to somewhere around her knees. "Five more minutes," she said under her breath.

Then a young bellhop approached her carrying a nosegay of yellow rosebuds. "Miz Phillips? Miz Celina Phillips?"

"Uh, yeah. I mean, yes, I'm Celina Phillips."

Extending the little cluster of flowers, he said, "Detective

McDermott asked that I deliver these and escort you to the car waiting outside."

"Now? . . . Oh, of course he meant now. You must forgive me, I'm just, well my goodness, I—"

"If you'll take the flowers, ma'am, I'll make sure you get safely to the car."

Rising slowly, she took the bouquet, then hooked her arm through the bellhop's and let him escort her outside. There in the porte-cochere sat a black limousine, the lights of Times Square dancing off it as if it were a black diamond. The driver, standing at the side of the car, nodded to her.

As she approached, he opened the door. "Ma'am, let me assist you."

Stunned, Celina took the help he offered and ducked into the car.

Matt reached for her hand and brought her all the way into the limousine onto a soft gray leather seat. He was wearing jeans and a starched white shirt, the collar framing his chiseled chin. The sleeves, rolled to just below the elbows, revealed muscular forearms shadowed with dark hair. "Good evening, pretty lady."

"Oh," she said. "I—I've never been inside a limousine before." She looked around. The windows were blacked out, but the interior was bathed in low golden light. A parade of dollar signs marched through her mind.

Matt was sitting opposite her, the corners of his mouth tipped up in a big smile. She picked up the scent of masculine cologne.

He lifted a champagne bottle from a silver bucket of ice

and poured a flute full of the golden liquid. He leaned forward and extended the glass to her.

She felt a flush crawl up her neck "Oh, my goodness. This must be costing a fortune, Matt."

He poured a glass for himself, then touched his glass to hers. "I don't do it every day. I don't have a car of my own, so this seemed better than a cab. Besides that, I thought I might be competing with a dozen guys, and I wanted to make a lasting impression."

"Gosh, I don't think I even know a dozen guys."

His eyes leveled on hers. "Really?"

As she looked into those dark eyes, she was sure she saw admiration there. She didn't know if her body would hold her happiness. She smiled as heat came to her cheeks. "No, I don't."

"Then I'd say that's their loss and my gain."

She shrugged, hoping she was reading his meaning clearly. "I'm sorry. I'm new at this. I don't know what to say."

"You've told me what I need to know." His gaze dropped to her glass. She hadn't yet taken a sip. "You don't like champagne?"

"I—I haven't had it often. I'm not much of a drinker. But I think I like it." She tasted a small sip, relishing the effervescence on her tongue.

"I don't drink a lot, either."

"You don't have a car?" She had both read and heard that many New York City residents didn't own a car.

"Don't need one. I live in the city. Everything I need is within walking distance. In fact, my place isn't far from here."

"Oh," she said again. "I can't imagine not having a car. Everywhere I go at home is too far to walk. My VW is old and beat-up, but it's taken me where I need to go for a long time."

She brought the glass to her lips for another tiny sip. From out of nowhere came the thought of the silky black underwear underneath her clothing and the reason she had bought it. She felt a new wave of nervousness. "How long before we reach the ballgame?"

"As long as you like."

She drew in a great breath, bolstering her courage. "Perfect." Leaning forward she placed her lips on his.

"Wow," he said huskily when they parted. "Is it the flowers, the limo or the champagne?"

"It's everything," she said softly. "It's the city, this car, these flowers and the champagne. But mostly it's you."

He reached to his right and pushed a button.

"Yes, sir," the driver said.

"Could you please take the *long* way to the Garden?"

"Certainly, sir. Would an hour be satisfactory?"

"An hour would be great."

He released the button, the window glided up and the next thing she knew, she was on his lap and lost in his kiss. The night had become a bottomless pool of possibilities, and Celina Phillips of Dime Box, Texas, was dipping her toe into the warm water. "Do we have to go to the ball game?" she asked.

"No," he said softly.

"Will—will you lose money on the tickets?"

"No," he said again, and his eyes locked on hers. "What do you want to do instead?"

"You could, ah . . . uh, show me your apartment? I've never seen a New York apartment."

A few beats passed. He continued to look into her eyes. "That can be arranged."

Matt's apartment was small and cozy and very masculine. Full of sports stuff. And it was very clean. Celina was impressed.

They had brought the bottle of champagne with them from the limo and almost all of it was still left. He set the bottle on the counter in the tiny kitchen. "Do you want some more?"

"Okay," she answered.

He pulled two goblets from the cabinet and gave her a sheepish grin. "I don't own champagne glasses. The ones in the limo belong to the limo company."

She laughed. "Guess what? I don't own any, either. And what's more, I probably never will."

He brought a glass of the golden liquid to her, removed her purse from her hand and replaced it with the glass. "How about some music? What kind of music do you like?"

She smiled up at him. "I'm a country girl."

"I don't think I have any country music."

"No George Strait? No Brooks and Dunn?"

His lips tipped up into a smile and he shook his head. "Country music. That's something you'll have to teach me."

She smiled back, feeling as if a smile had been permanently

affixed on her face. "Then play what you have, Detective."

He moved over to a CD player and put on something soft and sexy, with a lot of saxophone and piano. "Do you like to dance?"

"Believe it or not, I do. My grandmother taught me how. She and I have been dancing together since I was a little kid."

"Oh, yeah. She was a dancer, right?"

He drew her into a dance position and she looked up into his eyes. Few men were taller than she, but *he* was. Their bodies seemed to fit and she couldn't think of anything that felt as good as his arm around her waist. Still, she felt giddy and nervous. Nothing had been said, but they both knew why she had invited herself to his apartment instead of going to the basketball game.

He placed his cheek against hers and began to slowly move her around the floor. He smelled delicious, but she couldn't identify his cologne. She knew next to nothing about men's fragrances. "Who taught you to dance?" she asked him.

"Guess."

"Your sisters?"

"Yep."

They laughed together and she tried to remember if she had ever enjoyed herself more in a man's company.

"Are you sure you don't want to go to the game?" he asked.

She leaned back and leveled a serious look into his eyes. "I'm sure, Matt."

"God, Celina," he said softly and placed his lips on hers.

Their kisses became urgent in no time, and strange emotions were streaking through her mind and body. "I've never been a big fan of basketball," she murmured between kisses.

"Me, neither," he replied, trailing his mouth down her neck to the opening in her blouse. "But I am *your* fan."

"Matt, I should tell you . . ."

"Hmm?"

"I know coming here was my idea, but I'm not a . . . a terribly sophisticated woman."

"I know."

"I've—I've never been so forward, but I've never felt this way about anyone. I know you may not believe me, but—"

"You don't have to be sophisticated. Just be honest." He began to slowly unbutton her blouse.

"Oh, my gosh," she whispered, watching his nimble fingers loosen her buttons.

He pulled her close and kissed her again. His hand slid down and cupped her breast and his palm sent heat through the black silk of her new bra. A warm sensation she had never experienced began in her lower belly. She couldn't think what to do about it, so she pressed her body against his, wrapped her arms around his wide shoulders and threw herself into returning his kiss. His starched shirt rasped against her bare skin through the open front of her blouse. A low hum came from his throat and she felt herself being danced backward. She opened her eyes to a dimly lit room. His bedroom. A swarm of butterflies took flight in her stomach.

"I know you're nervous," he said softly as he peeled back the front of her blouse. "Just tell me if you want to stop."

★ ★ ★

Edwina glanced at the clock and saw it was only minutes from eight o'clock. She could hear the muffled sounds of Debbie Sue still talking and laughing. Not only could she not find an argument against going downstairs, she couldn't see even a hint of divine intervention. Hell, she could go down, perform and be back before Debbie Sue missed her. She raised her eyes toward heaven. *Patsy, bless your heart. I hear ya, hon. I'll do my best to make us both proud.*

She grabbed her fancy jeans and changed into a cute gold glitzy halter top she wore on special occasions. Stopping at the mirror she gave her makeup and hair a quick touch-up, then picked up the bright green piece of paper and jotted a note on the bottom: *DS, if I'm not back when you get off the phone, come get me. Karaoke calls! —Ed.*

She was in a hurry, but not so much that she didn't have time to grab two miniature bottles of Jose Cuervo Gold from the courtesy fridge. She knew for a fact that even Miss Patsy Cline wet her whistle before she performed. She emptied one miniature bottle into a drinking glass and belted it. A pleasant warmth seeped through her. Grinning, she emptied the second bottle into the glass and sipped half of it, then belted the other half. She had no doubt she would sound exactly like her idol.

Waiting for the elevator, she hummed to herself and practiced her dance step. Those designer shoes she wanted were as good as on her feet.

In a matter of minutes she was standing in the bar. The show had already started. A small group of people—maybe twenty—were present and seated at the tables arranged in a horseshoe around the stage. She recognized Frank Rogen-stein. She smiled politely at his nod, then looked away. She didn't want to make small talk. She was more interested in focusing on the stage and assessing the competition. A trio of drunken men in suits was onstage slaughtering Sinatra's "New York, New York." The one on the end attempting the high kicks wasn't winning any points, either.

Edwina walked over to the DJ standing just out of the spotlight. "How does this work?" she yelled, to be heard above the din.

"Hey, now, you look like a winner," he yelled back. "It's easy. I give you a book of songs. Choose the one you want to sing and it's showtime."

"The cash prize. How do you determine who wins?"

"I let the crowd choose. The singer that gets the loudest applause gets the loot." He reached for a photo-album-sized book. "Do you want to sing?"

"Sure." She took the songbook. "I'll just have a seat and make my selection."

She found a seat near the stage lights, leafed through the pages and was dismayed that among the hundreds of songs she saw not one Patsy Cline tune. No "Crazy," no "Sweet Dreams." *Damn.* She felt her chances of winning dwindling, but then she spotted a sure thing. Lee Greenwood's "God Bless the U.S.A."

Her eyes almost welled with tears thinking about the lyrics and all of the times she had heard it. She couldn't hear or sing it without thinking about her own personal hero and war veteran, Vic. When he had been an active-duty SEAL, he had bled real blood for the U.S.A. Now he was retired, but he still bled red, white and blue, and this song always had an emotional impact on him.

This was the one. And she would sing it with all her heart.

She would sing it so loud that Vic would hear it clear down in Texas. God bless the U.S.A. and those Jimmy Choo shoes.

"Ed," Debbie Sue called from the bathroom, "if you still want to go downstairs and sing, I'll go with you."

Talking to Buddy had been energizing. He had a way of making sense of the senseless and easing her fears. Even if they weren't married, and thank God they were, he would be her number-one best friend.

"Did you hear me?" She stepped from the tub and wrapped herself in a thick towel.

She opened the door and said again, "Ed? You asleep?"

Nothing. Not even sound from the TV.

Walking on into the room, she looked around in confusion. *Maybe she went to the ice machine*, she thought as she started back into the bathroom, but she stopped short at the sight of a bright green note on the bed pillow.

She quickly read it. Glancing at the clock, she made note of the time, 8:45. "Dammit, Ed," she mumbled.

She dressed hurriedly, then stopped at the vanity to put on some makeup, but when she saw the two empty shot-size bottles of tequila, she changed her mind. In all the years she had been friends with Edwina, she had learned two important things: Don't do anything to mess up her hair, and never let her out of sight when she's drinking straight tequila.

She almost ran to the elevator. As the elevator door closed, she mumbled to the walls, "I just hope I don't end up wishing I'd stayed in Texas."

"I'm sorry," Celina said, on the verge of tears.

Matt pulled up the sheet and tucked it around her. "Shh. Don't say that. You're wonderful."

Her purchase of sexy and sophisticated lingerie did not a wanton paramour make. Her inexperience with men had become glaringly obvious in no time and she had mostly embarrassed herself.

But he wasn't inexperienced. That, too, had become obvious. "No, I'm not. I'm klutzy and dumb."

"You're wonderful," he repeated and kissed her slowly and gently. "Celina, I don't want a sophisticated woman. What I want is a caring woman. And one who's honest."

Honest. That was the second time he had used that word. Had someone been dishonest with him? If so, whoever she was must be insane. There was no part of him that wasn't perfect, clothed or unclothed.

"I wish you didn't have to go back to Texas," he said and pulled her body against his. "I wish we had a chance to spend more time—"

"But I have to, Matt. Dime Box is my home. Granny Dee is my only family."

"You said earlier that you liked New York."

"I do. But in a serious conversation about it, I have to be

honest." She smiled. "There's that word again. Listen, New York is a fabulous place to come to, but I think I'd go crazy living here."

He gave her a rueful smile. "You've got this private-detective bug, too, don't you?"

"Not so much anymore. This conference has been an eye-opener for me. That session on blood spatter was awful. And I almost lost my breakfast during the film on serial killers. In all of my imagining of mystery solving, I never thought very much about the . . . well, the gruesome part of a murder investigation."

"Homicide is gruesome. No question about it. But you get used to it."

A shudder passed over her. "I don't even want to get used to it."

"Poor choice of words. I should say you get to where the puzzle and the challenge to find the killer override everything else."

"I don't think I'm tough enough to be a detective."

He buried his face against her neck and teased beneath her ear with his tongue. "You don't have to be. I can be tough enough for both of us."

"I do hate to leave you," she said, no longer able to hold back tears. "I never expected to meet someone like you in my whole life, and now that I have, I don't know what to do about it."

"Shh. Don't cry. Maybe we should concentrate on figuring out what to do about it together."

"I'm not crying because I'm sad, you know. I'm crying because I'm happy."

He leaned forward, kissed the tip of her nose, then gave her a big grin. "I'm happy, too."

"My grandmother has always told me not to waste my life being ordinary. I've never, ever felt less ordinary than I feel right now, Matt. I feel like a princess, like Cinderella. And it's you who makes me feel that way."

His hand came to her face and brushed back strands of her hair. "You're unbelievable. You're beautiful. You're smart and kind and gentle. Everything I've ever wanted in a woman, in the mother of my kids."

"Kids?"

"Do you like kids?"

"Well, yes. I don't know many, but—"

"I want a big family. I came from a big family filled with love." He trailed a finger down her arm. "I want the same thing in my future."

Celina could feel her heart swelling in her chest. "It would be wonderful to have a big family. I've never had anyone but my grandparents."

He brushed a kiss across her cheek, across her eyelid. "I'm great with kids. Just ask my sisters. My nieces and nephews think I hung the moon."

"So do I, Matt."

He leaned in and kissed her again, then moved over her. "It'll be better this time."

chapter seventeen

Edwina counted only five contestants besides herself. Feigning stage fright, she waved off the DJ's effort to coax her to sing, allowing the others to go before her. She wanted to be last. She wanted to—as they always said in show biz—end the evening with a big finish. While she waited, she had a straight shot of tequila with nothing but a lime and some salt, the way they drank tequila in Texas.

Besides the trio of drunks who had butchered Frank Sinatra, there was a visually challenged woman who couldn't see the words on the screen and spent most of her song adjusting her glasses. After her followed a young, clean-cut guy who couldn't carry a tune and a duet of young women who giggled more than they sang.

Finally Edwina's turn came and the eyes of the audience

landed on her. Hell, she wasn't even nervous. With the sassi-
ness of Shania Twain, she pranced up on the stage and took
her spot. The music blasted from the speakers and she began
to sing the Lee Greenwood favorite. The words flowed. She
had never sounded better, not even in the shower at home.

But one of the obnoxious drunks began to heckle her.
"B-o-o-o! B-o-o-o! Get off the stage! Where's the hook?
B-o-o-o!"

She stopped mid-lyric, planted a fist on her hip and gave
him a glare. Determined to not be deterred, she picked up
and continued.

"Get off the stage!" the man bellowed, but others in the
audience shouted him down and she heard them clapping.
She could see the drunk's friends trying to quiet him down,
but their laughing did little to convince her that they meant
business.

She looked to the DJ, but he just made a circle with his
hand, urging her to go on.

" . . . where at least I know I'm free—"

"You'd have to be free, sweetheart. Nobody would pay
you for it!"

Edwina saw red. Not only was he insulting her, he was
making light of the single most true-blue American ballad
since "The Star-Spangled Banner." Why, he was spitting
in Uncle Sam's eye and it ricocheted right into Vic's. She
stopped. "There's just way too much tolerance for bad behavior," she mumbled.

Ridding herself of the mike, she headed for the table
of drunks. From out of nowhere a woman walked up and

poured a drink over the loudmouth's head. Edwina was dumbstruck, but quickly recovered when she realized who her defender was.

Cher!

The gutsy Italian was all over the group, shouting cuss words even Edwina had never heard. The tirade started with their lack of manners and ended with the shortfall of their physical endowments. Cher ended with a flip of her hand, pivoted sharply and walked away.

The loudmouth stood up and yelled, "Fuck you, bitch!"

With no hesitation, Cher spun around, picked up a chair and threw it at him. Suddenly they were all on their feet, either punching one another, overturning furniture or moving to safer ground.

Edwina had never run from a fight in her life, especially when someone had come to her defense. An empty table sat close to the wall. She reached it in three strides, climbed on top and saw the perfect opportunity to jump and land on the back of the loudmouthed asshole.

She stepped back to give her leap full throttle. The table tipped and crashed to the floor. At the same instant, she felt something grab near the nape of her neck and she found herself suspended in midair, her feet inches off the floor. Twisting her body, she realized the strap of her halter top had snagged a hanging art object and she was pinned against the wall like a side of beef on a butcher's hook.

Debbie Sue thought it would take forever to reach the lobby.

Someone had been on the elevator before her and pushed

all the buttons, forcing the car to stop at every floor. She got off at the next floor and switched elevators. When the door finally opened into the lobby, she made a beeline for the bar. Her heart jumped to her throat when she saw ahead of her the hotel manager and two uniformed policemen.

Holy Mary, mother of God. The best she could hope for was that no one was hurt. Hell, she hoped no one was dead.

She jogged to the doorway and peered inside. Her jaw dropped. The usually dark bar was lit up. Furniture was overturned. Glasses and napkins were strewn everywhere and at least a dozen people were all yelling at once.

Two police officers were trying to restore order as the bartender, cocktail waitresses and the manager began to turn the chairs and tables upright.

Edwina was nowhere to be seen, and Debbie Sue was relieved. Perhaps she hadn't given her pal enough credit. Perhaps Edwina was already gone and had had nothing to do with whatever had occurred here.

Then she saw her. Hanging on the wall like a dress hastily stuffed back in the closet on a hanger. She appeared to be limp and lifeless, and for a brief second Debbie Sue wondered if she was even conscious. Then she saw movement. Edwina reached up and patted her hair. She was fine.

Debbie Sue threaded through the crowd to Edwina and looked up at her. "Whatcha doing?"

"Guess you'd get pissed if I said, 'Just hanging around.'"

"Ed, I'm not pissed, but I'd sure like to know what happened."

"Well, don't you think I'd like to know that too?"

"You don't look worth a damn as a picture on the wall."

"What am I hanging from? I'm afraid to move. I didn't want my top to get ripped off and then there I'd be. Topless and embarrassed."

"Yeah, Ed. You sure wouldn't want something embarrassing to happen. I can't believe I don't have a camera phone. I'd like to send this picture to Vic with the text message, 'Wish you could hang out with us in the hotel bar.'"

"Get me down from here before those cops come over here. They might arrest me."

Debbie Sue looked around. Right beside her was a turned-over table. She righted it and pushed it against the wall beneath Edwina's feet. Then she dragged over a chair. Close examination revealed that the strap on Edwina's halter top was caught on a massive iron sculpture of a tree. Beside it, a bronze plaque read THE TREE OF LIFE.

"Good Lord, Ed. You're hung up on the Tree of Life."

"This ain't no time for half-baked philosophy. Just get me down from here."

"I'm gonna have to untie your top, so hold on to it," Debbie Sue instructed. She began to loosen the knot at Edwina's neck. "The table is right underneath your feet, so you won't fall. Here we go."

As her feet touched the tabletop, Edwina grabbed her halter top and hopped to the floor.

"Quick. Tie your top back on and let's just sneak out of here," Debbie Sue said. "That manager and those cops look like they're really pissed."

"Cher started it," Edwina said, tying the strap of her halter top around her neck. "Some drunks insulted her and—"

"Tell me later," Debbie Sue said. "Right now, let's just get out of here."

They sidled along the wall, avoiding the confusion in the center of the room. They had almost reached the door when a policeman and the hotel manager blocked their exit with their bodies.

"Hold on there, girls," the cop said. "You're not going anywhere until I find out what happened here."

"You're guests here," the harried manager spat. "I've seen you around the conference area. This is unacceptable. You're going to have to leave the premises."

Stunned, Debbie Sue and Edwina stared at the manager.

"Now wait a minute," the officer said. "Don't be jumping to conclusions. You don't even know if these women did anything wrong."

"Yeah," Edwina cracked, "step back, Adolf. This is still the U.S.A., and we're innocent until proven guilty."

"But you don't understand." The manager clasped his hands together under his chin, a pained expression on his face. "I'm just the night manager. Mr. Pembroke's the general manager. When he finds out about this, he'll bust me back to bellhop. I've worked in every flophouse in this city for the past fifteen years, waiting for this opportunity. I can't let a barroom brawl ruin it."

He was almost in tears, and Debbie Sue felt sorry for him.

Edwina gave him a long, steady look and then told her side of the story to the cop. It was corroborated by others in the bar. Finally, the policeman persuaded the night manager to let the Domestic Equalizers go and concentrate on the real troublemakers.

"How dare that jerk make fun of you, especially when you were singing 'God Bless the U.S.A.,'" Debbie Sue said. "I'm glad I wasn't there. It would've been even uglier."

"I know," Edwina said, hoisting her chin with real indignation.

As they started to pass the manager, Edwina stopped. "We'll be expecting an apology from you before we leave, Adolf."

They walked on outside to the open lobby and Debbie Sue laughed. "That was great, Ed. You sounded almost regal."

"A girl has to do something to redeem herself when she's hung on the wall during a bar fight," Edwina said smugly.

"Wait a minute." Debbie Sue grabbed Edwina's hand. "You said Cher started it. I didn't see her in there. Did she get arrested? What happened to her?"

"A lot of people made for the exit when the fight broke out. I saw Frank Rogenstein take her by the arm and they left together."

"Frank Rogenstein, the detective?" Debbie Sue asked.

"The only Frank Rogenstein I know."

Debbie Sue gasped. "That bastard left without helping you?"

"Yeah, it kind of surprised me, too. But he was out of there in no time."

Just then a voice behind them called out, "Hey, lady, lady."

The two turned and saw a man approaching them. "Oh, I know him," Edwina said. When he came nearer, she said,

"Debbie Sue, this is the DJ in charge of the contest." She looked up at him. "Listen, I'm so sorry about all of that."

The DJ shook his head. "You don't owe me an apology. It wasn't your fault. This happens from time to time. In fact, you deserve the prize, I just wanted to give you this." He handed her two one-hundred-dollar bills and a fifty.

"Well, my stars." Edwina thanked the man profusely. After he walked away, she turned back to Debbie Sue, beaming. "You need to call your mom. I've got a title for her next song, 'I Lost the Fight for Your Love, but I Won a Pair of Jimmy Choo Shoes.'"

They laughed all the way back to their room.

"Wonder why something terrible is funnier later," Edwina said after they had locked themselves in their hotel room.

"I guess because you survived. Besides, sometimes laughing is the only thing you can do. You can regret it, but that doesn't change it. So the best thing is to laugh."

"I guess so." Edwina walked over to the bed and pulled back the bedcovers. "I'm worn out. I'll bet I don't have any trouble sleeping."

"Did you put the Do Not Disturb sign out? I'd like to sleep in tomorrow. We don't have to be downstairs until ten. We've been going nonstop. It'd be nice to lounge around a little."

"You're right. I'll put that sign out. Let's sleep in 'til, say, eight or eight thirty. "

"Perfect."

Edwina opened the door to place the sign on the outside. She closed it suddenly and stage-whispered to Debbie Sue,

"That detective is in the room next door. I just saw him going in. And Cher was with him."

"What?"

"Shhh. I said, that detective's room is next door and he just went in, leading Cher."

Debbie Sue gasped. "I thought he went out with Celina. I told you there was something you couldn't trust about that little shit—"

"No, no, dammit no. *Not* Detective McDermott. Detective *Rogenstein*."

"And Cher was with him? Ohmigod. What if she's in trouble? What if he's detained her for starting that fight downstairs? Or what if he's arrested her for soliciting?"

"Good Lord. It could be either one. I can't just go to bed. She defended me. She stepped up when not another asshole in the whole room did. I have to know if she's all right."

"What are you gonna do? Knock on the door and say, 'I'm sorry to bother you, but is my prostitute friend that started a fight on my behalf okay?'"

"I'm gonna do one better than that." Edwina rushed around the room throwing clothes, shopping sacks and newspapers everywhere. Finally she found what she was looking for and turned triumphantly, holding up the listening device they had acquired downstairs. "You and I, my friend, are going to test the Ear."

Debbie Sue laughed. "Good idea. Hook her up, boys, and let her rip."

chapter eighteen

" . . . came here . . . a drink . . . the offer, wasn't . . ."

"Yeah . . . I'll make good on it. What about *your* . . ."

" . . . no offer . . . end . . . bullshit performance . . ."

" . . . you jerk."

"What are they saying?" Debbie Sue said. "There's too much static. I can't hear."

"Me, neither," Edwina replied.

Debbie Sue looked up and saw Edwina fussing with the wire to her earpiece. It was entangled with her shoulder-length earring and her long acrylic nails.

"Don't listen yet," Edwina whispered. "I don't want to miss anything and I'm all screwed up here. I think they're arguing." She pulled and tugged at the wire. "Help me out, would ya?"

"Edwina, take the damn thing out of your ear. Then you can untangle it."

Edwina jerked the foam earpiece from her ear and began to fiddle with the earring and the earpiece. Debbie Sue continued to listen.

"Don't worry about it," a female voice that sounded like Cher's said. "Nothing's happened. Let go of my arm and I'll leave."

"Asshole," Debbie Sue muttered.

"What's he doing? What's he doing?" Edwina asked frantically.

"Shh."

"It won't be like . . . easy . . . those so-called private investigators, who, by the way, are a joke . . ." Rogenstein said.

Something told Debbie Sue he was talking about her and Edwina. "Asshole," she repeated.

"Dammit, what is he saying?"

"I don't know, Ed. I can't hear when you're yammering in my other ear."

Debbie Sue glared at Edwina. Now the woman had the earpiece and the earring untangled, but her earpiece was disconnected from the device and she was turning it every which way.

"I knew you couldn't believe that little bald-headed bastard when he said a nine-year-old kid could put this together," she mumbled, more to herself than anyone else. "It's supposed to be color coded. Dammit, there's no colors. Just show me some ever-lovin' colors."

Debbie Sue removed her earpiece, hung the wire around

her neck and went to Edwina's aid. "You and your friggin' Christmas ornaments you try to pass off as jewelry."

"Shush," Edwina hissed. "It just so happens I borrowed these from you."

"Oh. Well, in that case, I love them." Now Debbie Sue had the device reassembled and the earpiece plugged back into its proper receptacle. She handed it back to Edwina, reinserted her own earpiece and stepped close to the wall again.

" . . . corpse . . . laugh . . . stumble all over each other."

"Did he say 'corpse'?" Edwina whispered.

"Ed, you don't have to whisper. They can't hear us."

"I'm turning it up."

"Ed, no—"

Wheeee! A high-pitched sound pierced Debbie Sue's ear. Her eyes almost crossed. She yanked the earpiece free. "Ed, turn that fuckin' thing down! You 'bout busted my eardrum."

"Well, dammit, I didn't know. I was on the other end, too. It was no picnic for me, either." She pulled on her earlobe while she fiddled with the controls. "Here, I've adjusted it. Let's try again."

They resumed their listening positions. "My God," Debbie Sue said in amazement. "I don't know what you did to it, but it's like we're standing in the same room with them."

"We should definitely buy this. I don't care what it costs."

"Shhh, Ed, let me listen."

" . . . you're hurting my arm." Cher's voice.

"Holy cow. He must like it rough," Edwina said.

Thump . . . hump-thump . . . crash!

Debbie Sue heard an outcry that had to have come from a man. "I think you're right, Ed."

"That's it, Cher," Edwina exclaimed in a stage whisper. "Kick 'im in the nuts."

She made a swing with her fist and disconnected both wires from the device. The small recorder fell to the floor.

"Ed, forgodsakes!" Debbie Sue dropped to her knees, picked up the machine and reassembled it.

More thumps, then a gagging sound, followed by, "Police! Cheryl Angelo, Special Victims Unit. Frank Rogenstein, you're under arrest for assault on a police officer."

Debbie Sue's jaw dropped. She stared at Edwina. "Cher's a cop? I thought she was a prostitute."

Edwina lifted her shoulders and opened her palms.

"Now this is rich," Rogenstein said. "Two cops, *mano y mano*. Your backup should have been through that door by now. I'm guessing you're wearing a wire. . . . You didn't tell them you're up here, did you, cutie? Thought you'd be safe with ol' Frank, huh? Taking a little time off the clock is allowed, but it's really dumb to leave the safety on your gun."

"Oh my God," Edwina said. "Cher's got a gun?"

Thump-thump! . . . Thwack! Crash!

"Shoot him," Edwina cried.

"Ed, forgodsakes, will you shut up?"

" . . . rest in peace . . . better hooker than . . . a cop."

Silence.

Debbie Sue's heart felt as if it were bouncing in her rib cage. She looked at Edwina, blinking. Edwina blinked back.

"Debbie Sue, what did we just hear?"

"I—I don't know. I can't figure it out."

"Did it sound to you like they had a fight? Did he say 'cop'? Did he say 'rest in peace'?"

"I don't know," Debbie Sue said, trying to control the tremor in her voice. If she became hysterical, Edwina would, too. "Maybe he meant, 'Just lay down and go to sleep,' like, you know, 'Sleep well.'"

"Does that slimy guy seem like the type to tell a woman he's alone in a hotel room with to rest in peace as he tucks her in for a nap?"

Debbie Sue walked over and dropped to the edge of the bed. "Shit, Ed, I don't know what we heard."

"Well, let's just go knock on the door. Like, you know, we're going to visit."

"Wait, Ed, I'm thinking."

"Debbie Sue, I won't rest until I know if Cher is all right. She can't be dead."

"Cher is dead?" came a voice from the hall door. Celina stood there, her plastic key in her hand. "Oh, no. Poor Chastity. First Sonny on a ski slope, and now Cher. It really is the passing of a rock 'n' roll dynasty, isn't it?"

Edwina's brow squeezed into a frown. "What?"

"I remember 'I Got You Babe.' Granny Dee used to play it all the time."

"No, darlin'," Edwina said patiently. "Cher is the name of the woman we met in the bar. The one you thought looked like Gilda?"

"Oh," Celina said, laughing. Then her humor collapsed. "And she's dead? What happened?"

In broken sentences, Debbie Sue attempted to describe to Celina what they had heard. Edwina interrupted often. She, too, was shaky voiced. At the end of it, Debbie Sue said, "The damned Ear wasn't working right and Edwina kept talking, so we missed a lot of what happened. Maybe we should do what Ed said. Maybe we should go over there and knock and see what's going on."

"Too bad that Ear thing doesn't record," Celina said, chewing on her thumbnail. "You could play it back."

Debbie Sue looked at Edwina, who was staring back at her. "Does it record?" Edwina asked. "I don't remember."

Debbie Sue got to he feet, grabbed the box the listening device had come in and began to read the fine print. "Oh, my God," she said a few seconds later. "Once it's turned on, it records anything that happens, no matter what."

"Does that mean it was recording while we were screwing around with it?" Edwina asked.

"Sonofabitch, we've got the whole damn thing recorded."

Without another word Debbie Sue picked up the device and gingerly carried it to the desk. She set the small recorder down carefully and let out a deep breath. Edwina and Celina gathered closer. Debbie Sue sank to the chair and pressed REPLAY.

The entire recording lasted only minutes. At the end of it Edwina broke down in tears. "Debbie Sue, it sounds like he killed her. It sounds like he killed Cher."

Debbie Sue felt her brow tent with anguish and she couldn't hold back tears, either. "I know, Ed. That's what it sounds like."

"He killed her?" Celina said. She looked away.

"What should we do?" Edwina whispered. Debbie Sue could see her whole body trembling.

Finally Debbie Sue found her voice. She swallowed, her arm pressed against her stomach as if that would hold her together. "We have to call the police."

"Right. We should call nine-one-one." Edwina slashed away tears and running mascara with the back of her hand. Smudges of black stained her cheeks. "I'm gonna keep listening and make sure he doesn't leave the room."

Debbie Sue picked up the phone to dial, but Celina stopped her. "Wait, we should call Matt. He could tell us what to do. Or maybe he would do something himself."

"Maybe that's a good idea," Debbie Sue said.

"I have his cell number." Celina picked up her purse and began to dig inside. She came up with a business card.

Debbie Sue yanked the card from Celina and punched in Matt's number. After several seconds she hung up. "Fuck. It went straight to his voice mail. He must be on another call."

"Try again," Celina begged. "If you don't get him, leave a message. Tell him it's an emergency."

"Here," she said to Celina, rising from the chair. "You sit down here and you call him. If *you* tell him it's an emergency, he'll come running."

Celina took Debbie Sue's seat and placed the call. Minutes that seemed more like hours, passed. The three women sat and watched the phone as if their sheer will would make Matt answer.

At the ten-minute mark Edwina sprang to her feet. "I'm

not sitting here another minute. Even if she's not dead, the poor woman could be hurt. We should have already gone over there. I can't just stand here and act like I didn't hear what I think I heard when I know I heard it. When I look in the mirror I like what I see and I want to keep liking it. I'm going over there and check things out." Her hands flapped like bird wings. "Holy shit, I wish Vic was here!"

"If you think I'm letting you go alone, you're crazy," Debbie Sue said. "I have to look in the same mirrors you do. If anyone goes, we both will. There's power in numbers."

"And there's crap in my pants," Edwina said.

"What about me?" Celina asked. She, too, was in tears.

"You stay here and wait for Matt's call," Debbie Sue told her. "If we don't come back in, say, five minutes, come bang on the door."

Debbie Sue saw the young woman swallow hard and for the first time realized she might be afraid. If they hadn't enticed her here with a free room, she wouldn't have become a part of this. "Everything's gonna be okay, Celina. I promise. Just make sure Matt gets over here."

"Okay," she said in a tiny voice.

Debbie Sue linked her arm through Edwina's. "C'mon, Ed."

chapter nineteen

Debbie Sue and Edwina stopped at the door to Room 620 and drew a deep breath almost in unison.

"Okay," Edwina whispered. "This is it. I'm knocking. Ready?"

"Ready."

Edwina pounded on the door with her fist.

The door popped open so quickly Debbie Sue and Edwina both jumped.

"Ladies," Detective Rogenstein said with a big smile. "To what do I owe this pleasure?"

Debbie Sue traded glances with Edwina.

"I'd like to talk to Cher," Edwina said, a flutter in her voice.

Debbie Sue attempted to look past him, but he was too tall and too wide.

"Cher? Sorry, but I don't think I can help you. As you can see, I'm alone." He swung the door wide.

"Yep, that's right, Ed," Debbie Sue said. "Yep, he's alone. Okay then, 'bye. Sorry to have bothered you." She grabbed Edwina's arm and pulled her away.

Edwina freed her arm from Debbie Sue's grip and glared at Rogenstein. "I saw her go in there with you."

"Maybe you're confused. Too much to drink this evening, perhaps?"

Debbie Sue finally succeeded in dragging Edwina back into their own room and barricading the door with her body.

"Debbie Sue, get out of my way. We know for a fact—"

Before Edwina finished, Debbie Sue took her arm and led her to the chair on the far side of the room. She sat her down and pulled the other chair close to her. "What we know for a fact is that he's lying and people lie to cover up the truth. The truth is if he's done something to her, now he knows that we know."

"Oh, poor Cher." Edwina pressed a clenched fist against her mouth. "Debbie Sue, do you really think she's dead?" Tears shimmered in Edwina's brown eyes.

"I don't know, but—"

"I couldn't get hold of Matt," Celina said. "He didn't call back."

Edwina stood and stepped around Debbie Sue. "I'm not waiting. I'm calling nine-one-one and telling them to get the fuck over here."

Debbie Sue looked up at her best friend's face and her reddened eyes. Lines of black mascara trailed down her cheeks.
She couldn't remember the last time she had seen Edwina so
upset. "Let me do it, Ed," she said softly. "We want them to
know we're serious. I'm afraid you're too emotional."

Edwina squared her shoulders. Her chin quivered. "I'm
not too emotional. But you're right. You call. You know
how to talk to cops. I'd rather watch the hallway. I'd love it
if that arrogant sperm bank showed his fat ass."

"I wonder if I should call Buddy and discuss it with him?"
Debbie Sue said, getting to her feet.

"No," Edwina exclaimed. "If you call Buddy, he'll call
Vic, and the next thing you know, Vic will be on the phone
telling me to come home now. Or hell, who knows? A SEAL
team might even show up."

"Let's go ahead and call nine-one-one then," Debbie Sue
said. "That fucker next door is a professional cop. Let his
own kind deal with him. When the cops get here, they can
search the room. If Cher's passed out, they'll find her. If she's
. . . well, they'll find her, right?"

"Right," Celina said.

"Right," Edwina agreed. "And while you're doing that,
I'm gonna watch his door." She dragged a chair over and
opened the door a crack.

Debbie Sue punched in the three digits. The emergency
operator's voice came on the line. "What is your emergency?"

"My name is Debbie Sue Overstreet. I'm registered at the
Anson Hotel on Times Square, in room six-one-eight. My

husband is James Russell Overstreet, Junior, Texas Department of Public Safety trooper. I have this friend who's a prostitute. She went into the room next door with a guy and . . . What I want to do is report a murder in room six twenty—"

"How do you know it was a murder, ma'am?"

"Well, uh, I heard it."

"You heard a gunshot?"

"Well, no, not a gunshot. It was a big thud and some thumps and—"

"Your friend's a prostitute? Are you sure you aren't hearing some kind of bed play?"

Debbie Sue jammed a fist against her hip. "Listen, I'll have you know my husband's studying to be a Texas Ranger, and I know better than to call nine-one-one for nothing."

"I'm sending someone, but I warn you, ma'am, misuse of the emergency call service is a crime." The line went dead.

Debbie Sue jerked the receiver away from her ear and stared at it. "She hung up. Dammit, she acted like she didn't believe me."

"Yankee," Edwina muttered.

"Hmm," Celina put in, frowning. "I guess a big thump and some thuds doesn't necessarily translate to murder."

"Well, she said she'd send someone. They have to come, if for no other reason than to give me a ticket or something for misuse of the emergency call service. For the first time in my life I hope I'm going to be made out an ass."

"I couldn't agree with you more," Edwina said, returning to her lookout post.

"Listen, y'all," Celina said. "I just remembered the conversation last night about the possibility of a serial murderer of prostitutes. You don't think—"

"Oh, my God," Debbie Sue said. "Do you suppose? An honest-to-God serial killer right here under our noses."

Edwina closed the gap in the door and leaned against it. "Dear God. And he knows we know."

Debbie Sue began to pace. Celina grabbed a bag of potato chips and dropped into an easy chair. She began cramming chips into her mouth as if she were in an eating contest with a phantom opponent.

Edwina gave Debbie Sue a troubled look. "This doesn't seem like it's real." Her brow tented and she chewed on her lower lip. "I wonder if I'm losing my grip on reality."

"I think that already happened downstairs in the bar," Debbie Sue replied, and strode to the bathroom.

Ten tense minutes later, NYPD officers arrived. Edwina dashed up the hallway toward them, waving her arms and gesturing wildly. Debbie Sue and Celina followed.

"We heard the man in the room next to us choke a woman to death," Edwina cried. "Quick, get in there. She might still be alive."

The taller of the two policemen patted the air with his palms in a calming gesture. "Slow down, lady. Tell us what happened."

Debbie Sue and Celina skidded to a stop behind Edwina.

"We're detectives," Edwina said. "We're here for the private investigators' convention. We got this piece of audio equipment to try out and when we put it against the wall to listen in on the room next door, we heard the man in six twenty choking a woman. That's the story. Now, go check on her."

The shorter cop couldn't have been over five foot five or six, Debbie Sue observed. He looked up at Edwina, giving her the squint-eye. "Weren't you in the bar earlier this evening when the fight broke out?"

"Yes. Yes, that was me, but I had nothing to do with the . . . well, with what happened down there. You yourself heard my story and let me go."

"This device," the tall cop said. "Would that happen to be the Ear?" He looked down at his partner, his brow arched. "I've been reading about that equipment. It's cool, man."

"Excuse me, but could we get back to the woman who's dead or dying in room six twenty?"

"Yeah," Debbie Sue and Celina chorused.

Debbie Sue heard the distinct sound of the elevator door opening and shot a glance in that direction. The night manager appeared from around the corner, approaching them in a trot.

"Oh, fuck," Debbie Sue mumbled under her breath.

"Officers, I'm the night manager. May I inquire—" He stopped and landed a glare of incredulity on Edwina and Debbie Sue. "You two again? What's going on now? Is something on fire? What's the meaning of this?"

"Sir, these ladies have reported a murder in room six-two-zero."

"Murder!" The night manager's eyes bugged. "My God. First a fight, now murder?" He slapped his forehead with his palm, making Debbie Sue wince. "I'm finished," he gasped. "Done. I'll never work in a first-class hotel again. I'll be lucky to even rent a room in a hotel." His eyes darted among them. "My ex-wife sent you here, didn't she? This is revenge, isn't it?"

Edwina looked down at his nametag, then back up at the distraught man. "Homer, none of this is your fault. Surely things worse than this happen in big-city hotels every day."

Homer yanked a handkerchief from his breast pocket and wiped his sweaty brow. His shaking hands showed fingernails bitten to the quick, and Debbie Sue again felt sorry for him.

"Worse than thousands of dollars in damage to the bar?" he cried. "A possible murder in the hotel in the same night? You'd have to know Mr. Pembroke. He doesn't allow *any-thing* ugly to happen in his hotel. On his watch or off. He fired the last assistant manager because a guest complained of slow room service."

"Well, he shouldn't be so quick to jump to judgment," Debbie Sue said.

Edwina redirected her attention to the men in blue. "So? Can we get back to the issue? Let's go talk to this perp." She started for the neighboring room.

"You ladies stay right here," the taller cop said with authority. "My partner and I'll take it from here." He turned to the night manager. "Sir? . . . Homer, you have a pass key for this room, don't you?"

"Of course," Homer answered weakly.

"Would you accompany us, please, staying back and out of harm's way, of course."

"Sure. Why not? Maybe there'll be an exchange of gun-fire and I'll get shot."

Both men freed their weapons as they approached Room 620. Debbie Sue and Edwina stayed only a couple of steps behind. The taller cop rapped on the door and called out, "NYPD. Open up. We'd like to talk to you, sir."

The door opened immediately and Detective Rogenstein greeted them as if they were invited dinner guests, a cigar in his hand. "Hello, boys. What's up? They need me back at the station?"

Edwina gasped and Debbie Sue gave her an elbow to the ribs.

"Detective Rogenstein," the shorter cop exclaimed, clearly shocked. "I uh, uh, we—we're answering a call, sir. There must be a mistake of some kind. There's been a report of foul play in this room."

"*Frank* Rogenstein? *The* Frank Frogenstein?" The second policeman thrust out his right hand. "It's an honor to meet you, sir. I'm Pat McShane and this is my partner, Ed Fitzpatrick. I've been studying some of your cases for when I take the detective exams."

Edwina turned to Debbie Sue and Celina with a look of astonishment. "Why, they're gonna have an orgasm any minute. I wouldn't be surprised if one of 'em whipped out a camera and asked somebody to take their pictures together."

Rogenstein obviously heard her. A chilling look came their way before he continued his conversation with his admirers. "Have you, now? Well good luck to you, son. Keep studying and working hard. You'll get there. I started out as a beat cop myself. A long time ago, mind you," he added with a chuckle, "but the same work eithic I've practiced my whole career will work for you too. Now, how can I help you?"

"Sir, uh," McShane said, "it seems a call was placed to nine-one-one—"

"Sir." The hotel manager pushed between the two officers, picked up Rogenstein's hand and began to pump it vigorously. "Sir, I cannot tell you how sorry I am for this disturbance. All of this is a terrible mistake. Can I repay you in some way? A muffin basket, perhaps? Our chef prepares a delightful arrangement accented with tiny little fresh flowers—"

"I hate muffins," Rogenstein growled through a tight smile. "I don't even know what's going on yet."

Edwina stepped up beside the taller cop, glaring at Detective Rogenstein. "You know what this is all about. Don't think you can piss down our backs and convince us it's raining."

"Yeah," Debbie Sue put in.

"Ma'am," Officer McShane said sternly to Edwina, "watch your mouth. We'll handle this."

Detective Rogenstein leveled a look of contempt at Edwina, then turned a cruise-director smile back on the two cops. "I don't seem to be very popular with my neighbors, do I? Perhaps I had the volume on my TV too high?"

"Hah!" Edwina said.

"Your volume was just fine and we heard every word of it," Debbie Sue said, stepping up to support Edwina.

Celina came forward, too, and stood shoulder to shoulder

with them. "I personally didn't hear any of it, but if they said they did, that's all I need to know."

"We're sorry about this, sir," Officer McShane said to Rogenstein, edging the three women aside.

"No need to apologize for doing your job," Rogenstein replied. "Come in and check the room. If you didn't, I'd have to report you."

He allowed the two cops entry, but blocked the doorway as Debbie Sue and her two pals attempted to follow. "I hope you don't mind if I close the door," he said to the two cops. "There's nothing worse than a bunch of wannabes trying to tell professionals how to do their job."

He chuckled and the cops laughed, too. "Not at all, sir," the one named Fitzpatrick said. "They have no business in here. They've already caused trouble downstairs."

The door closed and Debbie Sue, her two friends and Homer were left standing in the hallway.

"Fuck," Debbie Sue said.

"Shit," Edwina added.

"Oh, dear God," Homer said, falling back against the wall beside the door. He slid to the floor, holding his head in his hands.

"I brought this," Celina said, holding up a glass tumbler. She stepped around Homer, placed the rim against the door and glued her ear to the bottom of the glass.

"Outta my way," Edwina said, "I brought *this*." She produced the Ear. She planted it on the door and handed one of the earpieces to Debbie Sue.

Homer began to boo-hoo into his hands.

"Take your time. Look around," Rogenstein's voice said. "Let me get some of these papers off the bed. I was getting ready for a session tomorrow and I've got notes strewn everywhere. I'm a presenter at the conference downstairs, you know." He chuckled. "That's what happens when you become a respected professional, boys. Everybody wants to hear what you've got to say."

Officer McShane's deeper voice said, "If you don't mind, sir, I'll just take a quick look in the bathroom. I mean, it *was* a nine-one-one call, so we should check."

Silence passed.

"So, what did you find?" Rogenstein's voice said a minute later.

"You're right, sir. All clear."

"Fuck!" Debbie Sue whispered. "He couldn't possibly have searched the bathroom that well. He was only in there a few seconds."

"Maybe it's a small bathroom," Celina said with a look of innocence.

Debbie Sue and Edwina stared at her.

"I was just thinking of our own bathroom," she said meekly.

"Find anything in the closet?" Rogenstein's voice said.

"No sir," the voice that belonged to Fitzpatrick said. "It's easy to see there ain't nobody here but you, sir."

"Don't forget to look under the bed," Rogenstein prompted.

"Yeah," Edwina agreed.

"That's a good place to hide a body in a motel," Rogenstein added. "That'll probably be on your exams, Pat. Don't forget where you learned the answer."

"But there ain't no under the bed," Fitzpatrick's voice said. "This mattress is laying on a solid base and it's nailed to the floor.

"I said in a *motel*, boys. *Motel*. Don't forget."

McShane's deep laugh was easily recognizable. "That's right, sir, you did. Problem is, we don't get to motels. We never get out of the city. But thank you, sir. I'll be looking for that on the exam."

A few more seconds passed.

"Well, looks like we're finished here," McShane said.

"Sorry to have bothered you, but it was a pleasure to meet you in person, sir."

"The pleasure was all mine, Pat."

The door opened and Debbie Sue and Edwina almost fell through the doorway.

Fitzpatrick attempted to steady Edwina to keep her from falling, but her flat chest smashed into his face. "Ma'am," he said, turning his face to the side to speak, "I guess you know we're finished here. I don't know what you heard that prompted you to call nine-one-one. I'm thinking it must have been a TV show or the radio. There's no dead body here."

"Just let me look for myself," Edwina said, untangling her-self from the cop, who was at least a foot shorter than she.

But the vertically challenged cop already had her by the upper arm and was guiding her toward her own room. "We've already done that," he said. "We've assessed the situation and determined there ain't no foul play. Any further attempts to disturb Detective Rogenstein will result in a harassment charge against you. Do you understand?"

"Yes, but—" Debbie Sue started.

"That goes for all three of you," McShane said, grasping Debbie Sue and Celina's arms and herding them along behind his partner and Edwina. "We don't want to come back here. If we do, we'll be taking all of you to the station house. Got it?"

The tall cop looked at each woman individually. Debbie Sue glared back with defiant eyes.

"Ladies, don't test us on this." He spoke more firmly than Fitzpatrick. "If you don't think you can leave Frank, uh, Detective Rogenstein, alone, we can go to the station right now, and you can tell your story to the detectives there."

"No, no, that's okay," Debbie Sue said. "We'll cooperate. You go on. We won't be bothering you any longer, Officer. And we won't bother Detective Rogenstein. Thank you for coming. We're going to bed now." Debbie Sue gripped Edwina's arm and continued dragging her backward. Celina followed.

Once the two cops had disappeared and the three of them were behind the closed door of their room, Edwina confronted Debbie Sue. "Why didn't we go to the squad house with them? We could tell our story to the detectives, and maybe someone would do something."

"Yeah, and while we're doing that, *Rogenstink* has all the time he needs to move the body. Ed, we can't let him out of our sight."

"You're right. Do you think you should go ahead and call Buddy? He'd know what to do."

"Hell, Ed. He'd probably have a U.S. marshal pick me up and put me on a plane home. What about you? You calling Vic?"

"I already said what I think about doing that." She shook her head. "This is all too crazy."

"Who's taking the first watch at the door?"

"I will," Edwina volunteered eagerly. "I won't sleep for years. I might as well make some use of all this insomnia."

"Hey," Debbie Sue said. "I lost track of Homer. Where'd he go?"

"Don't know," Edwina said. "He said something about getting a resume together and calming a monster. Don't know what that means in hotel lingo, but he seemed hell-bent on doing it."

Frank Rogenstein hadn't felt this alive in years. His life had become stagnant. Predictable. Artery clogging, in his opinion. The close call this evening had him giddy and euphoric.

Pressing his right foot against the edge of the mattress, he put his considerable bulk behind the effort and gave a push. The base of the bed had appeared to be solid but the frame was a housing for a foam base. Using his pocketknife, he had cut away a crude outline and placed the woman inside. He had barely had time to stuff the foam into his suitcases when the beat cops knocked at the door.

He looked down at the woman who lay just as he had left

her. No outcry, no signaling for help, just bulging, dead eyes staring into space.

He chuckled. "Well, doll face, we've had quite a night, haven't we? I'll figure out what to do with you tomorrow. Right now I'm going to catch a couple of winks. Hope my snoring doesn't bother you."

He chuckled again. He would have to remember this when he supervised the next crime-scene investigation.

In the next room, earpiece still in place, Debbie Sue dashed from the wall into the bathroom and retched.

chapter twenty

etective Matt McDermott sat on the edge of one of the beds in Room 618, looking into the faces of the three distraught women. Edwina was openly crying and her face had black eye makeup smeared from her eyes to her chin.

All three of them were still recovering from Edwina's having gotten her long, red fingernails tangled up with the listening device and earpieces, and accidentally erasing the tape they had recorded. Unfortunately, he had heard no more than three words on the tape, but both Debbie Sue and Edwina had given him an animated explanation of what they had heard.

It was almost 2 A.M. They all looked weary-worn, but Celina's eyes were sharp. She leaned toward him and took his hand possessively. "You believe us, don't you, Matt? There's no reason Debbie Sue and Edwina would make any of this up."

It wasn't that he didn't believe their story. Training and experience had taught him that aberrant behavior by even someone like Rogenstein was possible. But Frank Rogenstein, a serial killer? Nah, couldn't be. "The first thing I want to do is relocate all of you to another room. If there's really a killer on the loose in the hotel and he knows this is your room, you're not safe here."

Debbie Sue perked up. "That's all taken care of. I spoke to the manager when he was here. He's more than happy to move us, but it won't be 'til morning."

Edwina wiped her nose. "But we can't—"

A jab from Debbie Sue's elbow cut Edwina's words short. *What was that about?* Matt wondered.

"Don't worry, Matt," Debbie Sue said. "It's all taken care of."

Somehow Matt didn't feel reassured, but he moved on. "Second, I need to pull some information together. You said she identified herself as a cop and tried to arrest him? To be honest, I'm unfamiliar with an officer in our precinct named Cheryl Angelo, but I'm not acquainted with a lot of them who work undercover."

He didn't see the necessity of saying that if the word was out that an undercover cop was really missing, wheels were already turning and a search had already begun.

He glanced down at his watch, buying time and organizing his thoughts. Rogenstein and he had checked into the hotel together. The guy had brought a shaving kit and a suitcase. If he had really done what these women said, as far as Matt could see, he couldn't have disposed of the body yet. Today he would have to keep up normal appearances so as not to draw attention to himself, but if he had a corpse to get rid of, he would have to act, and act quickly. By evening at the latest.

"You ladies try to get some sleep," he told them. "I'll be back here at six o'clock."

The three women nodded, agreeing. Matt wasn't worried that Celina wouldn't do as he asked, but he gave Debbie Sue and Edwina a second look. Anyone could see that these two were accustomed to following their own paths. "You're to stay in the room until I get back. Don't open the door to anyone. I don't want to be distracted by worrying about you."

He felt a touch of uneasiness that he got no argument from them, but at the same time, he had no doubt they were discouraged and exhausted. Hopefully, they realized they had stumbled into something over their heads. He made a mental note to thank them later for their cooperation.

Rising from his seat he took Celina's hand and drew her to her feet. Putting his hand at the back of her neck, he pulled her closer to him. "You've got my cell number. Please call me if anything, and I mean *anything*, happens. And please, please don't let anything happen to you."

Celina smiled up at him. "I promise," she said softly. She walked to the door with him. "See you at six."

Matt stood in the hallway outside their door until he heard

the *snick* of the lock and the *click* of the deadbolt sliding into place.

He had a lot to accomplish in four hours. The most difficult thing would be convincing a judge to sign a search warrant for Room 620. He had gotten a judge's signature on a warrant application with less cause than what he currently had, but the subject wasn't the most highly decorated detective in the history of the city. Frank Rogenstein had connections and friends in extremely high places. He was capable of destroying the career of any cop involved if this turned out to be a witch hunt.

Edwina watched Matt's departure through the door's peephole. As soon as he was out of sight, she turned back to Debbie Sue. "Are you nuts? We can't move to another room. We have to watch Rogenstein's room. We have to make sure he doesn't leave with the—"

"I know, Ed, I know. I lied. I was too tired to argue. Matt had that Buddy Overstreet set to his jaw. Buddy would have said the exact same thing, and knowing me better than Matt does, he wouldn't have left here 'til I had been planted in another room in another part of the hotel and locked in from the outside."

"Oh, well," Edwina said. "I guess that's worth me losing a rib over. But next time you feel the need to get my attention, lighten up with the elbow. I'm skinny. I'm gonna be going home black and blue from all the elbow jabs. Then I'll have to explain to Vic where I got 'em."

"Sorry, Ed," Debbie Sue said. "Look, I'm gong to bed

now and see if I can catch forty winks before Matt comes back."

"Good idea. You sleep and I'll watch." Edwina returned to her post as lookout and opened the door a crack.

Debbie Sue pulled back the bedcovers and slid between the sheets. Celina was already in her bed and looking up at the ceiling, a dreamy expression on her face. "Celina, I couldn't help but feel there's something different between you and Matt tonight. Did y'all have a good time at Madison Square Garden?"

"It was the best evening of my life," Celina replied, snuggling further down into the covers. "Can you fall in love with someone this quickly? I mean, we haven't been around each other that much, but I feel, I feel—"

"Like someone should who's falling in love? Just don't confuse falling in love with *being* in love. There's a world of difference and a lot of hours getting to really know each other in between. The falling is magic, but take it from me, it's worth the plunge."

"Amen," Edwina said from the doorway. "Now, y'all get some sleep. Somebody's got to relieve me in a couple of hours."

Edwina shifted in her chair for the umpteenth time. At the last look at the digital clock on the bedside table, it was 3:50. She'd been nervously browsing through the most recent mammoth edition of *Vogue* magazine. She had scratched and sniffed every perfume ad, taken a test on her fashion sense and was reading the photography credits, when she heard the bolt slip out of its slot in Room 620. She pushed her chair back, stood and closed her own door to a mere crack, watching and waiting.

She dared not draw a breath. If Rogenstein made for their room, she intended to bolt the door and start squawking like a mad hen faced with a fox in the chicken house. She had decided early in life that if she was ever in dire peril, she wouldn't go out easy, and she sure wouldn't go out quietly.

But no one approached. She grabbed her hand mirror, stuck it through the door opening and looked up and down the hall. Frank was walking away all right, and he was empty-handed.

She looked back into the room at Debbie Sue and Celina sleeping. Her mind was tumbling and turning. She didn't have a clue what she should do. The same remedy kept coming to her repeatedly: *Follow him. Follow him.*

Didn't she owe that much to Cher?

She tiptoed to the dresser, picked up a room key and her cell phone, sneaked out the door and headed up the hall toward the elevators. Frank was nowhere in sight and the elevator was descending, so she assumed he was its passenger. She ran to the stairs, threw the door open and started down the steel steps, her wooden platform shoes clomping like horses' hooves, the hollow echo reverberating off the walls.

She heard a sound and stopped. She couldn't tell if she had heard something real or if her sleep-deprived mind was playing tricks on her, but the hairs on the back of her neck told her the door leading to the stairwell from the sixth floor had just opened and closed. Had Frank opened the door? Was he plotting to trap her here, where no one could see or hear them? Had he been hiding in the recesses of the hallway waiting for her to make a fatal error?

Edwina didn't know where the speed and agility came from, but she remembered her childhood. In that memory she was strolling home from school and for some reason she became convinced a monster was set to pounce on her from behind. If she dared look back she would be devoured. So she broke into a run and by the time she reached her home, she practically charged through the screen door, with her mother standing there looking on in bewilderment.

The next thing she knew, she was entering the hotel lobby in a dead run, legs and arms pumping. Before now, she hadn't known she was capable of what she had just done—descending the stairs four steps at a time, gripping the handrail and swinging her body to the next level like a trapeze artist. She had been magnificent. Olympics material, for sure.

The best part was that no one was behind her, and fifteen steps ahead of her was Frank Rogenstein. He pushed through the revolving doors and stood outside on the sidewalk, made bright as day by the lights of Times Square.

"Humph. I'll just see where that sucker's going," she mumbled to the air.

She trailed him at a distance, safe from detection, but never letting him out of her sight and paying no attention to her surroundings or the direction in which she walked. Her dogged determination paid off. Rogenstein entered a brightly lit corner store that proudly advertised WE SELL EVERYTHING! on a sign in the plate-glass window.

Pretty ballsy of the owners to make that claim, she thought. She didn't think even Wal-Mart could say as much.

She didn't dare go in and get trapped. She stood outside a few feet from the door and stared through the tall display windows. What wasn't sitting on the shelves hung from the ceiling and she didn't doubt that merchandise was crammed into every nook and cranny.

Only a few minutes passed and Detective Rogenstein came outside lugging a large trunk. It didn't take a genius to know how he intended to use the trunk. Picturing it stuffed with Cher's body, a shiver skittered up her spine and she caught a quick breath.

Frank hailed a cab and Edwina watched helplessly as he and the cab driver loaded the trunk into the cab's trunk and sped away.

"Ohmigod, ohmigod, ohmigod," she chanted, dancing in circles. All she could think was that she had to call Debbie Sue before Frank returned to the hotel and left the room with poor Cher's body.

She dug the phone from her back pocket and pressed the ON switch. The screen remained blank. Her stomach rose to the back of her throat. She couldn't remember the last time she had charged the phone. Then she realized she didn't have any money—or her purse. She couldn't even use a pay phone. *Shit*!

We Sell Everything might do just that, but she doubted they did it for free, and cabs didn't operate that way either. As to her exact location? She was standing at the intersection of God Knows Where and Boy Are You Screwed.

Dammit, girl. Think! And while she was thinking, she starting walking in the direction from which she had come. She had to get back to the hotel before Rogenstein, and definitely before six o'clock.

At an intersection she noticed that every other person had a cell phone stuck to his ear. A couple of people even had two. She remembered the admonishments from her friends in Salt Lick not to mix with New Yorkers, but hell, she had to do something. Figuring she had nothing to lose, she drew a deep breath and yelled, "Does anybody have a cell phone I can borrow to make one teeny-weeny call?"

To her astonishment phones magically appeared from everywhere. "Wow, this is really nice. I only need one. Here, I'll take this one. Thanks, everybody. Thanks so much."

When the light changed everyone moved except her and the cell phone owner, a young black man in baggy jeans and an oversize basketball jersey. A bill cap was perched sideways on his head.

He cocked his chin. "W'sup, tornado bait?"

Tornado bait? Is he talking about me? "Uh, I'm trying to stay one step ahead of trouble, but I think I'm losing the race."

She wasn't sure why she explained her situation to him except that he had been nice enough to offer his phone, and from the looks of him he might appreciate the circumstances.

"Oh, snap! Pass me an oar, you know what I'm saying? I mean, that's some whacked shit."

"Uh-huh. Well, I—"

Keying in Debbie Sue's cell number, she smiled at him as

the phone started ringing. A voice came on the phone. "Detective McDermott here."

"Oh, snap," Edwina muttered. She was no longer losing the race. The race was over and she was sucking everybody's dust.

"Edwina? Edwina, is that you?"

Edwina's heart dropped to her feet. Dammit, Matt wasn't supposed to be there yet. "Yeah, it's me."

"Where are you? I'm sending a unit to pick you up."

"Let's see, I'm catty-cornered from a cute little church. It looks really old. It's called St. Paul's Chapel. Do you know where that is?"

"Wow. You walked quite a distance."

Nobody had to tell Edwina she had walked quite a distance. Her feet were killing her.

"But luckily, you're not that far away," he added. He sounded serious. "You're at Ground Zero."

"No kidding? Oh, sweet Jesus. I was so afraid I wasn't going to get to come here before we left. Where were the buildings? Were they at this construction site that's all lit up? They were, weren't they? It seems so small. I just want to sit down and cry. This is so sad."

"Edwina, listen to me. Are you safe? Is Rogenstein anywhere around?"

"He left. He bought a big trunk in this store that sells everything and put it in a cab and drove away. I don't know where he was headed, but I didn't have any money, so I had to ask—"

"I'm sorry to keep interrupting you, but listen to me carefully. You are to come straight back to this hotel when the officers reach you. Is that clear?"

"Yessir. I'll wait right here for the officers."

"You've been foolish, woman. You could have become another victim."

"I'm sorry, Matt, but I lost track of the time. When Frank left the hotel, he seemed hell-bent on the direction he was going and I got carried away. What time is it, anyway?"

"It's five thirty. I came back a little early."

"Well then, it's not my fault," Edwina said indignantly. "You said six o'clock. I'd have been back by six o'clock."

"We'll discuss it when you get back here. The car should be pulling up any minute now."

Edwina disconnected and handed the phone back to her new street-savvy friend.

"Five-Oh comin' to haul yo' ass to lockup?"

Edwina thought a moment. "I don't think so, but they *are* coming to pick me up. He said a couple of cops in a cruiser."

The young man gave her a round-eyed look. "That is off the chain! You must be some Bonnie-and-Clyde motherfucker!"

"Yep, that's me all right. The chain's slipped off. Or on the chain, or whatever. That's me."

"I thought you was jus' some sad ol' wack-a-loon that was lost."

A police car pulled up to the curb. The officer on the passenger side got out and opened the back door. "Miz Martin,

Detective McDermott asked us to escort you back to your hotel."

Edwina entered the cruiser as if she were royalty. She glanced back at her new friend. "Thanks for the use of the phone. And take it easy, sleazy!"

"Backatcha, spooky lady."

"Backatcha, baggy pants."

chapter twenty-one

Edwina worried as the squad car approached the Anson Hotel. She didn't dread seeing Detective McDermott nearly as much as she did Debbie Sue. Her friend and partner would give her a ration of shit for sure. At the same time she wondered if Rogenstein had returned.

The hotel's porte cochere was congested with police vehicles. Uniformed men and women seemed to be everywhere. Had they been looking for her? They must have been. The last thing she had expected was that Matt and/or Debbie Sue would be so concerned that they would sound an alarm and get the whole NYPD involved. The best thing she could do was simply not put in an appearance.

Edwina leaned forward to speak to the two cops in the front seat. "Hey, guys, I don't suppose you'd want to take me back to Ground Zero, would you? I'm from out of town, you know. I didn't really get to look around as much as I'd like to."

The cop on the passenger's side turned halfway in his seat and looked at her. "Detective McDermott was direct about us bringing you straight to the hotel."

Mentally, Edwina winced. "Oh, yeah. There's that. Well, I mean, he's not your boss or anything like that, is he?"

When neither policeman replied, she slumped back in the seat.

The police car pulled to a stop in front of the hotel entrance and Edwina climbed out. "Thanks for the ride, boys. It was nice to meetcha."

"I'll walk you to your room," one cop said, sliding out of the passenger seat.

Somehow Edwina had known he would say that. She trudged wordlessly beside him, her mind whirling with questions. Rogenstein had left We Sell Everything long before she had. Had he already come back to the hotel, and was he here now? And if the answer to either question was yes, then what?

She stood silently as the elevator rose to six. When the door opened she said to her escort, "Thanks, shug. I've got it from here."

"If it's all the same to you, ma'am, I'll hand you over to Detective McDermott. That's what he told us to do and he was clear on the matter."

Police lined the hallway leading from the elevator to the room she shared with Debbie Sue and Celina, some on phones, some just leaning against the wall talking to one another. The scene was congested but fairly quiet, except for the frazzled, coming-apart-at-the-seams night manager, Homer.

Edwina tried to be inconspicuous, but Homer spotted her and marched toward her, his lips drawn thin. He was within a few steps when a hand suddenly grabbed his shoulder and pulled him back. It appeared Debbie Sue was hell-bent on reaching her before Homer did.

To Edwina's surprise Debbie Sue grabbed her in a big bear hug and rocked her back and forth, half talking, half blubbering. "Oh, Ed. You're alive. I pictured you dead. I've never been so happy to see anyone in my whole life. I couldn't stand it if something happened to you. What would I tell Vic?"

"Well, hon, that's so sweet of you. But I'm fine—"

"You're not hurt?" Debbie Sue held her at arm's length, her gaze running up and down her body. "Did he grab you and make you leave with him?"

"No, hon, I followed him."

"Shit." Debbie released her, scowling. "That's exactly what I was afraid of." Now the friend who seemed so happy to see her suddenly became the person Edwina had dreaded. "Shit, Ed. Have you taken leave of the good sense God gave you? Do you know what could have happened to you out there? How do you think we felt when we woke up and you were gone?"

"I tried to call earlier—"

"Did you even think about what could have happened to you? Will you please promise me you won't go off half-cocked again? From here on out we do things together, right? As a team, right?"

Edwina raised her right hand. "I promise. Where's a Bible? I'll swear on it. Now, do you want to know what I found out when I followed him?"

Before she could tell, Homer planted himself in front of Debbie Sue. "I'd like to know when you and your party will be leaving this establishment." Indignation made his voice tremble.

Debbie Sue swung her attention to Homer. "We've got a room 'til Sunday morning. That's when we leave, *Homer.*"

Edwina drew herself up to her full five feet and ten inches. "Just why are you in such a hurry to see us gone, *Homer?*"

Matt was suddenly standing between them. He addressed the night manager. "Sir, these women haven't done anything except be in the wrong place at the wrong time."

The manager pointed a finger at Edwina. "*That* one has caused an untold amount of damage in this hotel."

"But you wouldn't want to see harm come to her and her friends, would you?"

"Well, no. But there are policemen—"

"Yes, sir, I'm aware of that. I called them. Now that Mrs. Martin is back safe and sound, I'm going to send all of them on their way. Everyone else is going back into the room. All will be quiet again. Isn't that what you want?"

"Yes. Oh, God, yes." Shaking his head, Homer covered his face with both hands. "I just want some peace and quiet. And some order. Mr. Pembroke demands order. He comes in at nine o'clock sharp on Fridays and if he sees—"

"There's nothing for him to see," Matt said. "Thank you for your cooperation and understanding. I'll be happy to write a letter to Mr. Pembroke praising your professionalism and the extent to which you've gone to help the men in blue. Now, why don't you accompany these officers downstairs?"

One of the cops stepped up beside Homer and said, "Happy to help you, sir."

He settled a withering glare on Edwina and pointed a finger at her again. "*You*. You stay out of the bar, stay out of the restaurant, stay out of the lobby." He pounded his palm with his fingertip. "You stay in this room. Do you understand me?"

Edwina huffed and hoisted her chin. "Well, I never . . ."

After the uniformed cops and Homer left their sight, Edwina turned to Matt in awe. "You know, you're slick as bat shit. You're wasting your time as a cop. You could have been a used-car salesman."

"And you should have been a magician," he replied, without smiling. "Come into the room, Houdini, before you disappear again."

Edwina was thrilled to see a cart of food inside the room. *Breakfast!* She'd had no sleep, she was pumped on adrenaline and the long walk in the early morning air had kicked her appetite into full gear. She grabbed a plate and started heaping on muffins and pats of butter and fresh fruit.

Celina was sitting in a chair, her big eyes brimmed with tears. "Edwina, are you all right?"

"Look, y'all, cut it out. I'm fine. He never knew I was following him. Lord, I've been in worse life-threatening situations than that."

"You have?"

"Lord, yes. Every time a customer sits down in my chair and announces she wants something 'fun and exciting,' I know I'm in trouble."

Celina laughed then. "Oh, Edwina, you take the cake."

"Thank you, I think I will. I'll take this piece right here." She gave Celina a big grin as she grabbed a slice of white cake covered with strawberries and added it to her heaping plate.

Everyone calmed down and began to eat. "Tell us everything that happened," Matt said, pouring a cup of coffee for himself. "Don't leave out any detail. Anything could be important."

Edwina told of hearing Rogenstein's door open and seeing him walk up the corridor and of herself being overwhelmed with the urge to follow him. She told of his entry into the store that sold everything, his coming out with the trunk and stopping a cab. "The trunk's green. It has a large loop handle. Did he come back here? Have y'all seen him?"

"No, he hasn't been back," Debbie Sue said. "Or if he has, we missed seeing him. But then we were asleep until Matt showed up."

"So how's the investigation going?"

"I'm working on it," Matt assured her. "Under any circumstances there's red tape involved in getting a warrant, but in this particular case there are more concerns. Since we don't have the recording, I want to be sure everything's done by the book. I don't want something coming back to bite me."

"I still can't believe all of this is happening," Celina said, shaking her head. "I never in a million years thought coming to a convention to learn how to be a detective would end up with me involved in a real murder investigation."

Matt turned a grim look at her. "And you're right in the middle of a really big one, too. I hope you're enjoying the adrenaline rush."

She returned an angelic smile. "Honestly? I'm not. I think it's very sad and very scary. This isn't for me. It would come across as really exciting on paper, but being in it is a whole other story. I miss my library. Finding a book I thought was lost is enough excitement for me."

He turned to Debbie Sue and Edwina. "And you two. I suppose you love it."

"It has its moments," Debbie Sue said. "But today is the first time I've been honest-to-God scared and it wasn't for my own safety."

Edwina knew Debbie Sue was talking about her and was genuinely touched. "I'm sorry, Debbie Sue. The next chance you get to do something really lame, I won't say a word."

"Thanks, friend. Knowing our history, you won't have to wait long."

To Debbie Sue's dismay, Matt lectured them again on the dangers of getting involved in something they weren't qualified to handle. He preached statistics and gave more warnings than a father to a set of triplet daughters on prom night.

"I spoke to Homer," he said pointedly to Debbie Sue. "He doesn't remember a conversation with you yesterday about a room change, but he assured me he'll see to it this morning. I intend to stay here until that happens."

"There's no need for that," Debbie Sue said, chastened. "I confess I told you a fib. I promise not to do it again. Look, Ed and I have to give our session at ten o'clock, and we'll take Celina with us."

"If I know you two, you'll decide to stay up here in the room so you can eavesdrop or spy or whatever."

"Oh, we can't do that. If we don't fulfill our obligation to these conference folks, we'll have to pay for this whole thing, the airfare between here and Texas and the hotel bill. Holy cow, the courtesy bar alone could put Edwina and me both in bankruptcy. We've had experience with that."

He gave her an arch look. "You're changing rooms just the same."

Debbie Sue shot Edwina a look of desperation. When Edwina shrugged her shoulders, Debbie Sue turned her attention back to Matt. "We're going to need some privacy to get dressed. Can you at least wait outside the door?"

"That much I'll do. I'll be sitting in a chair by the elevators. When you're ready I'll escort you downstairs to the concierge."

He rose from his seat. Before leaving he stopped in front

of Celina, tilted up her chin and kissed her. "Be careful," he said softly. "Don't blindly follow these two."

"Awwww," Edwina said dreamily.

Matt glowered at her and started for the door. "See you in an hour," he said as he pulled the door shut.

Debbie Sue watched his departure through the peephole. When she was satisfied he was out of sight, she turned back to her roommates. "Okay. With all the cops around here, it's safe to assume that Rogenstein didn't come back here, right?"

"Right," Edwina agreed. "And he had that friggin' trunk. Somebody would have noticed."

"Maybe not," Celina put in. "This *is* a hotel. Would it be out of the ordinary for someone to bring in a trunk?"

"I don't think he's in that room. There hasn't been a sound from over there. With all the commotion in the hallway, if he was in there, he would have come out to see what was going on."

"If no one saw Mr. Rogenstein go in," Celina said, "maybe Cher left and no one saw her, either."

"I say we've got to go in and look around in that room," Debbie Sue said. "We've got to look closer than those two cops looked. Rogenstink had them bamboozled. If we don't find anything, great. We've satisfied ourselves."

Adrenaline was still rushing through Edwina's bloodstream. She needed action. "I'm for that."

"Okay. Any idea how we can get in there?" Debbie Sue asked.

"But what about the warrant Matt's waiting for?" Celina asked. "If Mr. Rogenstein goes on trial, wouldn't our entering his room without a warrant put the evidence in question?"

"If we were cops, I suppose it might. But we're not. We're private citizens just snooping around. We haven't been hired by anyone to do anything. At the worst, I suppose they could get us for breaking and entering."

"Hmm," Edwina said. "I'll bet Homer would like to do just that."

"Well, I'm willing to take that risk." Debbie Sue's tone had a ring of finality.

"You may be willing, sweet cheeks," Edwina said, "but it ain't gonna' happen. Not with 'Steel Jaw McDermott' waiting for us to relocate."

"Maybe he'll get a call and have to leave," Celina said as she chewed on her thumbnail.

"Oh, yeah," Debbie Sue said, and Edwina heard a plan in her tone. "That just might happen. Guess we'll just have to hope the wheels of justice turn smoothly. We're pretty much out of it at this point."

Edwina glanced at Debbie Sue, puzzled, but Debbie Sue gave her a wink.

"We might as well get ready to go downstairs," Debbie Sue said. "Celina, you take the bathroom first. Ed and I'll finish packing."

"Oh, okay. I'll hurry," Celina gathered her things and headed for the bathroom.

"No need to rush. We have plenty of time."

Once Celina closed the door and Debbie Sue heard the shower, she said to Edwina, "Listen, I've got an idea."

"Now there's a surprise. I'd be shocked if you didn't."

"I'd like to keep Celina out of this as much as possible. I think she's starting to get a little weak-kneed over this whole thing and I don't want to put her relationship with Matt in jeopardy. It looks to me like those two are in love whether they realize it not. You know that voice changer thingamajig you bought for talking dirty to Vic?"

Edwina's brown eyes narrowed. "Yeeaah?" she said cautiously. "What about it?"

"There's no way our real voices would fool Matt, so let's give that thing a trial run."

Catching on glinted like a light in Edwina's eyes. "What a great idea. Now, where did I put it?" She rummaged through the packages and sacks strewn about the room.

At last she lifted a small box triumphantly. "Hello. Here it is, and I know how to connect it. I watched the demonstration about ten times."

"Good." Debbie Sue reached for her purse. "Get it set to go while I look for Matt's card."

By the time Edwina had disconnected and reconnected the room phone to the voice-changing device, Debbie Sue had found the card and Matt's cell phone number and was waiting.

"Okay, it's ready." Edwina handed over the phone. "Do you know what you're gonna say?"

"Yeah, but don't look at me. This is a one-time shot and I don't want to start laughing." She hesitated before keying in the number. "You did watch when they adjusted the pitch on this thing, right? I don't want to sound like an old man or worse yet, a cartoon character."

"Yeah, yeah. I did it right. Go ahead."

"Okay. This is it. Here goes."

Edwina opened her palms and urged Debbie Sue onward. "So do it."

"I'm nervous, Ed. I mean, I'm lying to a cop."

"Yeah, I know. But it could be worse. You could be lying to Buddy. I'm turning my back. Have at it."

Debbie Sue punched in Matt's number before she lost her nerve.

Three rings later he came on the line. "Detective Mc-Dermott."

"This is Judge Longoria's assistant," Debbie Sue said into the voice changer. "Would it be possible for you to come to our office? The judge would like to talk to you about the warrant application you've presented."

Debbie Sue considered it dumb luck that Matt had mentioned the name of the judge earlier and she had remembered it. She listened as Matt asked questions.

"Oh, I'm sorry, detective, but Judge Longoria didn't give me any details. He only asked that I call you and ask you to come to his office immediately."

She waited and listened again. "I'm afraid an hour might be too late, sir. He's trying to leave town. I called and confirmed his flight out of Kennedy two hours from now, which means he'll have to be at the airport in an hour."

She waited as Matt groaned and agreed.

"Thank you, Detective. I'll tell the judge you'll be here soon. . . . Uh, what was that? My voice? Oh, I'm just a little hoarse. Sinus troubles. . . . Shrill? . . . It does? Well, I just never know what's going to come out when my allergies act up. . . . Yes, sir. Thanks, I will."

As Debbie Sue disconnected, Edwina turned around and stared at her in astonishment. "God love a goose, Debbie Sue, that was great. I'm pretty much awestruck right now. I didn't know you could think that quick on your feet."

"We don't have time for you to be awestruck. Lucky for us he bought it, even though I must have sounded like I had my tit caught in a wringer.

"Now there's a visual," Edwina said.

"Shut up, Ed. You've got to go downstairs and give our presentation. Alone."

"What? No way, José. Why do I have to go?"

"Because I'm in the zone and somebody needs to make sure we fulfill our agreement and don't have to pay for this hotel bill. Take Celina with you. She can sit by the fountain and keep an eye out for Rogenstein."

Just then they heard a light *rap-rap-rap* on the door.

Not bothering to use the peephole, Debbie Sue opened it a crack and saw Matt standing there. "Oh, hell. We're not ready yet. Is it time to go?"

"Ladies, I'm sorry, but I have to leave. I'll be back as soon as I can. I'll ask Homer to send a bellhop for your luggage in an hour and to make sure you leave your rooms."

Debbie Sue feigned concern. "Oh, Matt, is everything all right?"

"Judge Longoria has some questions. I've got to get to his office ASAP or the warrant may be down the tubes. Promise me you'll follow my instructions."

"Oh, don't worry about us. Celina's in the bathroom getting dressed or she'd tell you the same."

He appeared reluctant to leave but finally nodded and turned to go. Stopping in mid-stride he turned back. "You have my number if you need me, right?"

Debbie Sue summoned a beatific smile. "One of us has your card, I'm sure, but why don't you give me another just in case."

The detective fished a card from his leather badge holder and handed it to her. "Don't hesitate to call me," he said.

"Oh, don't worry, we won't."

chapter twenty-two

For the second time this morning, Debbie Sue watched Matt depart. Feeling confident he was gone, she started talking rapidly to Edwina. "Okay, let's get going. We don't have much time. Take Celina and go downstairs. You don't have to tell her I'm not doing the presentation with you. Just tell her we're counting on her to watch for Rogenstein while we're giving our program."

"Where will you be?" Edwina asked.

"I'm getting into that room next door one way or the other."

"Oh, no. Cher was my friend. I'm the one who should get into it."

Debbie Sue gripped Edwina's skinny arm. "Ed, listen to me. I'm a lot younger than you. I'm not as scared of stuff as you are and I don't get as rattled as you do. I'm the one to do it."

"Well, you're not doing it without me. I won't allow it. You just preached me a sermon about us doing things together."

"I know I did, but this is different." Debbie Sue grasped Edwina's shoulders firmly and forced her to face her. "Listen to me, Ed. This is the only way it'll work. You go downstairs and act like everything's normal. Celina watches for Rogenstein. She can call my cell if he shows up and I'll leave his room and come back into this one. It's ten steps away. I'll never be in any danger."

"Do I have to remind you of the last time you said words like that to me?" Edwina asked. "We were in the bottom of an open grave at night in Haskell, Texas."

"No, you don't have to remind me. Just remind yourself that realistically, when you stop to think about it, the odds of me getting into Rogenstein's room are pretty slim."

"Realistically, my ass. There's nothing realistic about this whole damned thing."

"Ed, hurry. Get Celina and get downstairs. The quicker y'all go, the sooner I can get to work myself."

"I don't have a good feeling about this, Debbie Sue. Not a good feeling at all. If Buddy finds out, he'll ground us forever. Any day of the week I'd rather face Frank Rogenstein than a pissed-off Buddy Overstreet."

"You won't have to face either one. Now, go!"

Edwina walked over and tapped on the bathroom door. "Celina? Ready to go, hon?"

Celina opened the door, a look of confusion on her face, "I'm ready, but are y'all? Neither of you has even been in the bathroom yet."

"Let me just give my teeth a quick swipe," Edwina said pushing past her and grabbing her toothbrush. She ran some water on the bristles, made a couple of up-and-down movements over her teeth and announced, "There, ready to go."

Edwina handed a card to Celina. "Look, you're gonna have to hang out at the fountain and watch for Rogenstein. I've written Debbie Sue's cell number on the back of this card. Call it from your cell at the first sight of him. Your phone's charged up, I hope."

"Oh, yes, it's been plugged in all night."

Debbie Sue was holding the door open, making sweeping motions with her hand. Edwina urged Celina through. "Debbie Sue, see you downstairs." Edwina gave her a huge exaggerated wink behind Celina's back. Than she stopped and wrapped her arms around Debbie Sue in a huge hug. "Promise you'll be careful," she whispered.

"I promise." Debbie Sue said, wishing she felt only half as assured as she attempted to show.

Once the two friends were gone, she gathered up half a dozen pieces of luggage and, struggling under the weight, moved them to the hallway. She went back into the room for her cell phone. Just as she picked it up, the University of Texas fight song blared. The caller was Edwina. "Ed, what's up?"

"I'm in the Big Apple Room. We're set to start in fifteen minutes."

"Okay."

"Frank Rogenstein is sitting on the front row sipping a cup of coffee and talking to everybody around him. I don't know what he's got up his sleeve, but he's smiling like a cat that just got in the cream jar. Bastard. He's probably come to flaunt himself at us."

Debbie Sue's heart plummeted. "Fuck. What if he's already moved the body? Why else would he be acting so smug? If we're too late, he'll never be caught."

"Maybe he's just an arrogant piece of low-class shit," Edwina spat in a stage whisper. "Maybe he's just a limp-dicked motherfucker who doesn't know when he's bit off more than he can chew. You get in that room, whatever it takes, girlfriend."

"Damn straight, Ed. I'll talk to you later."

The plan has to work, Debbie Sue told herself.

One way or another she had to make sure it would.

She hung up and keyed in the hotel's housekeeping number, then said a little prayer while she waited for an answer.

"Housekeeping. I help you?" said a voice in broken English.

"This is room six eighteen. I need someone to come to my room immediately with toilet paper." Debbie Sue forced her words to drip aggravation. "When the room was cleaned this morning they failed to leave a new roll and now I'm stuck on the toilet."

"Oh, yes, ma'am. I send someone as soon—"

"You'll send someone this very minute or I'm calling the

manager. I know him personally. For what I'm paying for this room the very least I should be able to expect is an adequate supply of toilet paper."

"Yes, ma'am. I send Angela right away."

"I don't care who you send. Just send someone now."

Debbie Sue disconnected, feeling like an overbearing bully. She had worked in a service job long enough to know how hard it could be getting along with pains in the ass. She made a mental note to write something favorable to someone about the housekeeping department. It was the least she could do after being so rude.

She scurried out to the hallway and stood and waited for the sound of the elevator's arrival. Within minutes she heard the *ping* and the glide of the doors. Then a young olive-skinned woman came around the corner carrying rolls of toilet paper.

At Room 618 the maid tapped on the door and waited. Debbie Sue busied herself with the luggage she had placed directly in front of Room 620.

The young woman knocked several more times. When there was no response, she used her card and opened the door slightly. "Housekeeping," she called out. Still there was no response from inside the room. Opening the door wider, she said in a loud voice, "Ma'am, I leave toilet paper here by the door. You need more, just call."

Before she left, she fished a walkie-talkie from her apron pocket. "Rosie? Is Angela. You say six eighteen?"

"That's right, six one eight," came the reply through heavy static.

"Okay. She no answer. I leave paper inside." Rosie said something else, but Debbie Sue couldn't make it out. "Two rolls. I leave two rolls. She be happy now?"

"She said she was stuck in the bathroom," Rosie said with a snicker. "Besides wiping her butt, that's all you can do."

Angela giggled. "Shhh, Rosie. Someone will hear."

As the maid started back toward the elevator, Debbie Sue said, "Angela? That's your name, right? I couldn't help but overhear you just now."

Angela smiled shyly. "Yes, ma'am, I am Angela."

"I'm in a little bit of trouble here. I'm in room six twenty. I'm checking out this morning and as you can see, I have all of my luggage here. I was about to go back in my room and get my purse and key when I accidentally let the door close behind me. Can you help me?"

"I don't know," the young woman said hesitantly. "You need to call front desk—"

"But I can't get back into my room to use the phone. If you could just open the door for me, I would be so grateful."

"Oh, ma'am, I cannot open a door—"

"I know, I know. I'm sure it's against rules. But I have a cab waiting outside and a plane to catch. I don't have time for the front desk to help me. At this time of day everyone is bound to be trying to check in or out and the desk will be swamped. Since you're already here, couldn't you please just open the door?"

"I call the front desk," Angela said, taking the walkie-talkie from her pocket again.

Money. Debbie Sue had money in her pocket. She dug inside it and pulled out the first thing she felt. "Angela, I'll give you twenty dollars if you'll just open this door now." She dug in her pocket again. "Look. Here, here's another twenty. Forty dollars total. I really am in a big hurry."

Angela stopped and eyed the two bills for what seemed like an eternity. "Okay, miss, I do. But please no tell."

"Thank you so much," Debbie Sue gushed, pushing the bills into the maid's hand and molding her fingers around hers. "This will be our little secret, I promise. You have really saved my life."

Angela stepped up to Room 620's door and swiped the card in the key slot. A little green light flashed and Debbie Sue grasped the door handle, opening the door and stopping just short of going in. "Thanks again, Angela."

"You welcome." Angela hurried away.

Debbie Sue didn't doubt the chambermaid was anxious to put distance between herself and the unlocked room. She had just broken what was probably the number-one rule for working in any hotel or motel. Never, under any circumstances, open a door for anyone to a guest's room, even if the guest says it's hers.

Debbie Sue felt remorse again. She hoped Angela didn't get in trouble, but her choice to unlock the door just might help catch and stop a serial killer. Sometimes you just gotta bend the rules a little and if you can't do it yourself, get someone else to do it for you.

Edwina was on a roll. She had deliberately started ten minutes late and now she veered from the scripted presentation.

She feared it was too short, too boring, but she had to be sure she used the minimum of an hour and she had to be sure Rogenstein remained in attendance.

She was winging it with stories, some true, some almost true, but all filled with humor. Despite being a nervous wreck, she was enjoying herself and making the most of the moment. And the audience was lapping it up. All but one, that is. Rogenstein didn't appear to be having as much fun as he had been earlier. Edwina realized smugly that by taking attention away from him she had most likely ruined his good time.

Then he appeared to be looking for something. What, the exit?

All at once he stood up from his front-row seat and started making his way to the end of the row. Edwina's thoughts raced. Finally, she did the only thing that came to her mind. "Ladies and gentlemen, please give a round of applause to one of the conference's special guests. Detective Frank Rogenstein of the New York City Police Department."

She started clapping and soon so did everyone in the audience. At first Rogenstein appeared flustered, looking both skeptical and questioning, but he warmed quickly to the ovation. Edwina had already seen he had a big ego and a narcissistic side. With all this adulation from a roomful of people, he would have no desire to leave. Praising him galled her, but she had to keep it going.

She didn't know where she got the mustard to go through with it, but she smiled and continued, "Detective would you please join me onstage? I'm sure everyone in the room would like to hear about your career and your stellar accomplishments. Maybe they'd even like to get some tips to make their jobs easier. How 'bout it, folks?" she asked the audience. "Wouldn't you like to hear from a seasoned NYPD detective?"

The clapping continued, and the detective, shaking his head and laughing with feigned resistance, climbed onto the stage. Edwina handed him the microphone and stepped behind a nearby acoustic panel. Shielded from view, she opened her cell phone and keyed in a single digit. After only one ring Debbie Sue answered.

"Where are you?" Edwina whispered urgently.

"I just got into his room. What's up?"

"Whatever your plan is, do it quick. He was leaving here, but now I've got him onstage talking. I don't know how long this will last. Do you see anything?"

"The trunk's in here, Ed. It's standing in the middle of the room."

"Holy shit. Have you looked inside?" Edwina could hear Rogenstein continuing to talk from the stage and glanced around the acoustic panel's edge to take a quick look.

"It's got padlocks on it. Oh, hell, Ed. I feel sick to my stomach."

Edwina could detect panic in her friend's voice. "Oh, no, you don't! Don't you dare hurl. You might compromise forensic evidence. Check to see if it's heavy. Rock it side to side."

A few seconds passed. Edwina could hear Debbie Sue's huffs and grunts. Finally she came back to the phone. "It's heavy, Ed. I can barely move it, much less rock it. There is definitely something in there."

"Or *someone*. What happens now?"

"Fuck. I don't know. I wasn't a hundred percent sure that even if I got in here I'd find anything. I sure didn't expect a heavier-than-shit trunk. Hell, it could have anything in it. Books, rocks, guns or who knows?"

Edwina rolled her eyes and beat her fist against her thigh, "*Assuming* you found a body in the trunk, what was your plan?"

"I was going to call Matt."

"Okay. Good plan. Do that now. Listen, are you okay? You sound kind of squirrelly."

"I know. I'm sorry. I just don't feel good. Just the sight of this trunk did something to me. Ed, he's been back to his room at some point and none of us saw him. Hold on, I hear somethin'. . . ."

"What? What is it?"

"Damn, that's creepy. Can you hear that, Ed?"

"I don't hear anything. What does it sound like?"

"It's music forgodsakes. Fuck! It's music! And it's coming from inside the trunk!"

"Oh, shit. What in the hell could that be?"

After a long pause Debbie Sue said, "Christ, Ed. It's playing 'Strangers in the Night.'"

Tears flooded Edwina's eyes. "Oh, my God, Debbie Sue. That must be Cher's cell phone. Hang up and call Matt quick. Rogenstein's just leaving the stage and I'm guessing he's headed for his room."

"Fuck, Ed. Try to detain him."

Debbie Sue disconnected, pulled Matt's card from her hip pocket and pressed his cell number. The phone rang once, twice, three times, and then she heard, "This is Detective Matthew McDermott. At the signal please—"

She disconnected. Damn, she didn't need to leave a message. She needed to talk to him. And now.

Just then her phone began its familiar Texas tune. *Matt, calling me back,* was her first thought. She flipped open the phone. "This is Debbie Sue."

"Debbie Sue, this is Celina. Detective Rogenstein just walked past me. I hid behind a ficus tree and watched. He got on the elevator and it's going up. He must be going to his room. Where are you? I thought you were supposed to be onstage with Edwina."

Debbie Sue didn't answer. She was trying to move the trunk from the room, but common sense told her she would never make it. She had always been a superb athlete and still kept herself in great shape, but she was no match for this friggin', ever-loving trunk.

"Debbie Sue? Debbie Sue, did you hear me?"

Debbie Sue was sweating like a racehorse on its final lap. She thought about the speed of the elevator. Her only option was to lock the door and hide. "Celina, I gotta go. I'm hanging up."

She looked around the room and confirmed that she was trapped in the worst kind of web, one that offered no place to hide. She was trapped like a bug with the spider approaching.

She dashed to the window, opened the curtains and looked outside. Unlike the room she shared with Edwina and Celina, this room had a window that opened onto a ledge, roughly two feet wide. The upside, if one could be found at this point, was that there were no bars on the windows.

The ledge was her only chance.

chapter twenty-three

Refusing to look down, Debbie Sue squeezed her body through the open window. As she stepped out onto the narrow ledge, she closed the window behind her with her left foot. She carefully straightened, securing her feet and pressing her sweating palms to the wall. Half a dozen pigeons sat between her and the balcony.

Below, pedestrians looked as if they were moving in slow motion. The din of the traffic came up and hit her like a wave. She felt small and helpless and she had an almost overwhelming urge to simply step off into space. The very thought turned her already shaky stomach shakier. She wasn't suicidal. What was wrong with her?

She hugged the wall, wondering how her life had come to this. Here she was, six stories above a bustling New York

City street, standing on a ledge not more than twenty-six inches deep, while twenty-six feet behind her a murderer approached.

And sixteen hundred miles southwest of her, Buddy Overstreet assumed she was safe.

If she weren't so damned scared and wired from adrenaline, she could laugh. Her final hours just might come down to a matter of numbers, because it looked like hers could be up.

Buddy's words came back to her and she felt tears sting her eyes. *Besides, didn't you say the place will be crawling with cops? At least I'll know you're safe.*

"Shoo," she said to the pigeons. "Shoo. Shoo."

The dumb birds only stared at her. *Fuck!* She didn't dare try to scare them off by waving her arms at them or kicking at them. One wrong step and she could end up as a pancake on the sidewalk below.

"Easy for you to be indifferent," she grumbled to the birds, "with me with no shotgun and bird season months away."

She carefully reached inside her pocket for her cell phone, pushed one number and waited.

"What's happening?" Edwina demanded. "Where are you?"

"Celina called and said Rogenstink was getting on the elevator. I couldn't get the trunk out of the room, so I locked the door."

"You're locked inside his room? Good Lord, Debbie Sue, he's got a key. I don't suppose you put on the deadbolt, did you?"

"I forgot about it. I'm not used to deadbolts. Anyway, he won't see me. I'm not exactly *in* the room."

"What the hell does *that* mean?"

"Well . . . I'm outside the room. On the window ledge. Me and a bunch of dumb pigeons."

A pause. Debbie Sue knew Edwina well enough to imagine that the lanky brunette was taking everything in, perhaps even looking for a place to sit down. Finally her voice came back. "Well, at least you're safe."

"I couldn't stay in the room, Ed, with Rogenstink on the way up and me knowing Cher could be in that trunk. And I just thought of something else. I have another plan."

"Oh, great. Now's a good time for it. What are you going to do now, whiz a spider web from your fingertips and swing from building to building?"

"Just cool it and listen to me. I don't have time to go into detail. Keep calling Matt. I couldn't get him on the phone, so keep trying him and tell him what's going on. Oh, and you might hook up with Celina and go outside and look up at me."

A humorless giggle came from Edwina. "Why? So we can wave good-bye?"

"Ed, is this really the time for sarcasm?"

"I'm sorry. I'm stressed to the max and scared shitless, which is really weird because I think I feel a case of diarrhea coming on. That combination tends to bring out my sarcasm. Why do you want us looking up at you?"

"So that others will too. You know, create a crowd."

"Aha! *That* I can do! Debbie Sue . . ."

"Yeah?"

"You're not afraid of heights, are you?"

"Shut up, Ed. If I wasn't before, I sure as hell am now."

"Please be careful. I can get a crowd together, but if you fall, I can't catch you." Her voice broke and she began to sniffle.

"Don't worry, Ed, you won't have to. And don't cry. Hell, this isn't much higher than the back of a horse."

"Emergency operator. What is your emergency please?"

"I'm standing six floors up on a ledge at the Anson Hotel in Times Square, just outside room six twenty. There's a bomb inside the room. The room number is six-two-zero. The bomb's in a green trunk. It's set to go off. A bomb. Room six-two-zero. Got that?"

Debbie Sue couldn't think of anything that would bring more attention than an impending suicide or a bomb threat. Or both. She knew there were serious penalties for making false emergency reports, but jumping wasn't that far off her radar at the moment, either.

"Miss, just remain calm," the operator said in a buttery-smooth voice. "What is your name?"

"It doesn't matter. Nothing matters. I can't go on. It's all over. I don't want anyone to get hurt. You better get someone to clear the hotel and the streets."

"Miss, my name is Betty. Won't you tell me your name?"

Debbie Sue pressed the disconnect, ending the call. Now she just had to wait and watch while she hoped Rogenstein didn't make an appearance before the fire and rescue units did. The only thing she knew for sure was that if Frank Rogenstein left this hotel, he would be taking that trunk over her dead body.

Possibly literally.

Detective Frank Rogenstein hummed to himself as he unlocked his door, the echo of thunderous applause still ringing inside his head. He was having a superb day. His little impromptu talk, "telling it like it is," in the session downstairs assured that PIs from all over the nation saw him as a hero. For that matter, he saw himself as a hero. He couldn't think of anything that could bring him down.

Everything was falling into place. Later today, he would leave with his "souvenir" and dispose of it at his leisure. He still wondered if she was really a cop. When he returned to the station, he would check that out. He plopped his suitcase onto the bed and began to neatly fold his clothes and pack them. He didn't give a second thought to the minor interruption of someone knocking at his door. Perhaps it was an autograph hound.

"Detective Rogenstein?" His callers were the two young police officers he had met earlier. McShane, the taller one, said, "Sir, we have to ask you to vacate your room immediately."

Standing behind the uniforms were several members of the elite bomb disposal unit and two restless dogs on leashes. Dressed in blast protection gear, the bomb squad members looked like robots.

"I was just packing to do that very thing. What's going on, fellas?" Peering out into the hallway he saw police, security officers and hotel employees knocking on doors up and down the corridor and room occupants spilling out of their rooms.

"It's a bomb threat, sir. We're moving everyone to street level until the building is declared safe."

"Nonsense. It's a prank. I'll be along in a minute. I just need to finish packing."

"Sorry, sir," the officer named Fitzpatrick said sternly. "We don't mean to alarm you, but the caller mentioned the bomb's in your room."

"In *my* room? Couldn't be."

Fitzpatrick reached for his elbow. "Please come with us and we'll see to your safety."

Rogenstein was bewildered. Then the lightbulb clicked on in his brain. *Those fucking bitches next door. Those Hicksville whores.* Did they really think they could bring him down? He was Detective Frank Rogenstein. He wasn't some dirt farmer who had stolen a pig. He wasn't a Saturday-night drunk you threw in the tank to sleep it off.

Smiling, he relented and started to reach for the trunk handle. "I'll just take my trunk with me. We'll all go downstairs together."

A bomb-squad member stepped forward and caught his wrist and a growling German shepherd planted itself in front of him. "Sorry, sir, but that isn't possible. The report says the bomb is in this trunk." He took a hard look at the trunk.

"Yep, that's it. A green trunk. Please remove your hand from it and step away. I'll have to ask you to follow the other hotel guests out of the building. Now, sir."

Rogenstein knew a refusal would bring about his arrest. The bomb squad had no sense of humor and not a human alive could defy their orders in a situation like this and get away with it. His mind was playing a movie in slow motion of a thirty-year career going up in flames. His retirement plan—hell, his very life—could be going with it.

He would have to do what he had done his entire life— make the most of the situation. One advantage to being an opportunist was that to further his own interest, with no regard for principles or consequences, he took advantage of all possibilities. Always.

Now, he did as asked and followed the officers out to the hallway. Watching the door close on Room 620, ironically enough, he knew he could be watching the door closing on the only life he could remember. He felt a sickness like none he had ever experienced.

He boarded the elevator with the other hotel evacuees and watched the numbers descend. When the doors opened on the ground floor, he became a part of the crowd that was making its way to the perimeters the police had set up across the street. When the crush of people went straight, he turned left and disappeared into the crowd that was gathering and looking up. He thought of an old adage he had heard before: Best to walk away and return to fight another day.

★ ★ ★

A subway ride gave Matt the opportunity to dwell on the negatives that had been creeping into his thoughts since receiving the call from Longoria's secretary. He had known from the outset that obtaining a search warrant in this case wasn't going to be easy, but a face-to-face with the judge? Typically if a judge dug his or her heels in, a phone call was all that was necessary.

But then the request for this warrant wasn't typical. This whole venture, accusing a senior, decorated member of NYPD could be a political nightmare. A career killer for sure. Still, if this was what it was going to take to bring a murderer to justice, he had to do it.

He reached the justice building and took the steep front steps by twos. Inside, as he waited for an elevator car, he took in his surroundings.

This magnificent old building housed one of the great loves of his life—the law. The law had stood the test of time and tempers in this country. It wasn't always perfect, it was sometimes downright ugly, but American jurisprudence was the best in the world. It protected citizens from criminal predators and inserted civility into an otherwise uncivil world. He loved it and he wasn't about to run from a fight to make sure that it was used properly and to its fullest, no matter the affiliation, reputation or VIP friends of a suspect.

Before entering the judge's suite, he adjusted his tie, smoothed his jacket and ran a hand over his hair. Judge Longoria was from the old school, and decorum was required in his presence. Matt had never met him, but he had

heard horror stories from those who had made less than favorable impressions on the magistrate.

He turned the knob, the massive oak door swung open and
he stepped inside. A professional-appearing woman whom
Matt guessed to be in her mid-forties stared at a law book
lying open on her left. Her fingers flew over the keyboard,
not even stopping as she looked up at him. She smiled. "May
I help you?"

Matt was at a loss for words. She hadn't missed a tap and
still continued, her fingers moving as if independent from
her body. "I'm Detective Matthew McDermott. I'm here to
see Judge Longoria."

"He should be here within the next twenty minutes, Detective."

"You mean he isn't here?" After receiving an urgent message, Matt was confused.

"No. But I just spoke to him. His session has ended for the
morning and he's on his way."

"Uh, mind if I wait?"

"Not at all. Mind if I keep typing?"

"Uh, no, of course not." Her fingers still hadn't missed
a tap. "If you don't mind me asking, how fast do you type?
I've never seen anything like that."

The woman chuckled as she pushed back from the computer. "I'm sorry, I'm trying to get into the *Guinness World
Records* for fastest typing speed. The judge doesn't mind my
practicing when he's out. The record is two hundred words
a minute, with no errors. I'm up to one hundred and twelve.
So you see, I still have a way to go."

"You mean you're going to get even faster? That's hard to believe. Please continue. I wouldn't want to interfere with your chances of making the record books."

The woman laughed pleasantly and returned to her task.

Matt took a seat on one of the leather couches and began leafing through magazines. Ten minutes gave way to fifteen. Twenty minutes later the judge hadn't appeared.

When the secretary stopped the marathon typing to take a phone call, Matt quickly got to his feet and approached her. "Did you did say the judge is on his way?"

"Yes, sir. I'm sorry he's late. He must have gotten stopped by someone. But he is coming. His briefcase and car keys are in his office, so he has to come here."

"What about his flight. Won't he miss his flight?"

"I don't know anything about a flight, sir. He and his wife are entertaining at their home this evening. I was on the phone the better part of the morning with caterers."

Matt chewed on the inside of his cheek. "Are you the only secretary Judge Longoria has?"

"I like to think of myself as his personal administrative assistant." She lifted her chin. "His *only* personal administrative assistant."

A dawning began to rise in Matt. "You didn't call me to come here to meet with the judge about a warrant, did you?"

"No, Detective, but I did send a courier to your station house with the warrant you requested."

"When? When did you do that?"

"It was about an hour ago," she said brightly.

Then it hit him. He had been had. "I've got to be the world's biggest idiot. Uh, thank you, ma'am." He started for the door, but stopped with his hand on the doorknob and looked back at the judge's assistant. "Do me a favor, if you don't mind. Don't tell the judge I was here. I don't want him to know how dumb I am."

He had been gone nearly an hour. He had to go by the station house and get the warrant. By the time he reached the Anson, closer to two hours would go by. God only knew what those three Texas women could get into in that amount of time.

He hailed a cab and made it to the police station in record time. Walking past the desk sergeant, he stopped and looked around. The reception room and the halls were usually filled with people, but no one was in sight. The eerie calm gave Matt a sense of foreboding. "Hey, Johnson. Where is everyone?"

The older cop peered over his half glasses. "They called all available units to the Anson Hotel. Some ditzy broad is out on a ledge, six floors up. Said she has a bomb in a trunk in one of the rooms. A trunk, no less." He shook his head.

"Sonofabitch," Matt growled. "Those damn women are going to be the death of me."

chapter twenty-four

D ebbie Sue could see the crowd below. They didn't exactly look like ants, but they looked like toy people hurrying around. Police had set up barricades to prevent onlookers from getting too close to the hotel. She spotted several fire trucks as well as other huge vehicles with NYPD BOMB DISPOSAL UNIT stenciled large enough to be seen even from her high perch. Her plan had worked.

With so much activity, where was Matt McDermott? She had been forced to leave him a message after several failed attempts to reach him. Her message had been short but as concise and to the point as she could make it in the allowed time: "*Matt, this is Debbie Sue Overstreet. I'm standing on the ledge outside room six twenty. The green trunk is in the room. I've called the bomb squad. Either call me or rescue me.*"

If a message like that didn't prompt him to call, she didn't know what would.

Did she dare go back into the room? Had Rogenstein been evacuated or had he talked his way out of it? Retrieving her cell phone she pressed Edwina's number. When Edwina answered, Debbie Sue quizzed her. "Have you seen Rogenstink? What's going on?"

"My God, Debbie Sue, the bomb squad's here. They're evacuating the hotel."

"I can't believe no one has tried to talk to me. I'm standing on the ledge, forgodsakes. They always try to talk to people on ledges."

"Feeling a little neglected, are we?" Edwina asked. "Did you hear me? There's a bomb in the hotel. Do you think Rogenstein would plant a bomb?"

"No, Ed, it was me."

"What? *You* planted a bomb?"

"No, dammit, I crawled out the window. I reported the bomb's in the trunk."

"That fucker. He'll do anything to destroy evidence. Even blow up the trunk."

"Fuck, Ed, you're making me want to jump. The trunk's not gonna blow up. I came out to escape Rogenstink."

"Debbie Sue, what are we talking about?"

"Listen to me carefully, Ed. I called in a bomb report so the cops would come and the bomb squad would open the trunk."

"Oohhh. Well, hell, Debbie Sue, I guess your plan worked. All of New York City is here."

Just then a large pigeon landed on the toe of her boot and left a large deposit. "Oh, fuck, Ed!"

"What? What is it?" Edwina frantically asked.

"Oh, nooo. Dammit to hell. I've got pigeon poop on my best pair of boots and I don't even want to feel what's in my hair. Plus, I'm going to have lung disease from all the crap I'm breathing up here. I gotta hang up, Ed."

Edwina began to hyperventilate even before she snapped the phone shut. *Jesus, Joseph and Mary!* How would she ever explain it to Buddy Overstreet if Debbie Sue got returned to Texas in a body bag? Or in a black-and-white-striped suit. She looked around the lobby for Celina. All hell was about to break loose and she wanted to be sure Celina was by her side.

"Edwina. Edwina, over here."

Looking to her left, she saw Celina running toward her with a troubled expression on her face. "Edwina, Debbie Sue hung up on me. Where is she?" She skidded to a stop in front of Edwina. "The bomb squad's here. Where's Detective Rogenstein? Where's Matt?" Celina's eyes widened and her voice rose in panic. "Edwina, why isn't Debbie Sue with you? Answer something quick, because I almost can't get my breath. I can't just go on and on like this."

"Come with me," Edwina said, grabbing her hand and tugging her along behind her, pushing through the crowd gathering outside the hotel. "Just keep calm. That'll help me out, because I'm trying not to lose it."

"Why? Oh, my gosh, what's happened?"

"We need to keep an eye on Debbie Sue and make sure she

gets back *inside*." They squeezed through the crowd gathered on the sidewalk.

"Where is she?" Celina asked.

Edwina looked up, shielding her eyes with her hand. The sight of Debbie Sue six stories up, doing her West Texas version of Naomi Watts in *King Kong* made her want to throw up. "Up there."

Celina followed her gaze and gave a whimper. "Oh, my goodness. There's a woman on the ledge."

"Celina, you're gonna make a hell of a detective."

"Oh, please, Edwina, tell me that isn't Debbie Sue."

"I wish I could, hon, but I'd be lying."

"Oh, my gracious goodness." Celina slapped both hands over her face, peeking out between her fingers.

"I'd recognize that mop of hair anywhere," Edwina added.

"Edwina. How can you act so calm? Aren't you scared?"

"Yep, I'm scared." Edwina stared so hard at Debbie Sue, her eyes began to ache. "But I know Debbie Sue. She's gonna be all right. Yep, she's gonna be all right."

"Your voice is shaking," Celina said, staring, too. "You don't believe that."

"Hon, I've got to. I've got to believe that ledge is plenty wide enough. Just like I've got to believe that Debbie Sue won't do anything stupid."

"Edwina, she's moving. Look, she's moving."

"Like I said, hon. Just keep believing that Debbie Sue won't do anything stupid."

Celina stepped in front of Edwina, her mouth agape. "You

don't call it stupid to step out on a ledge six stories up, with a serial killer on the other side of the only open window?"

"Nope, not really," Edwina said, looking past Celina's shoulder to keep her eye on her best friend. "Where Debbie Sue's concerned, I call it just another day."

Debbie Sue finally succeeded in shaking the pigeon off the toe of her boot. "Go deliver a message somewhere," she said as the bird hopped from her boot to the ledge.

Then, just to her left, she heard a male voice. "Hello."

She looked in the voice's direction and saw the head and shoulders of a man protruding from the window.

"Miss? Miss, my name is Lawrence Jacobs. I'm from the New York City Police Department. Why don't you come inside and talk to me? I'd really like to hear your story."

About damn time! She would bet a dime to a doughnut that he was one of those suicide intervention guys. She looked at her rescuer. "Okay Larry, I'm coming in. You talked me into it."

Detective Matt McDermott opened the door to the interrogation room and found it crowded with police and personnel from the fire department and the bomb squad. He entered just in time to hear Debbie Sue's closing sentence.

"I called nine-one-one and reported that a bomb was in the trunk because I knew he'd never be able to leave with it after that."

Debbie Sue looked in his direction. Her face lit up with recognition. He could also see relief.

"Thank God. Matt, come and talk to Larry. Larry, go talk to Detective McDermott. He'll clear this whole thing up."

The negotiator rose from his chair and walked over, motioning Matt out of the room. Once outside, he extended his hand. "Detective McDermott, we've met once before. I'm with Crisis Negotiations. I've been talking to Mrs. Overstreet for the better part of an hour. She's been telling quite a story. I'm torn between calling for a psych evaluation, taking her to Belleview personally or notifying the feds so they can transfer her to Guantanamo."

Matt lowered his head to hide a grin. "Has she explained anything?"

"Not really. She keeps talking gibberish mostly. Keeps saying she's a detective and she's married to a Texas Ranger. Also something about a SEAL team coming to her rescue."

"Well, believe it or not, she is married to a guy who's going to be a Texas Ranger if he isn't already. And she has a business partner who's married to a navy SEAL."

"No shit?"

"No shit. Has she made any requests?"

"A couple. And she keeps repeating them over and over. She wants to talk to somebody named Edwina and somebody named Celina. I don't even know if those are real people, or if they're personalities she's carrying around in her already crowded head. And she wants an oily rag to get bird poop off her ostrich-quill cowboy boots. The bird poop is real enough. Saw it myself. But I wouldn't know an ostrich quill from a porcupine quill."

This time Matt didn't grin. He laughed openly. "Celina

and Edwina are two doors down. Their story is the same as hers. And the oily rag's not a bad idea. I'd bet those are expensive boots."

The negotiator looked at the detective with a surprised expression. "You mean she's telling the truth? All of it?"

"Yep, all of it."

"Even the part about Detective Frank Rogenstein?"

"*Especially* the part about Rogenstein. When the bomb unit got the trunk open, the body of Special Agent Cheryl Angelo fell out. Rogenstein hadn't even bothered to try and hide the evidence. His fingerprints were everywhere. You'd think we would learn that nothing's impossible."

"You'd think. But Frank Rogenstein? I just can't wrap my mind around that one. What's he got to say?"

"We haven't been able to locate him, but we will. We've put out an APB. Posted his photo at all train stations, airports, ferries and subways. We've got his apartment staked out and his bank is going to alert us of any ATM transactions. We're trying to track his cell phone. As well known as his face is, it won't take long."

"Yeah, he's probably more recognizable than the mayor."

"Yep."

"So what do we do with these three women? Any charges going to be filed?"

"The guys upstairs are having a hard-enough time digesting Rogenstein being a serial killer and keeping the news from destroying the entire department. They don't need any more headaches. They want to release all three of them."

"Okay, fine with me," the negotiator said. "I'll tell this

one she's free to go." He backed away to re-enter the inter-rogation room.

"Before you go back in there," Matt said, "maybe we can find a rag with some oil on it for her boots. Maybe a wet cloth to get the bird poop out of her hair."

The crisis negotiator frowned. "What kind of oil?"

"Damned if I know. I don't even own any cowboy boots. But it might be fun to have a pair."

Matt stayed out of the reunion, leaning against the wall smiling. He was sure that a casual observer would think these three women hadn't seen each other in three decades instead of three hours and that they had been through some sort of ordeal and survived to talk about it. There was laughter, tears and hugging, then more of the same.

"I can't believe the risks you two have taken in the past twenty-four hours," Celina said to Debbie Sue and Edwina. "Do you have to go to such drastic lengths in every case?"

"This one was a little more personal than most," Debbie Sue replied, "but I think Ed will agree that when we sink our teeth into something we're not likely to turn loose without a fight."

"That's right," Edwina confirmed, "and I've got the ex-husbands to prove it."

When the laughter subsided, Matt walked up to the trio. "Ladies, why don't I arrange to ride with you back to the hotel?"

"What about Rogenstink?" Debbie Sue asked. "Has he been arrested yet?"

"Not yet, but we're making it awfully hard for him to remain a fugitive."

Celina's brow tented with concern. "But are we safe?" she asked him. "Debbie Sue and Edwina actually heard him murder that poor woman. As long as he's around—"

"I don't want any of you to worry about a thing." Matt put his arm around Celina, pulled her closer and looked deeply into her eyes only. "I'm not leaving your side until you get on that plane Sunday morning. For the next thirty-six hours you belong to me. Think you can handle that?"

"I'm willing to try," Celina said softly.

Debbie Sue cleared her throat. "Good, I feel better already. Let's get back to the hotel. I don't know about y'all, but I'm hungry and tired. And I'd love to take a shower."

"Don't forget a shampoo, 'Bird Poop Head,'" Edwina added. "Maybe with Lysol."

Matt rode with them back to their hotel. The closer Celina's departure time inched, the more he dreaded the moment. In just a short time, he had become far too attached to her.

The ride was quiet except for Debbie Sue's and Edwina's oohs and aahs. They were seeing parts of New York City they hadn't seen before and taking it all in.

Once they reached the hotel, Debbie Sue was surprised to see all signs of the morning's excitement gone. The emergency vehicles had departed and the barricades had been removed. Life moved on. *As it always does*, she thought. If anyone knew that life moved on after a traumatic event, she did. After all, hadn't she and Buddy buried a child? What could be more traumatic than that?

Detective McDermott reached for Celina's hand as the four of them entered the hotel.

"Let's get a new room for you ladies," he said. "I'll get one nearby."

Celina whispered something to him and giggled. Debbie Sue looked at Edwina and winked. The likelihood of Celina sharing their new room was remote, and Debbie Sue both envied her and worried about her. She had a sudden overpowering desire to see Buddy.

As Buddy flashed in her thoughts, she contemplated how she would tell him about all that had happened. She wouldn't keep it from him, even the part about the ledge. They kept no secrets and never lied to each other. But she worried if he would sit still for her to maintain the career she had come to love when he learned of her latest escapade. He still yelled occasionally about the mess she and Edwina got into in Haskell. She knew Buddy Overstreet's stubborn streak and she remembered what had happened when he demanded that she give up rodeoing.

Her thoughts were sidetracked as in their approach to the front desk they were suddenly surrounded by reporters and photographers, all shouting questions and taking pictures.

"Uh-oh," Matt said, "I should have brought you through the back entrance."

Celina clung to his arm in wide-eyed amazement while Debbie Sue kept looking away from the flash, refusing to answer questions. To her dismay, Edwina was taking every advantage of the opportunity, posing and smiling like a celebrity. She wasn't just answering questions. She was asking them as well.

"Which one of you actually crawled out on the ledge?" A reporter called out.

"She did," Edwina said, attempting to turn Debbie Sue to face the cameras. "Debbie Sue Overstreet. That's O-V-E-R—"

"What's going on here?" The commanding voice came from a vertically challenged but powerfully built man in an expensive tan suit. He pushed his way into the center of the commotion and said to the press, "Ladies and gentlemen, please allow our guests to move on. They've been through a terrible ordeal. I'm sure they'll be happy to speak to you later."

chapter twenty-five

With practiced skill, the man ushered all four of them forward until they soon found themselves standing in what appeared to be a private office. He took a place behind a massive desk that hunkered in the middle of the room and with a sweep of his hand, invited all of them to take a seat. Homer popped up from somewhere and was now standing just behind the man, wringing his hands, sweating profusely and looking down at the floor.

"Hey, Homer, how's it going?" Edwina said.

The man behind the desk gave Homer a thundercloud of a look, then turned his attention back to Debbie Sue and her friends. His mouth tipped into a reptilian smile and Debbie Sue knew instantly this was no social visit. "Allow me to introduce myself," he said. "I'm Otto J. Pembroke. I'm the general manager here. As I understand it, you've had an interesting stay with us."

"It's been more than we bargained for, that's for sure," Edwina said. "When we leave Sunday—"

"I'm afraid you're going to be leaving before Sunday. We've taken the liberty of securing your personal items and we'd like you to leave immediately." He continued to smile, but his tone left no doubt of the finality of his statement.

Panic shot through Debbie Sue. Their plane tickets were booked for Sunday. They didn't know of another hotel. And even if they did, they couldn't afford to pay for it. NAPI had paid for this one. She bristled. "You can't—"

"Oh, but I can." His smile was gone and his face had turned into a reddened mask of rage. "In less than two days you've been responsible for nine-one-one calls no less than three times. You've instigated a riot in our establishment and caused the destruction of one of our lounges. You took advantage of one of our housekeeping personnel by bribing her to allow you illegal entry into a guestroom in which you were not registered. You called the fire department *and* the bomb squad, forcing an evacuation of the entire hotel. And now there are men and women from the press everywhere."

Debbie Sue angled a glance at Edwina and saw her wilt under Pembroke's attack.

The lanky brunette friend said, "Well, when you put it that way . . ."

Debbie Sue stepped in before Edwina could capitulate. "Now, just a minute. It wasn't all our fault."

"The Anson is a refined hotel," Mr. Pembroke went on, lifting his head as if he smelled something foul. "We offer our guests the utmost in privacy and respect. Perhaps you'd be more comfortable at another establishment in the city. One that's more accustomed to accommodating your kind of people."

"Excuse me, Mr. Pembroke," Matt said, "but—"

Debbie Sue grabbed his arm, stopping him. She couldn't let Matt defend what she and Edwina had done. And she didn't intend to be insulted by someone nearly a foot shorter than she was.

She stood up and planted a fist on one hip. "You know, Mr. Pembroke, our *kind* of people are just plain country people. We don't have big-city ways, but we're smart enough to know one thing." She pointed a finger at the office door. "Right outside that door is the press. And they want to hear from us, any and everything from us. They'll want to hear how easy it was to bribe a maid with a measly forty dollars into opening a guestroom door. They'll get a big kick out of hearing how a window on the sixth floor was left unprotected, enabling anyone—man, woman or *child*—to crawl out onto an unprotected ledge."

"Yeah," Edwina piped up. "And I'm gonna tell 'em how this dignified hotel served so much liquor to customers in the bar that they dragged an innocent woman into a free-for-all."

"And most of all," Debbie Sue said, "they'll want to hear how three people responsible for bringing a serial killer to justice, after grave risks to their own lives, could be put out on the street like the day's garbage. And as for us staying in one of the lesser establishments, I'd say we're already there." She swerved a look among her three friends. "Let's go, y'all. We'll still have time to find another hotel after we've given our interviews to the press."

Mr. Pembroke's entire head had turned a vivid red. Beads of sweat had broken out along his brow. Rising slowly from his seat, he turned to Homer. "I believe there are two economy rooms available, are there not?"

"Yes, sir. We have two as of this morning."

"Fine, please escort our guest to their new rooms."

"Excuse me," Debbie Sue said, "but these *economy* rooms you're talking about—are those the best you have available? If you're not sure, I'll be happy to step out to the registrar's desk and check. I'm sure the press will maul me and force me to talk, but I'll do my best to get back here."

Homer jumped in, smiling for the first time since the meeting began. "That won't be necessary. The best we have is the Presidential Suite. And it *is* available until Sunday evening, when the emir arrives."

"Is that so? Tell me more, Homer," Debbie Sue said, grinning.

"The Presidential is on the penthouse level. It has a large living area with a private dining room and kitchen. There are two separate bedrooms, each with a private bath, and a spectacular view of the city." He looked at his employer. "That is, if Mr. Pembroke approves."

"Gee, I don't know," Debbie Sue said, frowning thoughtfully. "That sounds terribly expensive." She turned to the other three members of her group. "Do y'all think we can afford something like that? Maybe we should leave. . . ."

Mr. Pembroke stopped her with a rumbling noise from his throat. His smile was gone and little bubbles of saliva had gathered at the corners of his mouth. He ran his hand down the front of his suit and adjusted his pocket handkerchief. "Please allow the Anson to provide this suite to you and your party at no expense. It's our way of thanking you." He gave them his snakelike grin again. "If you'll follow Mr. Hess, he'll escort you. I'll have your luggage sent up immediately."

Debbie Sue sent him her best beaming smile. "Oh, my goodness. That is just wonderful, Otto. Thank you. We're all anxious to get to our suite. As you said to the press yourself, we've had a terrible ordeal."

Edwina grabbed his hand and pumped it vigorously. "Hey, thanks, Otto. You ever get out to Salt Lick, Texas, you be sure to look us up. Debbie Sue's got a spare bedroom and I've got a fairly new trailer house. We'll show you some Texas hospitality."

Before their luck had time to change, Debbie Sue walked toward the door. Homer, Edwina, Celina and Matt followed close behind. They walked wordlessly through the lobby and waited until the elevator door closed before breaking into raucous laughter.

"I must say, Mrs. Overstreet," Homer said, wiping a tear from his eye, "I've never seen anyone talk to Mr. Pembroke like that. It was worth everything just to have witnessed it."

Homer produced a key from his breast pocket and placed

it in a slot on the control panel. The elevator zoomed past the lower hotel floors and came to a stop at the penthouse level.

Celina stood aghast when the elevator doors glided open onto a foyer flanked by two intricately carved doors. She had reached Fairyland. She was sure of it.

Homer opened both doors in grand fashion and stood back.

And there it was. The Presidential Suite. Celina and her newfound friends walked in slowly, looking around in awe. Even Matt appeared dumbstruck by the opulence.

The cover of one of Celina's favorite magazines, *Architectural Digest*, had nothing on this suite. The décor was French Provincial, done in gold and ivory with splashes of navy. Vibrant impressionistic art hung in gold gilt frames. Overstuffed couches and wing chairs provided ample seating for a large group. From where they stood, they could see a formal dining area and a hutch full of gleaming dishes. Fresh bouquets of flowers were everywhere in exquisite arrangements and artful color combinations. Their fragrance touched her nostrils.

Her eyes tried to take in everything, but stopped at a pearl white baby grand piano elegantly filling a corner. Celina gasped and ran to it, with Matt trailing her. She ran her fingers over the piano's gleaming finish, touched two of the keys.

"Do you play?" Matt asked, coming to her side and smiling.

"Believe it or not, I do. Though not well. My grandmother had me taking piano lessons for years."

"Great day in the morning," Edwina said, approaching them. "What do you suppose something like this costs?"

"Several thousand a night, I'm guessing," Matt said.

"Get out! That's not right, is it? Homer, is he right?"

"To be precise," the night manager said, "it's three thousand, nine hundred twenty four dollars a night, without tax."

"Without tax," Debbie Sue echoed.

"And we have it for two nights?" Celina asked.

"Yes, ma'am. Tonight and tomorrow night," Homer answered.

Celina looked at each of her companions, who all looked at one another. Together they began squealing. Debbie Sue and Edwina ran from room to room, yelling out to each other their new discoveries, but Celina hung back with Matt.

As he was leaving, Homer handed the key to Matt. "I trust this will be safe with you?"

"Absolutely," the detective replied.

"Hey, y'all," Debbie Sue yelled from somewhere.

Celina and Matt, along with Edwina, followed her voice.

They found her gawking at a large, fully stocked refrigerator. "Look at this. Hell, I was just hoping for something with a bigger icebox and maybe some regular-size bottles of water. This thing is loaded."

"This whole experience is pretty amazing," Matt said. "It kind of dwarfs the treat I had planned for your last night in New York."

"You have something special planned for tomorrow night? Oh, Mattie," Celina gushed. "That is so sweet. Tell us what it is."

"Yeah, Mattie, tell us," Edwina said, grinning.

"I was hoping to take all of you to dinner at Tavern on the Green. It's a New York landmark located in Central Park. It really should be seen in the evening."

"Oh, how sweet," Celina said. "I've heard of Tavern on the Green my whole life. Thank you so much, Matt. We can't wait, can we girls?" Celina looked at her friends.

"You two should go alone," Edwina said. "You don't want to be dragging us old married women around with you."

Celina frowned. "I wouldn't think of going without you and Debbie Sue."

"Don't forget," Matt added. "I'm not letting any of you out of my sight."

"Ah, but did you mean that literally?" Edwina asked.

"Absolutely. Until you leave the city or Rogenstein is arrested, if you go, I'm there."

"Then you'll have to accompany me to Bergdorf Goodman tomorrow," Edwina said. "I'm not leaving here without a pair of Jimmy Choo shoes. I've got two hundred fifty dollars burning a hole in my pocket. With what I already planned on spending, that'll give me just enough."

Matt laughed. "I'm not an expert on shoes, but whatever your heart desires." He made a sweeping movement with his hand and bowed from the waist.

"I've got a great idea." Celina dug into the refrigerator, pulled out a bottle of champagne and handed it to Matt.

"I'll get the glasses," Debbie Sue said. "I saw some in this fancy dining room." She headed for the dining room, but Edwina stopped her.

"Just hold everything. They may not charge us for this palace, but are they gonna charge us next month's mortgage payment for what we take out of that refrigerator?"

"They wouldn't dare," Debbie Sue declared and continued toward the hutch in the dining room. Momentarily, she returned with four champagne flutes. "Let's have a toast."

Matt poured the glasses full.

"Sounds good to me," Celina exclaimed, enthusiastically picking up a glass. "What are we drinking to?"

"How about 'til two in the morning?" Edwina guffawed.

Debbie Sue gasped. "Ed, I'm serious. I want to have a moment of silence. I want us to make a toast to Cher. We only knew her for a few hours, but she was a colleague. She didn't deserve to end up in a trunk."

The four of them grew silent. They bowed their heads and closed their eyes. Then they opened them again. Celina sniffled.

Edwina wiped away a tear. "To Cher. She came to my rescue." She gulped down her glass of champagne.

"And to successfully stopping her killer," Matt added.

"And to a wonderful trip to New York and new friends." Celina said softly.

"Let's drink to all those things. Plus getting to stay in a hotel room that cost more than my trailer house," Edwina said. "Do you realize I've never done something like this in my whole life and probably never will again?"

"The fridge is full of champagne. Let's start with that and just keep on going," Debbie Sue said. "If we need more we'll call room service."

"Now you're talking, ledge walker," Edwina said. "Now you're talking. Like I said, 'til two in the morning!'"

The next morning, while Matt showered, Celina sat on the balcony overlooking Manhattan, sipping her morning coffee, a newspaper folded to the crosswords. For the first time in days she was alone with her thoughts. Her two new girlfriends were enjoying their own moments of solitude.

The dinner reservation Matt had made was for eight o'clock. Confusing feelings kept Celina from concentrating on the crossword puzzle. She was excited for an evening of fun and a romantic interlude, but what would happen for her and Matt after that? Her window of opportunity to explore that question was barely open. Tomorrow, her bus would leave within an hour after Edwina and Debbie Sue's morning flight.

There had been no talk of future plans between her and Matt or even the casual exchange of a desire to continue beyond her departure. From the way he looked at her, the way he behaved around her, she had to believe Matt felt the same thing she had come to accept. She was falling in love. She only hoped the opportunity to nurture those emotions would continue.

The intimacy they had shared cemented those thoughts for her. She didn't want to think about never again waking up beside him. She especially didn't want to think about not seeing him for long stretches of time. But his life was well rooted in New York, and hers in Dime Box. There were issues, like her grandmother, who was at a vulnerable time in her life. Celina couldn't just up and leave her, not after all Granny Dee had done and sacrificed for her. Why, without Granny Dee she would have grown up a ward of the state of Texas.

If anyone could appreciate her fears, it would be Granny Dee. As a young woman she had been through the same thing. How had she known her choice to leave New York City and move to Texas was the right one? Had she ever regretted her decision? How did one decide between following her heart or her head?

She reached into the pocket of her robe and pulled out her cell phone. She needed to hear the soothing reassurance Granny Dee would give her or the no-nonsense kick-in-the-pants she was just as capable of delivering. Waiting for the call to connect, she glanced at her horoscope for the day:

Feelings of security aren't what they seem. Someone has unfinished business with you. Watch your back.

She had no time to react to the ominous forecast. Granny Dee answered and Celina opened her heart.

Later, at Bergdorf Goodman, Edwina strutted in front of the shoe mirror admiring the Jimmy Choo foot candy that adorned her feet. She had never paid this much money for a single pair of shoes in her life. Hell, all the shoes she had purchased altogether in her life probably didn't add up to this much. But then this past week had been filled with a list of firsts. She wasn't that hard-pressed to add one more to it.

The price tag was astronomical for shoes, particularly

when she could get a pair with heels just as high at the Wal-Mart Supercenter in Odessa. Even with throwing in the money she had collected by winning the karaoke contest, the price would still lighten her pocket considerably.

She took another turn in front of the mirror. These shoes weren't just red with three-and-a-half-inch heels; they were *ruby* red and satin with three-and-a-half-inch heels. Just the thought of *ruby*, *red* and *satin* all in the same sentence was titillating enough to make Edwina's head spin. The real kicker was the half-inch red-and-black border of crystals that trimmed the vamp. Yep, this pair of shoes was in a class all its on.

"My God, Ed," Debbie Sue said. "Those are the prettiest shoes I've ever seen. I don't think I've got a pair of boots that'll top them. Not even my custom-made Luccheses that Buddy bought me. Where would you wear them?"

"Anywhere. Everywhere. Hell, at this price I'd wear them to work. Maybe I'd wear them to bed." Edwina turned on the ball of her foot and examined the back again. "On second thought, I'd definitely wear them to bed. They're sexy as all get-out, aren't they? And they match my teddy."

"Oh, hell yes. You should get them."

"But the cost. I don't know—"

"Look, I'd pay that in a heartbeat for a pair of custom-made boots. Why shouldn't you do the same? Remember that pair of boots I saw that time that were made out of anteater? And remember what they cost? I didn't buy them and I've always wished I had."

"But you'd wear those boots day in and out for a lifetime. I'd only wear these shoes occasionally, or until I'm too old to keep my balance in them."

Just then Matt walked up and let out a soft wolf whistle. "Wow, that's some sexy shoe. Edwina, you look like a million bucks."

Edwina turned immediately to the salesperson. She didn't bat an eye. "I'll take 'em."

chapter twenty-six

By seven o'clock that evening Matt had herded his bevy of beauties onto the elevator and out the hotel's revolving door.

The women were dressed in their best, smelling good and primed for a good time their last night in the city. All talk centered around the choices they expected to see on the menu, the attire each woman had chosen for the evening. The one thing they all had in common was the wish that everyone back home could see them.

Of course Matt wasn't intimidated. Hadn't he grown up in a houseful of sisters?

They were expecting to ride in a taxi, but he told them he had something else in mind. "I've rented two pedicabs to take us to the restaurant. I thought something a little different would be nice."

The three women only smiled politely, but no one questioned his decision.

"Do any of you know what a pedicab is?" he asked.

"Mattie, we don't have a fuckin' clue," Debbie Sue said, "but if you think we'll like it, we're all for it."

"I'm glad you have that much confidence in me. A pedicab is kind of like a rickshaw. Two people sit in the back of this little carriage that's attached to a bike and a person pedals it around. I thought about a horse-drawn carriage, but you Texas gals probably do that all the time."

"Oh, yeah," Debbie Sue cracked, "practically everywhere we go, we travel by horse and buggy. We hear tell there's an iron horse that runs on steel tracks coming our way soon."

"That, and water that flows from a pipe right inside your own house," Edwina added.

Matt laughed. "Okay, okay. Maybe I went a little overboard. I didn't mean to imply you were from the sticks."

Celina placed her hand on his arm. "We love it, Matt."

"You need to plan on coming down our way when we all get back home," Edwina said. "There's a lot more to Texas than cowboys and horses."

"Not much more that matters, but there is more," Debbie Sue added.

He covered Celina's hand with his and looked into her beautiful eyes. "Do you think I should plan a trip to Texas?"

She looked back with a smile, and he fell deeper. "I was hoping you had already," she said softly.

"Awww," Edwina said and gave a deep sniff. "That's so sweet. I could cry."

"Shut up, Ed," Debbie Sue said.

Matt squeezed Celina's hand. "We'll talk about it later. Meantime, ladies, your drivers await."

Two men dressed in biker shorts, tuxedo jackets and top hats approached and handed each of them a yellow rose.

"Ladies," one said, gesturing to the carriages that sat curbside.

"Hon, I'm afraid we're too heavy for you," Edwina said, eyeing the cab apprehensively.

"You'd be surprised how much we can pull," the young man replied. "We're a 'no weight limit' service. That's W-E-I-G-H-T, not W-A-I-T," he added.

"Then it's a go," Edwina said. "That's G-O, not N-O."

Everyone laughed. Debbie Sue and Edwina took seats in one pedicab and Celina and Matt sat down in the other. The drivers replaced their top hats with protective headgear and the pedicabs pulled away from the hotel.

During the trip to Central Park, Debbie Sue and Edwina laughed and asked questions of the cyclist. Soon they knew his name was Joseph and he was saving money for trips to California and Mexico.

Celina and Matt in the lead carriage turned frequently and waved at them.

Debbie Sue snapped pictures at every photo opportunity. Edwina used the exposed carriage as a chance to flash one foot in the air whenever possible to display her most recent red satin purchase. The air was festive, the mood was high and the evening was just beginning.

Captivated by Central Park, Debbie Sue looked up and saw the moon, full, huge and a brilliant yellow, hanging low in the sky and framing the silhouette of skyscrapers. The image was breathtaking. "Joseph. Joseph, stop for just a minute."

Their driver looked over his shoulder, concern showing in his face. "Is something wrong?"

"I've just got to get out and get this picture."

He braked and Debbie Sue climbed out. As she moved away from the carriage, seeking the best vantage point, Edwina said, "Aww, look." She strolled over to a couple walking a golden retriever and struck up a conversation.

"Is it okay, if I step away for a smoke?" their driver asked.

"Sure," Debbie Sue said, her attention focused on the camera. After snapping several shots, Debbie Sue put her camera back in her purse and joined Edwina, oohing and aahing over the dog. She, too, was a sucker for animals of any kind. The dog seemed to sense this and soon had both women wrapped around his paw.

"Hey," Debbie said to Edwina, noting that Joseph had returned to the bike. "We're falling behind. I can barely see Celina and Matt."

"Okay," Edwina agreed, bidding the dog and his owners good evening. They returned to the carriage, took their seats and the driver resumed pedaling.

After a few seconds, Edwina said, "Does it seem like we're going faster?"

"I thought that, too," Debbie Sue said, suddenly concerned for their safety. She glanced at their driver and noticed he was standing on the pedals, his legs pumping hard. She leaned forward. "Sorry to have gotten you behind," she shouted. "You keep going at this rate and we'll be passing our friends soon."

With no warning, the pedicab veered to the right, following a narrow trail, while the carriage with Celina and Matt continued straight ahead.

"Maybe he knows a shortcut," Edwina said.

The carriage hit a pothole and bounced Debbie Sue and Edwina out of their seat. Debbie Sue grabbed the side of the carriage and regained her balance. "Maybe so. But someone needs to tell him this isn't a race."

They zoomed at breakneck speed up the trail, which narrowed to a path. The carriage rattled and knocked and bounced them around. Enough was enough. "Joseph! Joseph! Stop pedaling!"

The bike swerved into a thicket of bushes and skidded to a stop so suddenly Debbie Sue and Edwina were thrown off the seat and into a jumbled heap on the floor of the carriage. Debbie Sue was stunned, but not so much so that she didn't notice their driver step off the bike and move away from it.

Debbie Sue climbed out of the carriage and marched after him. "Hey, Lance Armstrong, have your lost your friggin' mind? You could have hurt us."

"Surprise," a gravelly voice said.

Debbie Sue peered through tree limbs toward the voice. Instead of looking into the face of Joseph, the cyclist saving money for a trip to California and Mexico, she was standing eye to eye with Frank Rogenstein, fugitive and serial killer. Her heart, already pumping hard, dropped clear to her feet, but she summoned her courage. "Where's Joseph?" she demanded. "What'd you do with him?"

"Oh, is that his name? I think he's back there on the side of the road. He'll be okay, but he'll have a headache for a while."

Edwina stumbled toward them, adjusting her clothing. "Hey, Joseph, you got a death wish?"

"Funny you should bring that up," Rogenstein said.

Edwina looked up for the first time. Her mouth moved, but no words came out. Finally, she yelled, "Run!"

Before she could move, Debbie Sue grabbed her arm in a viselike grip. "Don't move, Ed," she said gravely.

"Best to listen to your smart friend," Rogenstein said, waving the barrel of some kind of gun in their direction.

"What—what are you going to do to us?" Debbie Sue asked.

"Gee, smart lady, you've had all the answers up to now. You tell me. What should I do with the two of you?"

Edwina said, "Well I think—"

"Shut up, you silly bitch!"

Edwina planted a fist on her hip. "Being rude isn't necessary. After all, you're the one with the gun."

"That's right. And you're the two that are gonna die. Now, walk over there into those bushes."

"No," Debbie Sue said firmly.

"What?" Rogenstein snapped, narrowing his eyes.

"What?" Edwina repeated.

"I'll have you know that this time next month my husband will be a Texas Ranger," Debbie Sue said. "If you harm a hair on my head, buster, you'll see what real trouble is. He's told me a million times that if I'm ever abducted that I was to refuse to leave with the abductor. Or the asshole, if that description fits better."

"And I'm supposed to be scared of a Texas Ranger? Where the hell do you think you are? This time next month your husband will be a widower," Rogenstein said menacingly.

Bang! Dirt and rocks stung Debbie Sue's shins.

He had shot at her! The sonofabitch had fired a shot at her feet!

"Now, walk," he said.

Furious, she grabbed Edwina in an impromptu hug about the neck and whispered in her ear, "When I fall down, run."

"Don't—" Edwina started to say.

"Break it up! Now! And walk!"

Debbie Sue felt tears rush to her eyes. "I just wanted to tell my friend good-bye." She sniffled, suddenly turned sharply and crumpled to the ground, grabbing her ankle. "Ow, ow. Damn, I've twisted my ankle."

"Get up!" the gun-wielding psychopath growled.

"I can't," Debbie Sue whined. "You'll have to kill me here."

Rogenstein came over and swung his foot backward to deliver a blow to her middle. Like lightning, Debbie Sue swung her own leg, strong and well muscled from a lifetime of controlling a horse while straddling its back, and struck Rogenstein's ankle with her Tony Lama stacked-riding-heel boot. With the other foot, she delivered a hard kick to his groin.

He choked and doubled over. Using the heel of her hand the way Buddy had shown her many times, she planted a blow to the bridge of his nose. He howled as blood gushed.

"Run!" she yelled at Edwina.

Edwina seemed frozen to the spot.

"Dammit, run!" Debbie Sue repeated.

Run? Edwina thought. Who the hell could run? She was wearing three-and-a-half-inch heels that had cost $750. She trotted on tiptoes as Debbie Sue passed her like an torch-carrying Olympic runner.

"C'mon, Ed. I've got the gun."

Edwina followed with tiny quick steps. When she reached the carriage, Debbie Sue was already climbing in.

"I'll cover us from the back of the carriage while you pedal."

Edwina scowled. "Are you crazy?"

"Ed, move!"

Something whizzed past Edwina's ear so closely she felt the hot sting, then she heard a *crack!* A gunshot?

"Sonofabitch," Debbie Sue cried. "He's got another gun! Edwina! Get on that fuckin' bicycle. Or I'll shoot you myself."

Edwina crawled onto the bike seat. She began pedaling as fast as she could, her heart racing, her eyes tearing. She was gonna die. She knew it. She was gonna die in her Jimmy Choo shoes, pedaling her ass through Central Park.

"That bastard," she yelled back over her shoulder. "If I ruin these shoes, I'll kill 'im with my bare hands."

"Dammit, just pedal, Ed! Pedal."

Edwina hadn't ridden a bike since childhood, but now she recaptured the hang of it. She lay over the handlebars, her mile-long legs pumping hard and fast, her knees bumping the handlebars. She would have bruises to kingdom come by the time this was over. Wind rushed past, flattening her hairdo. Still she pedaled. She spotted a curve ahead and attempted to brake, but the pedals spun in backward circles.

She turned and yelled over her shoulder again. "Debbie Sue, this sucker ain't got brakes."

"They're on the handlebars," Debbie Sue called back.

"How the fuck am I supposed to put my feet on the handlebars?"

"Dammit, Ed, don't stop. Just keep going."

They rounded the corner. She caught sight of Celina and Matt's cart ahead. Edwina felt the carriage tip behind her, but it righted itself.

Ka-whump!

Edwina was knocked to the ground, flat on her bottom, and the pedicab was weaving crazily across the roadway. It came to a sudden stop against a park bench. She was dazed, but she heard a struggle and the sound of someone gasping for air.

Off to her right, she saw Rogenstein sitting astraddle Debbie Sue. He had her in a strangle hold and the flailing of her best friend's legs was growing weaker.

Edwina forced herself to her feet, yanked off a shoe, lunged forward and jumped on the back of their assailant.

She pounded his head and shoulders with the stiletto shoe heel.

Rogenstein released Debbie Sue and turned on her. "You rotten bitch!" He leveled a gun at her face.

Edwina closed her eyes and instinctively turned sideways. She heard a shot and assumed she had been hit, but she felt no pain. Surprising. She thought getting shot would hurt more. Maybe she was already dead and it had been so fast there was no pain involved.

She dared to open one eye and saw Rogenstein on his knees in front of her. He had a surprised look on his face and a large hole in his chest. Looking up at her quizzically, he fell forward with a *shwump*.

Matt ran to him and kicked the gun aside. He bent down and felt Rogenstein's neck. "He's dead," he announced and pulled his cell phone from his pocket.

"Holy shit," Debbie Sue gasped. "Holy shit. Mother of God. Holy shit."

"Everyone all right?" Matt asked. "I've got medical on the way."

"I—I think I don't n—need it," Debbie Sue stammered. "Ed, are you okay?"

At some point, Edwina had broken into tears. "Oh, hell, I'm okay." She sniffled. "But do you think there's any chance that big store will take these back?" She held up for inspection what was left of her Jimmy Choo shoe and broke into sobs.

Matt had ordered Celina to stay with the other cyclist and wait for the police to arrive, and she had done exactly that. She was relieved and overcome with joy when he walked up with his arms around the shoulders of Debbie Sue and Edwina.

"It's all over," he announced solemnly.

"I heard shots," Celina said.

"Rogenstein's dead," Debbie Sue told her. "Matt shot him."

"Oh, Matt," Celina broke into tears and wrapped her arms around his middle.

A fleet of police cars arrived, sirens wailing, lights flashing. Innumerable police officers and other emergency personnel piled out of vehicles. Cops were everywhere, stringing crime-scene tape, talking on radios, controlling oglers.

Two ambulances came and soon left, one carrying the deceased detective and the other carrying the cyclist Joseph.

Hours later, Celina found herself, along with Debbie Sue and Edwina, in a police cruiser on their way back to the hotel. Dinner plans forgotten, they all decided that the privacy of room service, with an abundance of liquor, was all they really needed.

When room service brought their dinner, Debbie Sue and Edwina rolled their cart into one of the bedrooms and closed the door.

Behind closed doors Matt and Celina sat in a large garden tub filled to the top with foamy scented bubbles tinted golden by the glow of candlelight. A bottle of champagne and two glasses sat on the tub's rim.

"I can't believe this whole evening," Celina said. "When you left to check on Debbie Sue and Edwina, I could barely breathe. You don't know what it did to me when I heard that gunshot."

Matt pulled her closer and kissed her brow. "I'm fine," he said. "We're all fine. You don't have to worry. I know how to take care of myself."

"I know, but just the thought of never seeing you again . . ." She didn't finish her sentence. She chose instead to kiss him, squelching the words she was afraid to say.

Pulling away from their kiss Matt said, "Speaking of seeing me again, we were going to discuss tonight when I could make it to Texas. Remember?"

"Yes, I remember."

"I could get out of here in thirty days," he said and kissed her left cheek."

"Really? You mean on a vacation?"

He kissed her right cheek. "No."

"I don't get it."

"I mean forever, Celina." His lips brushed hers. His fingers touched beneath her chin and his eyes looked into hers. "If Texas is where you need to be, then that's where I need to be."

"Oh, Matt," she said, wrapping her arms around his neck. "I love you. I was afraid to say it. I was afraid you didn't love me back."

He laughed. "Know what? I love you, too. All of you. Back, front and everywhere in between."

They laughed together.

epilogue

*D*ebbie Sue and Edwina bid a fond farewell to New York City and returned to Salt Lick. On the plane ride home they made an agreement that they would tell only an abbreviated version of their week in New York. They wouldn't really lie, but they wouldn't give all of the details, either.

Debbie Sue had a hard time hiding *all* of her activities since the episode of her on the sixth-floor ledge made national news and police bulletins. The result was that she was forced to tell Buddy most of the truth, minus a few details. Buddy tried to be open minded, as did Vic, but both women sensed that any chance of the Domestic Equalizers ever leaving town together again hung in grave doubt. They resumed their careers as hairdressers and partners in the Domestic Equalizers, raising hell and the blood pressures of their spouses.

Buddy took the Texas Ranger exam and passed with flying colors. He was posted to the West Texas region, an assignment that allowed Debbie Sue and him to continue to reside in their home in Salt Lick.

Matt made good on his promise to Celina. He traveled to Texas and fell almost as much in love with Dime Box and its 381 inhabitants as he was in love with Celina. He applied for a job as a detective in Austin and was enthusiastically hired.

One of the first Texas Rangers he met was Ranger Buddy Overstreet. To his credit, Matt never mentioned the events during the week Buddy's wife spent in the city. Matt was sworn to keep the peace, and he could see that telling Ranger Overstreet the details of the New York City caper involving the Domestic Equalizers would have resulted in the direct opposite.

Celina and Matt married a few months later. The bride was given away by Granny Dee's new husband, Dewey. Debbie Sue and Buddy and Edwina and Vic traveled to Dime Box for the ceremony.

Celina moved the library to a new location in its own building and founded an annual book festival honoring Texas authors. Prompted by her relationship with the authors, she wrote a romance novel based loosely on her trip to New York City, where she had found adventure and love. It became a *New York Times* best seller.

Hotel manager Otto Pembroke was unable to keep the week of mayhem caused by the Domestic Equalizers' visit a secret. Someone leaked the story to the New Yorker Hotel's board of directors, and Pembroke was reassigned to the hotel chain's struggling link located in Death Valley, California.

Homer Hess became the new general manager, and the hotel flourished under his watchful eye. He was written up in numerous publications and received many awards, most of which lined the walls of his large, cushy office.

Still later, Debbie Sue and Edwina were contacted by the Manhattan Police Women's Association. A reward of a thousand dollars had been offered for the capture of Detective Frank Rogenstein. Because of their heroic efforts, Debbie Sue and Edwina were presented with the reward.

They happily accepted the money and Edwina again became the proud owner of a pair of Jimmy Choo shoes. Ruby-red satin trimmed with black and red crystals.

"It just goes to prove," she told Debbie Sue over an ice-cold margarita, "you can take the girl out of the country, but you can't strip a killer pair of designer shoes off a country girl's feet."

"Amen," Debbie Sue said. "I'll drink to that."

A⁺

AUTHOR INSIGHTS, EXTRAS, & MORE...

FROM

DIXIE CASH

AND

AVON A

Some Further Fun
with Debbie Sue and Edwina

Sometimes Debbie Sue and Edwina are so busy with Styling Station patrons, they don't have time to answer the Domestic Equalizers' telephone. They have been forced to make a decision on which business should receive their first priority. Since the salon is their bread and butter, the decision wasn't a hard one.

After having an automatic telephone answering system installed, Edwina recorded their outgoing message:

> "Thank you for calling the Domestic Equalizers.
> If you *think* your lover is cheating, press one.
> If you *know* your lover is cheating, press two.
> If you're looking through a window *watching* your lover cheating, hang up and call 9-1-1. Nothing spoils a romantic interlude faster than the cops showing up."

Edwina's weekly advice column in the *Salt Lick Reporter* continues to be wildly successful. She has acquired a reputation among the locals for being an expert on relationships.

Dear Edwina,

Should I go through my husband's pockets?

Don't Trust Him

Dear Suspicious,

First of all, is he in or out of the pants? . . . If he's in the pants at the time, he'll like it if you've got your hands in his pockets. But if the pants are on the floor (and aren't they always?), that's another story.

The last time I looked, there were no locks on pockets.

Edwina *"I'll Look in Yours if You'll Look in Mine"* Perkins-Martin

Dear Edwina,

I can't decide if I should:

- *a) get married*
- *b) have children*
- *c) get my education*

What do you think I should do?

Can't Decide Which One

Dear Wishy-Washy,

Who ever said life is a multiple-choice quiz? What's wrong with "all of the above?" Why limit yourself when you can do it all?

Edwina *"Don't be Wishy with Your Washy"* Perkins-Martin

Dear Ms. Perkins,

Any suggestions on what would help P.M.S.?

Two Personalities

Dear 2P,

P.M.S. is tough. I highly recommend G.I.N. or R.U.M.
Works every T.I.M.E.

Edwina *"Pardon My Sarcasm"* Perkins-Martin

Sometimes Edwina doesn't receive enough letters to fill her column. In that case, she resorts to filling in with some of her own poetry:

Ode to a Rodeo Cowboy

by Edwina Perkins-Martin

I like your tiny butt in jeans,
I like you when you're riding things.
I don't care if you treat me bad.
Just please don't leave me feeling sad.

Sometimes you're cocky and you're rude,
Others say that you are crude.
A cowboy is so hard to tame,
But I can beat you at your game.

I'll be sweet and sexy too,
You won't know just what to do.
You'll be mine in record time,
Then I'll leave you without a dime.

And when you're broke and feeling bad,
You'll remember the times we had.
I'll write a book and say mean things,
You'll wish you'd never given me a ring.

Dear Readers:

Thanks for reading our latest edition of the Dixie Cash stories of Debbie Sue and Edwina.

Since there is a pretty good chance we will meet and talk with few who read the books, I would like to answer some questions that are asked of us everywhere we go.

1. How do two people write a book together?

Jeff and I live about sixty miles apart. We do everything by email. I don't think we could do it any other way. We tried working together in the same room, but we both wanted to tap away at the keyboard. The one not typing usually ended up reading a magazine or watching TV. Or worse yet, snacking. Or we got distracted by gossip and online shopping. We decided the writing worked best if we were apart.

I'm the one who makes up the story and characters. Jeff does the editing and rearranging and adding to what I've written. Or not. Then she sends the pages back to me for a second go-round. Here's an example of how it works: I send her fifteen pages; she sends me back five. I send twelve; she sends back nine. Some writers want to make the *New York Times* Best Sellers List. I just want to get back the same number of pages I sent to my sister in the first place.

2. How did you come up with the name Dixie Cash?

Our publisher wanted a name that sounded "Southern." Dixie came to mind. How much more Southern can you get than Dixie? Everyone agreed on that one. And Dixie just sounds like somebody from Texas, right?

I suggested Couch for a last name because that's what I intended to use the advance money to buy—a new couch. But then, through a series of discussions in New York and a long list of other suggestions, Cash was settled on for the last name. That was okay with me. Cash works for me!

3. Where do you come up all your zany characters?

That's the easiest question of all to answer. We were raised by them. If not that, then we ultimately befriended, bedded or wedded all of them. They are fictitious characters, of course, but parts of them are real people who have come and gone in our lives. Oh, sure, some changes were made to make them appear saner and more normal, but you read it here in black-and-white—they're alive!

4. Is there really a Salt Lick, Texas?

Salt Lick is not a real town, but it's fashioned after a West Texas small town named Wink, which is located between Odessa and Midland. These days, like many West Texas towns, it has almost dwindled away.

Dwindling and surging is pretty much the history of Wink. After oil was discovered in 1926, the population skyrocketed from single digits to roughly 6,000 residents. In 1929, Wink took its place alongside Kilgore, Borger, Ranger and Beaumont as one of those wild "boomtowns."

The ensuing years brought Wink many ups and downs, including organized crime and more population gains and losses. Now, I would be surprised if it's as large as Salt Lick's fictitious population of 1,200.

Wink does have claims to fame. Besides being one of the original Texas oil boomtowns, it has an old movie theater, "The Rig," that is listed on the National Register of Historic Places. Wink was the boyhood home of the one and only inimitable Roy Orbison, and boasts the Roy Orbison Museum. For those of you who don't know who Roy Orbison was, for the love of God, close this book and go download some of his music. Expand your music library and your mind!

5. Did you always want to be a writer?

I never entertained the thought of being an author, although I did long to write sitcoms or to be a joke writer for *Saturday Night Live*. No one loves great comedy more than I do and I have often thought I could do it better than whomever I'm watching or hearing. My sister, on the other hand, had a hankering to write books from the time she was a little girl. She loves books like I love big earrings and anything liquid that contains liquor. Her home looks like a library. She writes beautiful prose and steamy sex, and then I come along and junk it up with trash.

6. Are you both really from Texas?

Yes, we were both born and raised in West Texas. I've never lived anywhere but Texas and I don't want to live anywhere else. I love it to the point of being corny. In reality, it's no better than anyone else's place of birth, but it's just *mine*.

Jeff was also born in Texas, but spent years of her adult life living in foreign countries like California and Oregon and Idaho.

But do I need to point out that after all of that tomfoolery, she's back in Texas? We have a sister who's holding out in Florida, but we'll get her back here, too, one of these days.

Despite my love for Texas, I *could* be persuaded to own a summer home in a cooler climate.

7. Will Debbie Sue and Edwina continue getting into scrapes and doing pratfalls?

They will as long as you keep buying the books. Jeff and I both hope you continue to enjoy these ladies as much as we enjoy telling their stories. They are dear to our hearts and have become permanent residents in my home. I frequently find myself having conversations with them and my son fears they are replacing him in my affection.

8. Are there any plans to make these books into movies?

Jeff and I plan on it all the time, but so far we haven't found a sucker. We constantly discuss which Hollywood hotties we would cast as our characters, which book would make the best movie and how we'd spend the money if that magical event should occur. If you've read the books and have suggestions, then by all means, let us know what they are.

9. Country-western music is mentioned often in your books. Is country music really that popular in Texas?

To quote Edwina, "Is a snake's ass close to the ground?" Country music is as much a part of Texas as cowboys, good horses and saying "y'all." It's hard to describe just how really cherished good country music is in our state, and if you aren't listening to it now, then you're fixin' to listen to it.

10. The question that will inevitably come from the publication of this book is, Do either one of you own any Jimmy Choo shoes?

And my answer is, "No, not currently."

But if Mr. Choo ever decides to make a full-quill ostrich cowboy boot with a twelve-inch shaft and a walking heel, I just might.

Hope to meet y'all in person soon,
Pam (Dixie Ca$h)

Trivia from the Book

By now you've read the book and you've seen the town of **Dime Box, Texas**. This is not a fictitious town. It really exists.

Dime Box, east of Austin, is on Farm Road 141, twelve miles northeast of Giddings. It was founded sometime between 1869 and 1877, when a settler named Brown built a sawmill near what is now State Highway 21. Until a government post office opened in 1877, settlers deposited outgoing mail and a dime in a small box at the mill for weekly delivery to Giddings.

The Brown's Mill post office closed in December, 1883. When it re-opened the following spring, frequent confusion of Brown's Mill with Brownsville caused the town to be renamed Dime Box.

In 1913, when the Southern Pacific Railroad built a line three miles southeast of Dime Box, the original settlement became Old Dime Box, and the new railroad station became Dime Box. Both towns are still on the Texas map. The presence of the railroad encouraged growth, and the community's estimated population increased from 127 in 1904 to 500 in 1925.

The town received national attention in the 1940s when a CBS broadcast kicked off the March of Dimes drive from Dime Box.

The number of residents remained between 300 and 500 throughout the middle years of the twentieth century and was estimated at 313 from 1972 through 2000. In the late 1970s oil was discovered in the Dime Box area.

The most recent census shows the population of Dime Box to be 380, but it doesn't say how many oil wells there are.

One thing we know for sure. It's the home of Matt and Celina.

Dixie Cash is Pam Cumbie and her sister, Jeffery McClanahan. They grew up in rural West Texas among "real life fictional characters" and 100 percent real cowboys and cowgirls. Some were relatives and some weren't. Pam has always had a zany sense of humor and Jeffery has always had a dry wit. Surrounded by country-western music, when they can stop laughing long enough, they work together creating hilarity on paper. Both live in Texas– Pam in the Fort Worth/Dallas Metroplex and Jeffery in a small town near Fort Worth.

Dixie Cash